THE LAST
AFFAIR

Also by Brandon Massey

Novels
Thunderland
Dark Corner
Within the Shadows
The Other Brother
Vicious
Don't Ever Tell
Cornered
In the Dark

Collections
Twisted Tales

Anthologies
Dark Dreams
Voices from the Other Side: Dark Dreams II
Whispers in the Night: Dark Dreams III
The Ancestors (with Tananarive Due and L.A. Banks)

THE LAST AFFAIR

BRANDON MASSEY

Originally published under the pseudonym
Rachee

Dark Corner Publishing
Atlanta, Georgia

Bathed in pale summer moonlight, the woman rested her forehead against the cool windowpane and watched the Oldsmobile cough and sputter like a sick dog across the curving driveway, dragging closer to the estate. She could not see the driver from her vantage point on the second floor, but she already realized that he had lied to her. During their Internet chats, he had claimed to be a successful physician. Would a wealthy doctor drive an obsolete car that was badly in need of a tune-up?

She drew her lips, dipped in cherry-red lipstick, into a disapproving line. Men and their lies.

The car grumbled to a stop in the huge, circular driveway. The headlamps faded to black. The driver switched on an interior light and examined his face in the mirror.

She still couldn't get a good look at him. Hurry up and get out, she thought, her stomach wound tight as a spool of wire. She had been in similar situations dozens of times, and it never got any easier. Few things caused more anxiety than that slice of time between the anticipation of how a new man might be—and the revelation of how he was.

Finally, he cut out the light, pushed open the door, and climbed out of the car.

In his online photograph, he'd appeared to be at least six feet of tantalizing chocolate, with refrigerator-wide shoulders; in the photo, he'd worn his shirt unbuttoned, too, giving a tempting peek at his rippling abs. Coco Adonis—that was his online handle.

Judging from her initial impression, Coco Adonis had transformed from a handsome prince into a frog, like an obscene perversion of the romantic fairy tale.

Although it was difficult to discern his exact features in the darkness, the man seemed to stand several inches below six feet. He did have broad shoulders, but the button-down shirt he wore displayed the swell of an ample gut.

He looks like a troll, *she thought.*

She felt a twinge of disappointment—which was quickly replaced by a rising tide of anger.

The man yanked up his ill-fitting slacks around his belly and began to waddle toward the front door.

She turned away from the window and crossed the bedroom. It was an enormous, lavishly appointed master suite, boasting a king-size bed draped with silky crimson sheets, plush white carpeting, a sitting area with leather club chairs, and a marble fireplace. Scented candles, arranged around the perimeter of the room, cast dancing golden light.

She glanced in a long oval mirror that adorned a wall. Her reflection revealed that she possessed every exquisite physical trait that she'd described in the profile she posted on the Internet. Flawless bronze skin. Hypnotic, honey-brown eyes. Long, thick black hair. Firm, melon-sized breasts. A taut waist. An ass that had reduced grown men to begging little boys. Legs that could incite a three-car pileup in downtown Atlanta.

She had never posted her photo online—privacy was important to her—but she never lied about herself, either. Instead, she liked to role-play. It was acting, not lying. There was a difference.

Her character for the evening was the dominatrix, a favorite of hers. She wore a glove-tight black leather miniskirt, her legs encased in crotchless fishnet panty hose. A leather halter top accentuated her ample cleavage and left her flat stomach exposed. A thick, studded collar encircled her neck Four-inch black stilettos, the heels almost sharp enough to pierce flesh, adorned her feet.

She picked up the studded, leather cat mask from the table beside the bed. She slid it on.

The doorbell chimed—rich, melodic notes that floated throughout the mansion.

She swept her gaze across the room, to ensure that everything was in place. The most important item for tonight's activities—a black, molded plastic case—lay on an upholstered chair near the bed, waiting to reveal its contents.

Satisfied, she left the bedroom, walking with the grace of a panther on the prowl.

She paid no attention to the mansion's sumptuous furnishings. The crystal chandeliers, the authentic African-American artwork, the decorative antique vases and sculptures, the soaring ceilings, the baby grand piano in the sunken living room. None of it meant anything to her.

After all, she didn't live here.

In the foyer, she looked in the mirror and double-checked that the mask was snug on her face, and then she opened the front door.

The man gaped at her. He had a pug nose and small, fish lips that were out of place in his moon face. Acne scars pockmarked his dark brown skin. His heavily lidded brown eyes might have been dreamy if they belonged to another man, but had the effect of making him look as if he were in dire need of a nap. His wore his hair in cornrows, the dry braids flecked with dandruff.

The individual in the online photo had borne a passing resemblance to Morris Chestnut. This fool in front of her hadn't just lied—he had lied flagrantly and shamelessly, as if trying to win a prize for telling the most over-the-top lie.

It would have been funny if she wasn't so pissed off.

"Damn." His lecherous gaze crawled up and down her body. He licked his lips. "You weren't lying about yourself, girl. You're fine as hell."

Although she was angry, she had to admit that she wasn't really surprised by his deceit. Most of the men she encountered on the Internet lied about something: their appearance, their profession, their marital status, their sexual orientation. Always something. On the Internet, honesty was as rare as a red diamond.

But she continued to use the Web as a means to meet men because it was the best way to satisfy her urges. It offered her a measure of necessary secrecy.

"You don't look like your photo." She poked his belly. "Too many Twinkies?"

"Oh, that was an old pic, college days, you know." Chuckling self-consciously, he rubbed his stomach as if to mold it flat.

"I see."

He still couldn't admit the obvious truth: It wasn't a picture of him. But that was a man for you—he would lie until the end of time.

It was a warm night, tempered with a cool breeze, and the wind pushed the scent of his cologne—it was cheap and he had splashed on too much—into her face. She wrinkled her nose.

"You gonna let me in or what?" he asked. The stilettos gave her a six-inch height advantage on him, putting him almost at eye-level with her breasts. He kept his gaze on her cleavage and wetted his lips again, mesmerized.

She bunched her hands on her hips. This man was dishonest, he stank, and he had no manners. She should have slammed the door in his face.

But for all his faults, he was fresh meat, and she was hungry.

"Come in." She beckoned him inside.

"All right, that's what I'm talkin' 'bout." He stepped into the foyer. Turning around, he gawked at the house. "You really live here? What kinda work do you do?"

"What's your name?" she asked him. "Your real name?"

"Tyrone," he said.

"Tyrone," she said, slowly and carefully. "Now that you're here, do you want to talk or fuck?"

He spluttered as if choking on a chicken bone. "You for real?"

"When I want conversation, I call a girlfriend," she said. "When I want to fuck, I call a man. Are you a man or a girlfriend?"

"Well, damn." Tyrone scratched his head. "Can't a brother take a minute to get comfortable? I don't even know your name."

"Man Eater," she said.

"Man Eater, yeah, right. Not the name you use online. I mean, what's your real name?"

"I don't think you're ready for this." She reached for the doorknob. "Good-bye, Tyrone. Drop me a line after you've grown past drinking mama's breast milk"

"Wait!" He put his hand on her arm. "I don't want to leave yet, seriously."

"Then shut up, get your funky ass to the bedroom, and take a shower."

His eyes widened at her insult. "But I took a shower before I left."

"And you got smelly again by drowning yourself in that cheap cologne. I'm not going to touch you until you shower. It's up to you."

"Fine." He shrugged, looked around. "Where's the bedroom?"

"Upstairs. Door at the end of the hallway."

Huffing, he shuffled toward the grand spiral staircase. He turned to glance at her.

"What's up with all the black leather and the mask and shit?" he asked. "And you telling me what to do like I'm your goddamn stepchild? You into some kind of dominatrix shit?"

There was a gleam in his eye as he asked the question. If she wasn't a dominatrix, he wanted her to be, that gleam said.

She pointed upstairs. "Get in the shower. Now. "

While Tyrone showered in the master bathroom, she searched through the clothes he'd left piled on the bed. They reeked of that terrible cologne, but she found his wallet. She riffled through it.

His Georgia driver's license verified his name as Tyrone Parker. He had thirty dollars in cash, a couple of credit cards, and a photo of a girl maybe four years old and a homely, pumpkin-faced woman who was obviously the kid's mother. The child, bless her heart, had Tyrone's sleepy eyes and fish lips. There were two more snapshots featuring the girl.

During their chats, he'd professed to have no children. Anger simmered in her.

This episode with Tyrone wasn't important to her—she had critical activities on the horizon—but she hated for a man to lie to her, especially when there was little to be gained from dishonesty. If you must lie, then at least do so for a good reason.

The truth was, she didn't care that he had children, didn't care that he was probably married, and didn't care that he wasn't a doctor. She didn't even care all that much about what he looked like. She'd had sex with ugly, unemployed men who had wives and several children, and she'd done it simply because she wanted to at the moment.

But don't promise her a trip to Tahiti, and then, at the last moment, reveal that you were actually taking her to Tuscaloosa. She had no patience for such dishonesty.

And no mercy.

She had deposited the wallet back in his pocket when Tyrone came out of the bathroom. He had wrapped a towel around his waist. Droplets of water streamed off his skin and pattered onto the thick carpet.

"You still dressed?" he asked her.

"Of course I am." Rising, she crossed her arms over her chest. "First, I want to see your package."

"My what?"

She sighed. Was this Sex 101?

"Drop the towel, Tyrone. I want to see what you have to offer me tonight."

He looked around warily, as if concerned that she was filming this episode with a hidden camera. "Can I get in the bed first?"

She stepped up to him, grasped the edge of the towel, and in one swift movement, snatched it off his body.

"What the hell's the matter with you?" He tried to cover himself, but she had seen all that she needed to see. She shook her head.

He'd lied about his length, too. He'd claimed to be swinging nine inches. He was maybe a third of that.

But at this point, another lie didn't matter. She was going to get hers. And Tyrone was certainly going to get his.

"I get a lot bigger when I'm hard." He massaged himself.
"Get in the bed," she said.

He hurried to the mattress and quickly burrowed under the covers.

"These sheets feel nice." Grinning, he patted the pillow beside him. *"Come to Daddy, baby."*

Smiling faintly, she unzipped her leather skirt, slid it down her legs, and stepped out of it, keeping the stilettos on. She wore no panties. The cool air kissed the outer folds of her clean-shaven flesh.

"Whoa, you shaved your pussy?" Tyrone watched her, his lips parted, like a boy living his ultimate fantasy.

She strutted to the bed. She produced a wrapped Trojan condom from a pocket near her breast and tossed it onto Tyrone's chest.

"Put it on," she said.

As Tyrone tore open the package and fiddled with the condom, she slid her fingers inside her pussy and gently stroked her clit. She kept her gaze on Tyrone, but she wasn't seeing him. She visualized that Tyrone was someone else—a fantasy man, someone she really desired.

Imagination was a coping mechanism. She'd lived a difficult life and would've died without the ability to create her own illusions, her own reality.

Her imagination was so vivid that she could see her dream lover's face superimposed over Tyrone's. The promise of making love to him made her moist.

I'm ready like Freddy," Tyrone said, his annoying voice temporarily disrupting her fantasy.

She bounded onto the mattress and pulled away the sheet. She straddled Tyrone and inched down slowly onto his dick. Her imagination, in high gear, placed her ultimate man's handsome face and chiseled physique over Tyrone's ugly face and out-of-shape body.

She began to ride him, clenching and unclenching him inside her, loving the sensation of his pulsating dick rocking against her walls, thrilling to the feeling of his balls rubbing *against her. Aroused by his smooth, sculpted muscles she traced circles across his chest. She tilted her head back, her long hair swinging, and she opened her mouth and let a purr slide out of her. . . . .*

"Oh, shit!"

Tyrone 's exclamation shattered her dream.

It had been less than two minutes, but Tyrone was shouting and trembling, ecstasy washing over his face. He climaxed with a shout: "Goddamn!"

As Tyrone panted and spasmed, she rolled off him and onto the mattress, putting several inches between them. He tried to embrace her—maybe his wife had trained him to always hold her after an orgasm instead of immediately falling asleep—but she slapped his hands away.

"What's wrong with you, girl?" he asked. "That was the shit!"

"That was two minutes."

"Hey, I got mine." He folded his hands behind his head and grinned. "You shoulda got yours."

"I think I might just do that." She swung out of the bed.

He propped himself up on his elbows. "Where you going?"

She went to the bedside chair, where the large black plastic case lay.

"Hey, now that a brotha's put it down, take that damn mask off!"

Ignoring him, she opened the case.

It contained a variety of polished metal instruments and well-oiled leather accessories. She always brought these items along with her when meeting a man. A woman had to be prepared to do whatever was necessary.

She removed a pair of handcuffs. Turning, she dangled them in the air like a treat. "Let's play a game first," she said.

"Ahh." Tyrone laughed. "I knew you were into some freaky shit!"

She winked. She approached the bed, swinging the handcuffs from her finger.

"Want me to put my hands up, Officer?" He grinned.

"You got it. You're under arrest!'

Chuckling, he pressed his wrists together and inserted them between the polished wooden rungs of the decorative headboard. She leaned over him and snapped the cuffs on his wrists, imprisoning his hands behind the sturdy wood.

Mirth sparkled in his eyes. *"What did I do wrong, Officer?"*

"You lied."

"Huh?" A shadow flitted across his face. *"Lied about what?"*

Standing over him, she ticked off the lies on her fingers. *"Number one, you aren't a physician. Two, you used someone else's photo in your profile. Three, you're married or at the minimum involved seriously with someone. Four, you have a kid."*

His eyes darted around the room. *"I. . . . I ain't got no baby."*

"Whose child is that in all those pictures in your wallet?"

"You went looking in my wallet?" Indignation spiked his voice. *"Who the fuck gave you permission to dig through my shit?"*

"I had to verify my suspicions. Besides, if you hadn't lied it wouldn't be a problem. But you did, and now it's a huge problem—for you."

"What the fuck are you talking about?"

But she spun around and returned to the case. There was such a variety of tools to choose from. What was she in the mood for tonight?

"Let me loose." Tyrone rattled the handcuffs, but they were police-issue cuffs, and the heavy oak headboard barely budged. *"Let me go, bitch!"*

She selected two items. Firstly, a pair of dental forceps, the same tool used by dentists to hold a patient's mouth wide open, enabling easy access to the teeth and inner reaches of the oral cavity. She placed them on the nightstand.

The second instrument she chose was a pair of pliers.

The diagonal cutter kind, ideal for snipping wires— and other things.

She turned back to the bed.

Tyrone's eyeballs swelled like balloons. His words came in explosive gasps. "What. . . what the. . .fuck are you doing?"

"I'm going to teach you that there are consequences to your actions," she said calmly. "Men like you think you can simply lie to a woman, say whatever you want, and get away with it. Well, I don't tolerate that kind of treatment from a man."

"You crazy bitch!"

She snatched away the bedsheets. He tried to twist away, but the handcuffs kept him from going far. Laughing, she swiped at him with the pliers.

He flinched. "Get the fuck away from me!"

"I should pull a Lorena Bobbit on you," she said. She placed the cutters at the base of his scrotum. Tyrone froze, quaking. She traced the sharp ends of the pliers along the shaft of his dick, which, not surprisingly, had gone as soft as warm butter.

"Tell me the truth," she said. "Do you have a daughter?"

Fat beads of sweat rolled down his face. "Okay! I have a daughter! Her name's Imani! She's four! All right, I admitted it, now get those fucking things away from me!"

She paused with the pliers poised above the crown of his dick. "Are you married?"

His chest rose and fell at a frenzied pace. "Yeah, I'm married, okay? My wife thinks I'm hanging with my boys tonight. Now will you take that thing away from me?" He struggled against the handcuffs to no avail. "Please?"

"In a minute." She pursed her lips. "Where do you really work?"

"I'm a supervisor at a Verizon store," he said. His panic-wet eyes pleaded for mercy. "I'll hook you up with a new phone, great service plan, as many free minutes as you want, girl. Just let me go, all right?"

"Do you apologize for lying to me?"

"Yes!" He shouted so loud that his voice cracked. "I'm really, really sorry. I didn't mean to lie, but I just wanted to have some fun, that's all, I didn't mean to hurt nobody."

"Is that right?" She smirked.

"Yeah . . . yeah." He nodded fervently.

She looked from his sweaty, scared face to the pliers, studied their glass-sharp edges.

"It's funny," she said, "the things a man will say when he's helpless. He'll say anything to get out of the situation. He'll tell you whatever he thinks you want to hear."

"Listen, baby, I'm being for real. I'm truly sorry."

She crawled onto the bed and straddled him once again.

"I don't believe you've learned your lesson," she said. She reached for the forceps.

"Get off me!" He thrashed beneath her, kicking his legs, trying to throw her off, like a rodeo bull bucking against a cowboy. She stayed on top of him easily, laughing and whooping, waving her arms through the air, enjoying the ride.

"Fuck you," he said hoarsely. Cold sweat pooled on his chest. He was breathing hard, worn out by struggle. He tugged again, weakly, at the cuffs. They were as unyielding as ever.

She brought the forceps near his mouth.

"Open wide," she said.

Fresh terror lit up his eyes. He clamped his lips shut, denying her access.

"You're only making this harder on yourself" she said.

She stabbed the pliers against his throat.

He yelped, and while his mouth was open, she drove the forceps inside, the metal clicking against his teeth. He tried to seal his lips, whipped his head back and forth, but she had gained a secure hold. Using the forceps, she pried his mouth open . . . wider . . . wider. . . until his protesting jaws wouldn't extend any farther.

"Say aaahhhh," she said.

A garbled scream roared from the bottom of his throat.

Holding the forceps in place with one hand, she grasped the pliers with the other. She inserted them in his mouth. She captured his wriggling tongue between the gleaming blades.

"You won't lie anymore," she whispered.
And cut.

* * *

A half hour later, she drove away from the mansion in a white Mercedes CL 600 coupe. She had changed into jeans, a University of Georgia T-shirt, and Nikes. She had pulled back her hair into a bun, and had slid a pair of wire-rim glasses over her nose. She resembled a grad student, perhaps a brainiac working on a Ph.D. Another of her calculated looks.

"Southern Girl," a classic jam by Frankie Beverly and Maze, played on the car's satellite radio hookup. She sang along, snapping her fingers.

Although it was nearly midnight, for her, the evening was young. She was on her way to see another man: an Atlanta Falcons player—a juicy Mandingo brother—who was so enamored of her that he had bought her the Mercedes she was driving.

A woman can have a lotta power over a man, but she gotta learn how to use it. Or she's gonna be used, hear me?

Those sage words, spoken by her aunt so many years ago, echoed in her thoughts. She had the power—and she was enjoying it.

After teaching lying Tyrone a lesson in honesty, she had unlocked his handcuffs. He would never tell anyone what had happened; she had sworn him to silence. Men didn't respect women. But they respected pain.

Understandably, he'd been in a hurry to get away from her.

She had kindly preserved the severed tip of his tongue in a Ziploc bag and advised him to have it reattached at a hospital emergency room. She assured him not to worry. She understood, quite well, the current capabilities of modern medicine.

As she drove down the road, her Georgia license plate, SEXYDOC, *glimmered in the coppery glow of the streetlamps.*

Chapter 1

"Do you love me?"

Kevin Richmond was raising the glass of Merlot to his lips, anticipating the taste of the red wine swirling around his tongue, when his wife, Lauren, asked the question. He hesitated. The wine's aromatic bouquet—earthy flavors of plum and black cherry— tempted his nostrils. It was a fifty-dollar bottle of Merlot, a fitting accompaniment to their dinner at Bones, one of Atlanta's best steak houses. They were there to celebrate his wife's thirtieth birthday, and the evening had been going perfectly.

Until she'd asked the question.

Bones was a power-dining restaurant, a place to which Kevin regularly brought his firm's most important clients. The atmosphere was unabashedly masculine: smoky lighting, hardwood floors, brick walls covered with photos of celebrities, and red leather booths. Waiters attired in starched steward jackets hurried from table to table, in pursuit of the hefty tips sure to be left by the well-heeled Saturday night crowd. It was the kind of clubby establishment where even the doorman remembered your name.

There, sitting at his favorite comer booth, Kevin usually felt confident. Like a mover and shaker. Like the kind of man in full control of his life.

But Lauren's unexpected question robbed the air from his lungs.

Not the words themselves, per se, but the underlying context of her inquiry. If Kevin had learned one thing in his thirty-two years on this earth, it was that if you wanted to truly understand a woman, you had better learn how to read between the lines.

She suspects something, he thought.

And in the next heartbeat, he wondered: *But how could she?*

Lauren leaned forward, arms crossed over her bosom, elbows pressing against the white linen tablecloth. A runner-up in the Miss Georgia pageant a decade ago, she was a strikingly beautiful woman—soft caramel complexion, chocolate doe eyes, flowing auburn hair, a statuesque figure born to grace a fashion show runway. But concern—or maybe it was suspicion—knitted her fine features.

Kevin finally discovered his voice.

"Of course, I love you, baby." He set down the wineglass and gestured toward the small, distinctive blue box from Tiffany's that lay on the table, near Lauren's manicured fingers. The gift, which Lauren had opened only fifteen minutes ago, contained a four-carat diamond tennis bracelet. "Isn't that proof?"

"Yes," she said. "In a certain sense."

Like him, Lauren was an attorney. She practiced corporate law at one of Atlanta's largest firms, was well on her way to make partner in the near future. And she was a smart woman, almost frighteningly so. With her sharp mind, honed by her legal training, she could make even the most innocent-sounding question segue into a blistering interrogation.

With no clue where she was leading with this, he decided the best defense was to play stupid.

"I'm not sure what you mean," he said. "But a gift like that, dinner at a nice restaurant—and, most of all, two years of a happy marriage—sure sounds like love tome."

"Then you're happy with our marriage?"

Why was she asking him these questions? He couldn't determine if she was really suspicious of him or was merely seeking feedback on the state of their union.

"I'm very happy, yes," he said. "Aren't you?"

"Sometimes, I wonder. . . . " Lips pursed, she glanced away. "I don't know."

Kevin's confusion was giving way to a slow-boiling annoyance. But he masked his feelings. Getting angry with Lauren could prevent him from discovering the root of the issue.

He reached across the table and took her delicate hand in his. Perspiration dampened her palm.

"What's on your mind?" he asked gently.

"Sometimes, I wonder, Kevin."

"What do you wonder about?"

"I wonder if you love me for who I am. Or for what I am."

Now he was frowning. "I don't follow you."

"That might have been too ambiguous." She slipped her hand out of his and clasped her hands together, as if seeking to fortify herself. "I'll put it like this—why do you love me?"

"Ah, I get it." Nodding, Kevin took a sip of his wine. As gorgeous as Lauren was, she sometimes suffered bouts of insecurity, proof that even stunning beauty wasn't an impenetrable armor against the weapons of the world. In fact, Kevin's experience with beautiful women had taught him that they were perhaps more prone to suffering low self-esteem than average-looking women, because they believed—rightly so, in many cases—that they were valued solely for their looks, and that as they aged and their beauty faded, they would lose their standing in the shallow eyes of society.

That's what this was all about. Lauren had turned thirty today, which for a lot of women triggered a midlife crisis. She was anxious that she was slipping, losing her appeal to him.

Kevin was relieved.

Her questions had nothing to do with suspicions of his fidelity.

"This is about you turning thirty, right?" he said. "Well, baby, I think you're getting more beautiful every day. You don't look a day over twenty-five."

A smile broke up the worry lines on her face. "That's sweet. But you still haven't answered my question. Why do you love me?"

"Because you can look great in an evening gown or a pair of knock-around jeans."

"That's my body, not me." But she gave him a smile. "Why else?"

"Because you can cook your ass off."

Another smile. "That's only due to good home training. Why else?"

"Because you lift me up when I'm down, you've got my back in good or bad times, you're the yin to my yang. *You complete me, baby,*" he finished, quoting a line from *Jerry Maguire,* one of her favorite movies.

"That's better." She squeezed his hand. "And since I 'complete you,' you would never cheat on me, would you?"

Kevin had been taking another sip of wine. He almost—*almost*—lost his composure and spat it out. But he caught himself, swallowed the wine, summoned a broad smile, and replied:

"I would never cheat on you, sweetheart. You don't ever need to worry about that."

"Good, that's a reassuring answer." Lauren had been watching him closely. Now, nodding as if satisfied by his response, she leaned back in her chair, picked up her own wineglass, and savored a sip.

A moment later, their waiter arrived and offered the dessert menu. Kevin could have kissed the guy in gratitude for taking Lauren's attention off him. They fussed over the selections for a bit, then decided to share a slice of cheesecake.

After the waiter departed, Lauren excused herself to visit the ladies' room. Admiring looks followed her across the restaurant. Lauren was the caliber of woman who drew attention everywhere she went.

As he watched her leave, a balloon of tension slowly deflated in Kevin's chest.

He had dodged a bullet. Lauren had nearly trapped him with a classic litigator's tactic: lull him into a false sense of security with a relatively comfortable series of questions—and then suddenly lunge in for the kill with a shocker designed to provoke an immediate reaction of innocence or guilt. He had passed the test.

But it wasn't over yet. The truth was obvious: Lauren *was* suspicious. Something—he didn't know what—had planted a seed of doubt in her mind. She wasn't going to let this slide yet. The woman could be relentless when she wanted to get to the bottom of something, whether it was a crucial legal matter or a problem as ordinary as new charges on their telephone bill. He had always been attracted to her analytical nature—so long as he wasn't the target of her investigations.

Kevin drained the remainder of his wine, the warm alcohol dispersing the tension that had gathered in his gut. He reached for the bottle and found that it was empty. It was just as well. He was in the mood for something much stronger, anyway.

Matter of fact, he was ready to get the hell out of there. The clubby atmosphere was suddenly suffocating. He fidgeted in his seat.

Lauren returned to the table. "You look ready to go."

"Would you mind? We can take the cheesecake with us."

"Sounds good."

Kevin signaled the waiter and asked him to box the dessert in a take-out container, and to bring the check.

Already, he was plotting how he could prevent Lauren from learning the truth.

Chapter 2

After leaving the restaurant, they drove through the trendy Buckhead section of Atlanta in Kevin's Jaguar XK convertible coupe, cruising with the top down, listening to a classic soul station blast out the hits. It was a humid July evening, the kind of night that lured Atlanta's countless freaks out to play. Peachtree Street, Buckhead's main artery, pulsed with decadent life: glittering nightclubs, upscale restaurants, jammed sports bars, sparkling high-end cars—and an endless parade of exposed female flesh that strutted along the sidewalks, drawing the eye of every male in the vicinity.

Kevin ignored the provocatively dressed women flashing past and kept his attention on the road. When he was with his wife, he was *with his wife*. He rarely paid so much as a casual look at another woman. It was a matter of respect.

Lauren was quiet as they drove home. Gazing absently at the passersby, she tapped her fingers to "After the Love is Gone," by Earth, Wind, and Fire. It was an old-school favorite of Kevin's, but he couldn't help wondering if the song might apply to the state of his marriage.

His worries aggravated him. On a night like this, he should have been feeling as if he were on top of the world. He was a successful young black man married to a brilliant, lovely black woman, and they were living a life lifted from the glossy pages of *Ebony*. He'd come a long way from the projects and the rough childhood he'd spent with his crazy, druggie mother and here-today-in-jail-tomorrow father. He had achieved more in his life than anyone, with the exception of his grandmother, had ever expected him to. He should have been basking in his accomplishments, feeling secure in his success.

But he felt only a nagging anxiety that threatened to give him indigestion.

He decided that as soon as they arrived home, he would take preventive measures to regain control of his world.

They lived in a high-rise loft condo in Midtown, located within walking distance of Piedmont Park and within ten minutes of their respective law firms. Like many of the new condos in Midtown, the place had once been a warehouse. Savvy real-estate developers, cashing in on a booming in-town market, had renovated the building into a luxury condominium that attracted a bevy of young professionals who wanted the benefits of urban living.

Kevin pulled into the cavernous underground garage and parked in his assigned slot, next to Lauren's silver BMW sedan. They took the elevator to their unit on the fourth floor.

They had moved into the place a year ago. It was almost two thousand square feet, with soaring ceilings. Hardwood floors. Warm modern furnishings. Pricey vases and sculptures and original pieces of African-American art.

When Lauren shut the door, Kevin took her by the shoulders and pushed her against the wall, right next to their framed engagement photo. He kissed her deeply.

"Ooh, Kevin." Redness bloomed in her cheeks. "What's gotten into you?"

He nibbled on her earlobe, which some women hated, but she loved. As she shivered with pleasure, he whispered: "I want to *show* you how much I love you, baby."

"First, let me get out of these clothes and go take a shower." She began to squirm out of his arms.

He stopped her, slid his hand to the back of her dress. "I'll get you out of these clothes." He found the zipper and smoothly pulled it down. "And there's no point in taking a shower until afterward, 'cause I'm gonna make you sweat."

She laughed, a bit unsteadily. "Oh . . . okay, then."

He lowered his lips to her neck, flicked her skin with his

tongue. He loved the sweet taste of his wife; it lit a fire in him, intensified his desire. He inhaled deeply. She wore a jasmine-like fragrance that was accentuated by her own unique, womanly scent, a delicious combination that made his head swirl.

He rolled her strapless dress down her shoulders, grasped her bra, and easily unhooked it. The bra fell away, revealing her pert breasts, the black berry nipples rigid, ready for his touch and tongue.

Seeing her arousal turned him on more. His erection throbbed eagerly, strained against his slacks.

He smothered her nipples with his mouth, suckled on them hungrily. She arched her back, letting him go deeper.

"You drive me crazy," he whispered. "You know that?"

Moaning, she raked her fingers down his back.

Kevin bent, grabbed her legs, and swept her up into his arms. Lauren was a tall woman, standing five nine without shoes and weighing maybe 140 pounds, but Kevin, with his muscular, six-foot-three physique, carried her easily. Giggling like a schoolgirl, she kicked off her heels. He carried her down the hallway and into the family room. A large picture window offered a panoramic view of the Atlanta skyline, the twinkling, golden lights of the buildings the only illumination in the room.

He laid Lauren on the soft chenille sofa and began to roll her dress down her body.

She looked at the cushions with concern. "Get a towel, honey. I don't want to leave a stain."

"If we stain it, I'll have the fabric treated." He tossed her dress to the floor.

She lay before him wearing only her panties. She covered her breasts with her hands.

Lauren had a gorgeous body. But she disliked being nude. It was one of those things about her that had always puzzled him.

He unbuttoned his shirt and dropped it on top of her dress. He knelt in front of her and buried his face between her breasts. He kissed, sucked, licked, nibbled.

"Hmm." Lauren ran her hands through his close-cropped hair.

Kevin moved his attention from her breasts to the smooth plane of her stomach. He threaded a line of tender kisses down her abdomen, winding up at her panty line—and the moment of truth.

Hesitating for only a second, he grasped the edge of her panties.

"What're you doing?" she asked.

Keep going. I need to do this for her.

He pulled down her panties and leaned forward. Her crisp pubic hairs brushed his nose, and the scent of her moist, eager sex filled his head like the sweetest perfume.

Almost there.

"Kevin!" she said.

He parted his lips and extended his tongue toward her warm center.

One lick and she'll never go back.

"Stop it!" she shouted. She clubbed the side of his head as if he were a misbehaving dog.

He pulled back and rubbed his stinging temple. "Woman, have you lost your damn mind?"

"You know I don't do that nasty stuff!" She pushed off the couch and snatched her dress off the floor. She quickly wrapped herself with it.

"I just wanted to make you feel good," he said.

Disgust contorted her face. "Putting your mouth down there would *not* make me feel good. It's gross, and you know I don't like it!"

Kevin pinched the back of his neck, massaged the muscles that had knotted back there. They'd had this argument before. He had worried that this was going to happen again.

He fell into the rut of repeating the old, tired points.

"How can you know you won't like it if you've never tried it?" he asked.

"Because I *know* I won't like it. It's a turnoff to me. I don't want your mouth on that part of my anatomy, and I'm not putting my mouth on that part of you, either. I've told you that before, Kevin. Why don't you get it?"

"If you'd only be a little more open-minded, willing to explore things, you might discover that you enjoy it."

"No. I'm not going to enjoy it because I'm not going to explore it. Yes, I know, you had this wild, crazy sex life before I came along—"

"Let's not go there."

"—but you knew what I was all about from the start. You know I'm not into any of that kinky stuff. You married me for who I am—not for who you thought you could turn me into."

"Turn you into? What the hell are you talking about?"

"You're trying to turn me into a freak!" she said. "I know all about those whores you used to date before we got together. Those nasty girls who'd do God knows what with you."

"That's history," he said, and glanced away. He picked up his shirt. "Anyway, will you listen to yourself? You sound like a damn nun."

"Wanting to be with my husband in a proper, Christian way makes me sound like a nun?"

He couldn't win this argument. There was no hope of her compromising what she claimed were her Christian beliefs about appropriate bedroom behavior. Lauren's parents had drilled into her brain what good Christian wives did— or did not do—in the marriage bed. Oral sex was not on the list of approved activities.

He might as well be talking to an oak tree.

"I'm not in the mood to debate with you, Lauren. I *was* feeling romantic."

"Shame on me for spoiling the mood, then." She ran her fingers through her hair, shrugged. "Anyway, I'm going to take a shower."

She walked out of the room. Soon after, he heard the patter of the shower in the master bedroom.

So much for his plan. He'd hoped that giving Lauren some oral pleasure would make her feel so good that she would forget all about their conversation at dinner, that she'd be so pleased with him that she would set her worries aside.

He saw his plan now for the foolish notion that it was. Sex could be used to manipulate a lot of women—but not Lauren. She didn't even enjoy sex all that much. She considered sleeping with him to be her wifely duty, like doing the laundry. Nothing more, nothing less.

Kevin slid on his shirt and walked to the wet bar at the edge of the kitchen area. He poured a shot of Hennessey in a snifter. He took a sip; the cognac spread like molten lava throughout his body.

Liquor in hand, he strolled through their home, stopping at the doorway of the master bathroom. Lauren was in the large, beveled-glass shower stall, scrubbing her skin with a sponge. As if she felt filthy.

You knew what I was all about from the start. . . . .

She was telling the truth. He had met Lauren three years ago, at a Christmas party hosted by the Georgia Association of Black Women Attorneys. Struck by her incredible combination of beauty and brains, he'd asked her out to dinner, and on their first date they'd had a frank conversation about sex.

Listen, you need to know something about me up front, she had said. *I'm sexually conservative. It may sound forward of me to tell you this so soon, but I've learned the hard way that it's best to let a man know what I'm all about from the very beginning.* . . .

Her revelation had thrown him for a loop. But he had pursued her anyway, and proposed after only six months. She was a good-hearted woman, a fine wife, and would make a wonderful mother to their future children.

They were great together. Until they entered the bedroom.

Fury burned in his chest, as though a furnace had opened inside him. He wanted to fling his glass against the wall, break something. It was so damn unfair, as if God was playing a cruel joke on him.

He doused his anger with another shot of Hennessey.

He flounced onto the sofa and threw back half the snifter's contents in one gulp. Vertigo spun through him. He closed his eyes and dug his hands into his slacks, touching himself.

Caught up in an erotic fantasy of his wife willingly taking him into her mouth, he fell into an uneasy slumber.

Chapter 3

Sometime later, Lauren tapped his shoulder. He jumped awake, startled.

"What?" he asked, his voice slightly slurred.

"Are you coming to bed?" She wore a long, frilly blue nightgown that left no skin exposed, like something from the Victorian era. "It's a few minutes after one."

He yawned. "I'll be there in a bit. You go ahead to sleep. Happy birthday, baby."

"Okay." She smiled briefly. "I do love you, Kevin, you know. In spite of our differences."

"I love you, too," he said automatically. "Good night."

She bent and kissed him on the cheek, hesitated as if uncertain whether she should do something else, and then walked away, leaving him alone.

Kevin took another sip of Hennessey and gazed out the picture window at the glimmering skyline.

How many people were having great sex in all those buildings out there, at that moment? Or waiting for a hookup?

Or planning a sexcapade?

Although there was a television in the room, he kept it off. He sat on the sofa for several minutes, taking small sips of cognac, contemplating the night and the possibilities it offered for those who desired to take advantage of them.

Then he crept to the bedroom. Lauren was asleep, in her customary sleeping position: on her left side, her back to the doorway, pillow bunched under her shoulder.

Kevin padded down the hall and climbed the staircase to the loft.

As part of their marriage arrangement, Lauren was free to decorate their condo in any manner she wished. Except for the loft. The loft was his private space.

Serving as his home office, den, and workout area, its decor could be best classified as Contemporary Bachelor Pad. It had sandy area rugs and a black leather couch he'd dragged from his old apartment. A weight bench, a barbell, several sets of dumbbells, and plates of heavy weights. A flat-screen TV and a DVD player housed in an entertainment center, the shelves jammed with DVDs of action flicks. A Panasonic turntable, circa 1985, and a milk crate full of vinyl records, most of which he had taken from his mom's house to keep her boyfriends from stealing them and selling them on the street. A funky lava lamp that had once stood on the nightstand in his bedroom; the shimmering red light had bathed the flesh of many a lover.

The lamp now stood on a glass computer desk. He flicked on the light.

He went to the crate of records, pulled out a George Clinton album, and placed it on the turntable. The bass line of "Atomic Dog" began to thump from the Bose speakers. Kevin turned the volume down, so as not to awaken Lauren—but he kept it loud enough to mask the sounds of what he would be doing.

He settled in the leather chair and turned on the laptop computer. Sipped more Hennessey.

He got no pleasure at home. It was time to seek satisfaction. Elsewhere.

Chapter 4

The computer's operating system required a password before allowing access to its programs. Kevin typed in the password—*sexmebaby*—and the display changed to reveal a scene of the neon-drenched Sunset Strip in Las Vegas. Kevin had visited Sin City for his bachelor's party—which took up an entire weekend, actually—and the memory of the trip invariably sent a pulse of bliss through his body.

Oh, the women he'd seen.

Online, Kevin clicked on the FAVORITES tab of his Web browser. He scrolled down to the customized Pro Sports links folder.

A collection of over two dozen dating Web sites appeared: Match.com, BlackPlanet.com, BlackSingles.com, Ebony Connection.com . . . . the list went on.

He concealed the sites within the Pro Sports folder in case Lauren ever gained access to his computer. She disliked sports and would never visit a sports Web site.

A married man enjoying extramarital run could never be too careful.

Kevin picked a Web site that he'd recently begun to frequent: Sexcapades. Although many sites focused on singles seeking marriage partners or monogamous relationships, this particular site was based on a simple concept: giving you an opportunity to explore the freak in you, with those of a like mind. All ethnicities, sexual orientations, and fetishes were represented. Were you a brother with a thing for Asian chicks? They had what you needed. Were you a woman seeking a lesbian orgy? They had the hookup. Did you want someone to beat your ass with a cat-o'-nine tails?

They had it.

Most importantly, confidentiality was guaranteed.

Kevin logged on with his user name—Supershaft— and password, and was taken to his WELCOME screen. A mailbox in the left-hand corner announced that he had three new messages.

Kevin hadn't included a photograph in his profile. But women constantly contacted him, based solely on his bio.

SUPERSHAFT

I'm a 32-yr-old, 6'3" Nubian Prince, with mesmerizing bedroom eyes and lips born to caress female flesh in the tenderest of places. I'm blessed with nine supple inches of chocolate joy that will melt in your mouth and anywhere else you'd like— but only after the night is through and your pleasure is complete. I'd love a walk on the wild side with a compatible female. As one of ATL's rising young professionals, I understand the desire for complete confidentiality.

Kevin clicked on the mailbox to read his e-mails.

The first was from Kitty Cat.

Hey, Supershaft,
Love your profile, baby. Why no pic? I want 2 talk 2U and see what we might like 2 share. Check me out and drop me a line if interested.

Kevin clicked on the link to read Kitty Cat's profile. She'd included a photo. Kitty Cat was a twenty-something white girl who desperately needed sunrays, and had dishwater-blond hair. She wore a black cat suit that wasn't the least bit flattering to her flabby figure, and her hands palmed her 44D breasts.

He was an equal opportunity lover, but she wasn't his type at all.

He deleted the message and opened the next one, from Queen Tee.

Wassup, Superman? I'm a cutie from ATL needn some of that all-night dick you say U got. Holla.

As he read the message, he was frowning. She sounded real street, misspelling his name and tossing around crude language. A little too hood for him. He wasn't into the around-the-way girls anymore, but he checked out her profile anyway.

"Oh, hell no," he said.

Queen Tee was a cocoa-skinned cutie and wore a skimpy red bathing suit that displayed a nice figure, but lurid tattoos covered her skin; she had platinum fronts in her mouth, and her tall, purple-dyed hair looked like a traffic accident.

Delete.

He moved to the last message. It was from Black Venus.

Greetings, Supershaft,

I read your profile with great interest. I'm a thirty-something, professional sister in ATL seeking a brother who is willing and able to explore the, shall we say, forbidden side of sensuality. Do you think you're man enough for the challenge?

One more thing: Like you, because of what I do, privacy is essential.

Kevin was intrigued. She sounded like his kind of woman. A professional sister with a taste for the wild side. Like Lauren without the ice maiden attitude.

His heartbeat picking up speed, he clicked on her profile.

Black Venus didn't have a photo. But she described her appearance: *I'm a tall, beautiful, black goddess with honey-brown eyes and long dark hair. I will not post or send a photograph. I don't have to. You've seen me before—in your dreams.*

Kevin was grinning. She was arrogant as hell. She was either as gorgeous as she claimed to be—or lying her ass off. There was no way to be sure.

As a general rule, he refused to communicate with a woman who wouldn't supply a photo. There were too many liars on the Internet. He'd been burned a couple of times by women who represented themselves as attractive, and had been anything but. He didn't like to waste his time.

But Black Venus had captured his attention. She had a haughty attitude that appealed to him.

He started to hit the REPLY button, and then saw that the ONLINE icon next to her name had lit up, indicating that she was logged on to the site at that very moment.

He clicked the button to send her an Instant Message.

Chapter 5

A small dialogue box appeared in the middle of Kevin's screen.

SUPERSHAFT: Hello, my sister. I see we're both home on a Saturday night.

A few seconds passed, and then she responded.

BLACKVENUS: Yes, I'm home. I'm enjoying a glass of Chardonnay before retiring to bed. You received my message?

SUPERSHAFT: I did. I'm interested. You sound like my kind of woman.

BLACKVENUS: What kind of woman would that be?

SUPERSHAFT: Beautiful, smart, erotic, adventurous. And discreet.

BLACKVENUS: I'm all of those and then some. You'll never meet a woman like me.

SUPERSHAFT: Oh, and I forgot to add, confident. ☺

BLACKVENUS: That's what I like to call it. ☺ So . . . . what are you going to do for me right now? I'm wearing a red silk negligee and this wine has made me tipsy.

Kevin drew another sip of Hennessey. This woman had skipped all of the meaningless small talk that characterized most initial chats, and got right to the point. He liked that.

Heat began to spread through his groin. Tingling, he resumed typing.

SUPERSHAFT: I take you to the bed, slip off your negligee, and massage that long, lovely body of yours with warm scented oils. Stroke away all of your tension and worries and leave you floating on a cloud.

BLACKVENUS: Mmmm. That feels delicious, thank you. Now that you've soothed me, what are you going to do next?

SUPERSHAFT: I turn you onto your back and tongue you down from your temple to your toes.

BLACKVENUS: Oooh, yes, yes.

SUPERSHAFT: I'm tracing my tongue up your body, ever so slowly. I slip my tongue into your warm pussy and savor those sweet juices.

BLACKVENUS: Yes, baby. And they are sweet. Sweet as nectar.

Yes, Kevin was thinking. *Yes, yes, yes.* He unzipped his slacks, dug into his boxers, and caressed his pulsating erection. He had only words on the screen, but his imagination had conjured a dream woman.

SUPERSHAFT: I keep punishing you with my tongue and my lips. You rake your fingers across my head, screaming 'cause it feels so good.

BLACKVENUS: Mmm . . . . so good! But I've got to have a taste of you now. I roll over, push you onto your back, and wrap my lips around your throbbing dick.

SUPERSHAFT: Your lips feel so good, baby. You're a pro at this.

BLACKVENUS: I lick the tip of your dick, lash it like my tongue is a whip, and then I move down and kiss your balls and slowly suck them into my mouth, like lemon drops.

SUPERSHAFT: Damn, you're going to give me a heart attack.

BLACKVENUS: Don't come yet, lover. I'm nowhere near finished with you.

SUPERSHAFT: I'm holding on, baby. I can take whatever you dish out.

BLACKVENUS: Good. Because I'm crawling onto the floor and sticking my juicy ass in the air like a bitch in heat. I want you to hit it. First with a whip, then with your big Mandingo dick.

SUPERSHAFT: Good thing I came prepared with my Indiana Jones bullwhip. I pop that motherfucker against your ass cheeks. WHAP!

BLACKVENUS: Ooohh! Tears are running down my cheeks. Do it again!

SUPERSHAFT: WHAP!

BLACKVENUS: My skin is burning, but oh it feels so wonderful. You know how to put a bitch in her place, baby.

SUPERSHAFT: WHAP!

BLACKVENUS: OOWWW!!!!!!

SUPERSHAFT: I throw the whip down, and now I stab my dick in your ass like a sword. I'm going deep!

BLACKVENUS: Oh, it hurts, it hurts . . . so good . . .

SUPERSHAFT: I'm giving it to you raw, girl, BAM-BAM-BAM, you ain't never had no dick like this, have you?

BLACKVENUS: Never, oooh. My knees are shaking . . . I think . . . I think . . . I'm coming . . .

SUPERSHAFT: I feel my nuts about to blow, too. Oh, shit!

Kevin sat in the chair, breathing hard. A hand towel lay on the corner of the desk, which he'd used earlier to wipe his sweat while exercising. He grabbed the towel and cleaned the sticky mess off his lap.

As good as it had felt, it was a damn shame when a married man had to resort to cybersex to get his rocks off. He could only imagine what Lauren would think about what he'd done. Not that she would ever find out.

He drained the last of his Hennessey. Another message appeared in the dialogue box.

BLACKVENUS: I really enjoyed that. Thank you.

SUPERSHAFT: Ditto.

BLACKVENUS: Your performance has earned you a reward.

SUPERSHAFT: Reward?

BLACKVENUS: Check your mailbox.

A new message appeared in Kevin's in-box. It was from Black Venus.

It was a photo of a woman, from the neck down, lying sideways on a plush, red chaise longue in front of a backdrop that resembled scrolling white clouds. She wore a black lace teddy and stilettos. She had bronze skin so smooth it appeared to be polished, and a long, slender body. Her breasts were perfect, her waist was taut, and her legs were the stuff of fantasies.

Even though Kevin had just experienced an orgasm, he felt himself getting aroused all over again.

SUPERSHAFT: Is that you?

BLACKVENUS: Yes. It's 100% me, no airbrushing or alterations of any kind—excluding cropping my head out of the shot, for obvious privacy purposes. ☺

SUPERSHAFT: Wow. You're stunning.

BLACKVENUS: Thank you. I rarely share photos with online friends . . . but I have a good feeling about you.

SUPERSHAFT: I appreciate it. One good turn deserves another. Hold on a sec.

He opened a folder on his hard drive. He happened to have a similarly head-cropped shot of him sitting on a Kawasaki motorcycle, wearing an Atlanta Hawks jersey and shorts, his muscles oiled up and pumped. He sent it to her.

BLACKVENUS: You're quite a specimen. My, my, my. You've cut off the head, too—how funny.

SUPERSHAFT: Like I say, discretion is vital.

BLACKVENUS: Do you still have your bike?

SUPERSHAFT: Yep. Ride it every weekend. Wouldn't give it up for anything.

BLACKVENUS: Maybe you can take me for a ride someday?

SUPERSHAFT: That could be arranged. In the very near future.

BLACKVENUS: I'll get back to you on that tomorrow. I'm exhausted. See, your loving was so strong you put a sister to sleep. ©

SUPERSHAFT: Have a good night. I'll expect your message tomorrow.

BLACKVENUS: You'll get it. Night.

Black Venus went offline. Sighing, Kevin closed the dialogue box.

He returned to the e-mail and studied her picture.

If that was really her in the photo . . . . he couldn't bear to think of it. The thought was almost painfully exciting.

A woman like her could get a married man in serious trouble.

Chapter 6

After concluding her online chat, the woman logged off the Web site and sat in her leather chair for several minutes, sipping Chardonnay and studying the photo of Supershaft that she had downloaded to her hard drive.

Supershaft . . . . aka Kevin Richmond.

She smirked.

Kevin's body looked fantastic. Although he had cropped his head out of the photo, she would never forget his handsome face, either.

His face had haunted her for years.

She turned off the computer. It was time to unplug and deal with the real world for a while.

But oh, how she enjoyed the Internet games. She'd introduced herself to Kevin as Black Venus, but on other dating sites she was known as Man Eater, Sweet Temptation, Ebony Queen, Princess Africa. Different handles for different purposes.

Her real name was Eve Kennedy.

Eve pushed away from the desk and stretched, her red silk negligee swaying over her glorious body. She was wearing the same garment that she'd told Kevin she had on during their cybersex session. She never lied about herself.

Her two dogs, roused by her movement, yawned and pulled themselves to their feet. They were Presa Canario hounds, male, muscular, and full-bodied, their thick heads reaching her waist. The canines, descendants of Roman war hounds, were singularly fierce and loyal companions. One dog, white, was named Snow; the other one, black, was Storm.

Snow and Storm watched her, their dark eyes curious.

Eve glanced at the ornate wall clock hanging on the other side of her study. It was almost two o'clock. Almost time for bed.

But first, she had to complete a household task. She left the study and went to the bedroom, the dogs trotting dutifully behind her.

She lived in the Grant Park neighborhood of Atlanta, in an old, rambling Victorian that she'd furnished to meet her tastes. The house offered five spacious bedrooms and hardwood floors. She'd filled it with rosewood furniture, and colors in lush reds, burgundies, and blacks. She preferred dark tones: they were sensual, mysterious, powerful. Like her.

In her bedroom, she wrapped herself in a Merlot-tinged robe, slid on a pair of soft Burberry slippers, and padded downstairs, to the kitchen.

She stored two brands of dog food in the expansive pantry, each sealed in large plastic containers: a cheap brand, and a special, designer food. While Snow and Storm watched her, licking their chops, Eve filled a large plastic bowl with the generic kibble and took it to the basement door at the end of the kitchen.

"I'll feed you afterward, boys," she said, and the dogs wagged their tails eagerly.

The stone-walled cellar below was dark and smelled like every bit of the house's eighty years. She liked it that way. Like a dungeon.

She turned on the light—the staircase was lit by a single, bare bulb—and wound her way down the wooden steps.

Boxes of junk—stuff that belonged to the prior owner—sat in the shadows, draped in cobwebs and dust. A red door stood in a far corner of the basement, barely visible in the murk. She took a set of keys from the hook on the wall and unlocked the double dead bolt.

The chamber contained an iron cage, large enough to confine a man.

The stench of feces and urine blew out of the black, enclosed space. There was a mutter; then, shuffling feet.

Flanking her, Snow and Storm growled deep in their broad chests.

Eve knelt and dumped the dog food into a metal bowl that was bolted to the iron bars, close to the floor.

There was a thin cry of hunger or anguish-—she wasn't sure which—and then the noise of flesh hitting the stone floor, and nails scrabbling forward.

Eve stepped back, swung the door shut, and engaged the lock.

But she could hear, faintly, the crunching and snapping of frenzied eating.

Dog food for a dog.

Her canines following her obediently, Eve returned upstairs. While her dogs ate their expensive kibble, she soaked in the large, claw foot tub in the master bathroom. There was nothing like a bubble bath at the end of a long day.

She slid her fingers to her pussy and lovingly stroked herself.

She thought about Kevin.

She couldn't wait to finally meet him again.

Chapter 7

Before heading to bed, Kevin took a long, hot shower. He had to rinse off the fuck-funk, as one of his brief, live-in exes had called it. That girl was so jealous that sometimes when he would come home in the evenings, she would run her nose across his genitals as if she were a cat sniffing for a mouse. She said that if he ever cheated, she would smell another woman's scent on him. He'd cheated on her plenty of times, but her nose never found him out—because he was careful to clean himself thoroughly after the deed was done.

Sweet and innocent Lauren, of course, wouldn't dare put her face "down there," but he showered all the same. Old habits died hard.

Finishing his shower, he shuffled into the dark bedroom, bare-chested and wearing silk boxers. He liked to sleep in the nude, especially in the sultry Georgia summers, but that bothered Lauren. She'd expressed concern about brushing against him in the middle of the night and feeling private parts that she didn't want to explore without being wide awake.

Lauren, baby, what am I going to do with you?

Standing beside the bed, Kevin watched her sleep, her features revealed in the soft lights trickling through the window. His heart stuttered. Awake or asleep, her flawless face resembled a porcelain doll's.

Kevin wished he were the kind of man who could be faithful to one woman. Lauren deserved a man who would be committed to her, mind, body, and soul—the holy trinity of fidelity. He gave Lauren his mind and soul, but not his body.

She didn't want his body the way he wanted to give it to her. And he'd learned, over the years, that he was *unable* to pledge his flesh to a single woman.

His appetite for sex was too strong.

He'd been introduced to the world of sex at the age of thirteen. Tawanda, a chocolate beauty who lived next door, had been his tour guide. Although Tawanda was only fifteen, she had the body and sexual experience of a woman ten years older—and she was insatiable. During the summer that they hooked up, they spent hours rolling on the twin bed in her family's basement, her teaching him about a female, showing him what felt good to her, and then having her way with him, giving him blow jobs and coaxing him into countless positions. His experiences with Tawanda opened his eyes to the vast array of carnal pleasures, and he began to view every attractive girl as a potential conquest.

By the end of the summer, he was cheating on her.

Tawanda loved sex so much she was probably a nymphomaniac, but now that she'd awakened his appetite, he hungered for a taste of something different, something new.

His love for various female flavors had followed him throughout high school, college, his twenties, and into his current life as a thirty-two-year-old married man. An ever-evolving medley of sexual adventures kept life fresh, interesting. Like dining at a gourmet restaurant at which the menu changed daily.

Monogamy, on the other hand, was the equivalent of eating Hamburger Helper every day for the rest of your life.

Kevin got into bed beside Lauren. He kissed her shoulder. She turned away and burrowed deeper in the sheets—rejecting him even in her sleep.

Sighing, he rolled onto his back and laced his fingers behind his head, gazing at the shadowed, hand-textured ceiling.

He could never tell Lauren the truth. In his past relationships, he'd sometimes told his girlfriends about his sexual preferences, that even though he was with them, he had to see other women in order to satisfy his needs. His revelation had ended a couple of relationships—but other girlfriends were actually cool with it. In a city like Atlanta, where the ratio of black women to black men (straight men) was rumored to be ten to one, man-sharing was a concept that a lot of sisters embraced, so long as their needs were being met. He always explained that his affairs were based strictly on sex, not love. He reserved his love for the main lady in his life.

But that argument would never fly with Lauren. She viewed sex and love as inextricably linked. Sex, in her mind, was the celebration of the union between a husband and wife, and should be practiced solely in the marriage bed. No exceptions.

Yet for all her high-minded talk, Lauren had not been a virgin when they'd married. She had experience; there were times when he sensed that she had a whole *lot* of experience actually, and that she was holding back on him out of some misguided notion that being freaky with her husband was dirty. There were depths to her that he yearned to explore, but he didn't dig for details.

If he pressed her, then she would inquire about his background, too, and he didn't want to tell her more than she already knew. Earlier that night, she'd made a caustic reference to his "wild" sex life, based on a few details he'd told her when they had begun dating, and he regretted that he'd ever disclosed anything.

The less Lauren knew about his secret life, the better.

Chapter 8

Lauren was awake, pretending to be asleep, when Kevin finally came to bed.

Earlier, she had tiptoed out of the bedroom and into the hallway. She'd heard Kevin in the loft, playing a George Clinton record. She caught, underneath the music, the sound of his fingers clacking against the keyboard, in quick staccato bursts.

He was either working, or surfing the Internet for leisure. She was willing to wager that the latter was true. He was a hard worker, but he wasn't that fanatically committed to his job.

Why would a married man be awake at two o'clock in the morning, cruising the Web for fun?

She had her theories.

Lauren was not a jealous woman; a jealous woman would not have been able to endure a marriage to a man like Kevin. Kevin was gorgeous, charismatic, successful, well-mannered, the kind of man women desired to bring home to their daddies. With all of the brazen sisters out there in ATL, she would've been a fool to think that Kevin wasn't regularly tempted to stray from the marriage bed.

And she knew his past. When they'd begun dating, she'd asked around about him; Atlanta, for all its millions of residents, was a small city in many ways, and very cliquish. With access to the same network of black professionals of which Kevin was a member, she'd found out that he was a straight-up playa from the Himalayas. Her girlfriends had warned her to stay away from him.

But she'd stayed with him anyway, and married him, too. She'd thought she could change him, thought she could make him a one-woman man.

After all, *she* had changed. She was no longer the wild party girl she'd been in her late teens and early twenties, when she had driven her parents crazy. As she'd neared thirty, she realized that if she wanted to settle down, marry, and have a family, she would have to give up running the streets. She'd assumed that she could tone down Kevin, too.

A few days ago, she learned that she was deluding herself.

She'd come home after a long day at the office, tired and wanting to do nothing but fall into bed. Already home, Kevin was watching a Braves game and drinking a beer. She went into the bedroom to change clothes, and while she was in their large, walk-in closet she found a small cell phone lying on the carpet, underneath a row of Kevin's business suits.

She picked it up, examined it.

It wasn't Kevin's primary cell phone, the one he used for taking calls from her and his family and friends. And it wasn't his work cell, either.

She opened the lid. Pushed a button.

But the phone was locked and could be accessed only with a code.

Lauren put the phone back on the floor, exactly where she'd found it. She undressed and went to take a shower.

When she returned to the closet afterward, the phone was gone.

Kevin, realizing that he'd dropped the phone on the floor, had apparently put it away somewhere.

Lauren didn't say anything about it. The seed of suspicion had been planted, and questioning him about the phone would only have forced him to concoct a possible lie.

There were much better ways to get to the truth.

Beside her, Kevin began to snore softly.

She looked over her shoulder at him, this gorgeous man, her husband, whom she loved with all her heart.

Soon, it would be time to put her theories to the test. Soon, it would be time to find out the truth.

And take whatever measures were necessary.

Chapter 9

The next morning, Kevin and Lauren went to church.

They attended Rebirth Baptist, located in the southwest suburb of East Point. Like many black churches in metro Atlanta, Rebirth was a megachurch, boasting fifteen thousand members and a church campus that sprawled across two hundred acres. Services took place in a magnificent, domed cathedral that had the capacity to accommodate ten thousand worshippers.

Rebirth was a world away from the cramped, crumbling chapel that Kevin's grandma had used to drag him to every Sunday when he was a kid, a dusty place full of sad-faced poor folk and old people suffering from debilitating ailments. An impressive slice of Atlanta's black elite attended Rebirth: lawyers, physicians, executives, entrepreneurs, entertainers, athletes. The senior pastor, a self-proclaimed bishop, had been voted one of the most influential black people in America by *Ebony,* and was a frequent guest at the White House.

For a man with upper-class aspirations, Rebirth was the place to be. Kevin had begun attending when he graduated from Emory Law School, when he finally felt *qualified to* attend. Joining had been a savvy career move; he'd snagged a load of lucrative clients there, heavy hitters who felt comfortable doing business with a fellow Christian.

As he drove to the church, he and Lauren didn't speak much, music playing on the local gospel station the only sound in the car. Last night's disagreement hung over them like a mushroom cloud. He was hopeful that attending church would improve his wife's mood, as it usually did. He hated conflict between them.

Kevin swung his Jaguar coupe into the enormous parking lot at a quarter after ten, fifteen minutes before the start of the next service. A sea of sparkling luxury automobiles surrounded him. He found a parking space, grabbed his leather Bible case, and climbed out of the car, smoothing down the jacket of his tailored Armani suit. Then he went to the passenger door and helped Lauren out.

In a flowing peach dress that fell just below the knee, Lauren was stunning. Although Rebirth wasn't her family church—that would be an old, tiny chapel in Savannah, where she grew up—she fit right in here with the beautiful people, as if she'd been a member all her life.

They streamed inside the cathedral, exchanging cheerful greetings of "Good morning, praise God," as they moved along, and found their regular pew seats near the front of the gigantic sanctuary, toward the end of the aisle. Even in a church as large as this one, people tended to sit in the same spot every Sunday.

In the minutes before the service officially began, while Lauren busied herself filling out a check for their monthly tithe, Kevin casually looked around at all of the stylishly attired women.

Some of the sexiest freaks in the city went to church, and this one, especially. Hoping to collar a man of means and get her praise on at the same time. It was common to see the same female who bounced her assets at a strip club on Saturday night jumping for Jesus on Sunday morning. Or to run across a Bible-toting woman who'd posted a tantalizing photo and naughty profile on a dating Web site.

Kevin had used to regularly fish the church waters for sexual partners, but since he'd been married, he'd had to cut that out. He had to maintain a measure of discretion.

But it was so hard to keep from looking. These sisters *were fine.*

"Is this seat taken?"

Startled by the familiar voice, Kevin looked up.

An ebony-hued woman in a yellow dress had appeared in the aisle beside his seat. She gave him a friendly smile. She had lustrous, shoulder-length braids and the fit, sculpted body of a dancer.

Although she was gorgeous, Kevin's insides recoiled. He *knew* her.

He was about to tell her that the seat was taken, but his voice caught in his throat.

"Have a seat," Lauren answered, face sunny. She'd finished sealing the check in the offering envelope and had been studying her Bible, her mind on things above, not concerns about attractive, single women sitting next to her husband.

"Thank you," the woman said, and settled into the seat. He smiled tightly at her. What was her name? Vivian, Vanessa? He couldn't remember. It had been months since their encounter—several women ago.

Her perfume engulfed him like a fog. It was a familiar fragrance—Coco Chanel—and though he couldn't recall her name, he suddenly remembered his experience with her. Initially meeting on the Internet, they'd arranged their rendezvous at the Westin, downtown. They'd enjoyed three hours of hot, invigorating sex. She had wanted to see him again, he seemed to recall, but he had brushed her off—he rarely saw the same woman twice. He couldn't risk forming an emotional attachment to these women, and vice versa.

Hopefully, she wasn't mad at him. Maybe she didn't remember him.

But he doubted that. A woman usually remembered a man with whom she had shared her body.

Humming a gospel hymn, the woman had opened one of those Bible study workbooks on her lap, and started writing on a blank page. She nudged him slightly with her elbow.

Frowning, he glanced at what she had written.

Hey, stranger. It's Valerie, remember? Is that your wife? Tap your knee once for yes, twice for no.

Valerie, that was right. She was a dance instructor.

Looking away, Kevin rapped his knee once with the palm of his hand.

Valerie scribbled more words: *You said you weren't married. But that was a little while ago. Maybe you settled down with her after you and I met?*

Cold sweat matted his forehead. He didn't like this line of questioning.

He tapped his knee once.

I think about you a lot. I don't care if you're married. I want to see you again.

Here we go, Kevin thought. Could there have been a worse time for this?

He glanced at Lauren. She was involved in a chatty conversation with an older woman seated next to her.

Kevin tapped his knee twice.

Valerie wrote: *I can do you better than she ever could.*

Her words sent a charge of desire through his veins. She was telling the truth. Sex with her had been mind-blowing. She'd done things Lauren refused to do—and done them exceedingly well.

But he couldn't knowingly get involved with a woman who attended the same church. He already had to dodge enough women here.

He hit his knee twice.

But she wrote, quickly: *Let me change your mind. Meet me at the back of the bookstore in five minutes.*

Before he could respond, she had gotten out of her seat and was striding away down the aisle.

Kevin drew a short breath, looked around. A young man in a bright blue suit was approaching the podium. He was the worship leader.

Service was about to begin, an electric current rippling through the congregation.

"Hallelujah!" the worship leader proclaimed in a booming voice. "It's a blessing to be in the house of the Lord this morning!"

The massive video displays mounted above the stage flashed

images of cherubim and white doves, the band—the church had a ten-piece band, like a group performing at an arena—struck up a much-loved praise song, and the hundred-member choir let loose an opening chorus that shook the rooftops and brought the congregation to its feet.

Lauren leaped out of her seat and applauded, too, crying out praise in a high-pitched voice that exceeded any shriek of pleasure she'd ever released in their bedroom.

Kevin sat still, unmoved. He was thinking about Valerie. His dick stiffened.

Let me change your mind . . .

As the crowd began to clap and sing along with the choir, Kevin murmured in Lauren's ear that he had to use the men's room, and then he slipped out of the sanctuary.

Chapter 10

Walking to the church bookstore, Kevin greeted several people who knew him. Among his many duties at the church, he was one of the leaders of the men's ministry, which gave him a high level of visibility in the congregation. A lot of people there either knew him personally or knew of him.

Which was another reason why he should avoid another encounter with Valerie. If she regularly attended Rebirth, it could present a problem to his image—to say nothing of the danger to his marriage.

He entered the Sow a Seed Bookstore. "Sow a seed" was one of the bishop's popular catch phrases about tithing and planting spiritual seeds that would be harvested later as material prosperity. The good bishop himself was a busy gardener: His dozen or so books and DVDs were featured throughout the store, ensuring a continuous reaping of wealth.

Kevin looked near the back. Valerie, standing near a door, waved at him.

He walked to her. "Hey, we need to talk."

Putting her finger to her lips, she ushered him inside and closed the door behind him. Books and boxes of books were piled everywhere. She led him to a dimly lit comer, where a folding chair sat against the wall.

"Hey, baby," she finally said, and hugged him, pressing her firm breasts against his chest. "I've missed you. It's been almost six months."

"Are you a member here?"

She nodded. "I've been going here for two years. I'm the assistant manager of the bookstore, part-time."

"I had no idea," Kevin said. But visiting the church bookstore wasn't exactly high on his list of priorities.

"I usually attend the seven o'clock service," she said. "That's probably why you've never seen me. Besides, this is a huge church, you know."

"Still, a lot of people here know me, Valerie. They know I'm married."

"And?" She reached for his belt buckle.

He didn't stop her, but he said, "I can't fool around with another church member. Even one as fine as you."

"Uh-huh, that's what your mouth says. But your little friend here is saying something else."

She slid his slacks down his legs. His erection throbbed at the seams of his boxers.

He glanced at his watch. "I told my wife I was going to the men's room. I've gotta get back."

"Three minutes," Valerie said. She pressed him into the folding chair, and knelt in front of him. "That's all the time we need to get reacquainted, baby."

She rolled down his boxers and took his dick in her mouth, hungrily. In seconds, he was gasping, his legs trembling. Valerie drew him in and out, skillfully using her tongue and lips to caress his shaft and crown, making soft, mewling sounds of pleasure as she worked him.

"Jesus," he breathed. He grasped her braids as if they were handlebars. He came hard, the orgasm buckling through him like a deep earth tremor, and Valerie held him between her lips still, sucking down his juices.

He shuddered, the aftereffects of the climax slowly subsiding.

Why couldn't Lauren do something like that for him?

Sighing, Kevin finally withdrew. She opened her purse and handed him a tissue. He cleaned himself, then rose and quickly snatched up his boxers and slacks, while she popped a Tic Tac in her mouth and reapplied her lipstick.

"That was great," he said. "Thank you."

"Told you." She smirked. "I want to see you again."

"I don't think we can do that."

"We did it before."

"That was before I knew we went to the same church."

"We can work it out. I can be discreet. I know you can, too— like you were the first time."

She'd probably known then that he was married. Maybe she had seen him around church, asked around about him. Women could be sly.

"I can't talk about this right now, okay?" he said. "I have to get back to my seat."

He hurried out of there, ignoring the hurt stamped on her face. He'd been up front with her. It wasn't his fault that she refused to play by the rules.

He reached his seat as the worship leader was leading the choir into yet another song. The praise and worship segment was a major part of the service at Rebirth, orchestrated with all the flair and energy of a Kirk Franklin concert. Lauren was clapping her hands and singing, beaming with joy.

She glanced at him when he came to stand beside her. There was a question in her eyes. *What took you so long?*

"My stomach was upset," he muttered, by way of explanation, and rubbed his belly.

Lauren turned back to the stage.

A couple of minutes later, Valerie returned to her seat beside him. She studiously avoided looking at him, for which he was grateful. Lauren wasn't a fool. Given a clue, she could put two and two together, and the sum would *be fucked,* for him.

He had to keep the truth about his sex life hidden from Lauren, no matter what.

But halfway through service, as the bishop was preaching, ironically, about avoiding temptations of the flesh, Kevin glanced at Valerie's Bible workbook and saw that she had written another message.

You know you want some again. I'll let you hit it from the back. I put my number in your pocket. Call me, okay?

He fished inside his pocket, felt the card she must have inserted in there while his head had been thrown back with ecstasy. Lust spread through him.

He shouldn't call her. But he probably would. Just as he shouldn't—but probably would—hook up with Black Venus sometime soon.

He couldn't help it.

He looked at Valerie, caught her eye, and tapped his knee one time.

Chapter 11

The worship service concluded around twelve-thirty. Kevin took Lauren's hand and guided her out of the sanctuary, doing his best to ignore Valerie's luscious form as she disappeared in the crowd—but not before she threw a glance over her shoulder and winked.

He was already missing her. Well, his body was, anyway.

In the lobby outside the sanctuary, cliques were forming. Businessmen chatting with other money-minded folk; sisters talking to other sisters; married couples communing with others. Men and women were busy hooking up, too, exchanging phone numbers and cards. Churches had surpassed nightclubs as the best place to arrange a tryst.

"Wait, I see Charmaine over there," Lauren said, signaling at one of her sorors. "I'll be back."

"Meet me outside in fifteen," Kevin said. Lauren would be talking with her friends for at least that long. It was a post-church ritual.

"Brother Kevin!" a baritone voice boomed, behind him. A heavy hand fell on Kevin's shoulder.

Kevin knew that voice; he turned. Oliver Holmes, head of the men's ministry and his longtime mentor, grinned at him.

"Morning, Oliver," Kevin said.

They shook hands. Oliver gave him a bone-crusher handshake, as he always did.

In his late fifties, Oliver was a stout, barrel-chested man, six two, with maple-brown skin, a wide, clean-shaven face, and a round head as hairless as a bowling ball. He wore a blue

The Last Affair

Brooks Brothers suit and wire-rim glasses. His eyes danced behind the lenses. Oliver had the youthful exuberance of a man half his age, and the bright orange tie he wore with the conservative suit was a nod to his flair for drama, for the unexpected.

Not only was Oliver the leader of the men's ministry, but he was, more importantly to Kevin, a senior partner at the corporate law firm at which both of them worked, specializing in mergers and acquisitions—Kevin's concentration as well. Because of Oliver's campaigning on Kevin's behalf, Kevin was on track to make partner by year's end.

"Did you enjoy the bishop's sermon today?" Oliver asked. "Avoiding temptations of the flesh?"

Kevin nodded. "It was deep. Gave me food for thought."

Kevin and Oliver had frequent discussions about the challenges of being a married man. Oliver, widowed five years ago, had been married to the same woman for over twenty years. He'd confided to Kevin that in the early days of his marriage, it had been difficult to resist the temptations of other women. While he'd never confessed to cheating on his wife, Kevin concluded that he probably had. He was a man, after all, and in Kevin's opinion, it was damn near impossible for a virile man to be one hundred percent faithful.

Still, Oliver's admittance of the weakness of his flesh, in his youth, had prompted Kevin to share his own ideas about the importance of a man satisfying his sexual needs. Kevin hadn't told Oliver that he had ever cheated on Lauren, but Oliver wasn't a fool.

"It's important to do the right thing, Brother Kevin," Oliver said. "Isn't always easy—matter of fact, it's much *easier* to sin. But the Lord doesn't give us a burden that we can't handle. We need only admit that we need His guidance."

"Amen to that," Kevin said, absently, his gaze on a shapely sister who was strutting past.

"Amen to what?" Oliver asked.

Kevin blinked. "What you just said."

"You weren't listening to me! Can you pry your eyes from

64

God's beautiful creations for just one moment?" Oliver's thunderous laugh echoed down the corridor, drawing looks from passersby. Oliver was loud and theatrical, at church and at work. Before pursuing a law career, he'd taught drama classes in high school and been a regular on Atlanta's theater scene, which Kevin found easy to believe—Oliver reminded him a lot of James Earl Jones.

Sweeping his arm forward, Oliver placed his hand on Kevin's shoulder and drew him closer. He lowered his voice, conspiratorially. "How's your mother?"

Kevin was so startled by the abrupt change in the topic of conversation that he nearly flinched.

"Um. Well, Mom is all right."

Oliver's gaze probed him. Kevin fidgeted and glanced away, looking for Lauren. He was suddenly ready to leave.

"When was the last time you spoke to her?" Oliver asked.

"About a month ago, I guess."

Oliver gave him a withering look. *You're a pathetic excuse for a son,* that look said. *And you need to do better.*

Oliver's opinion meant a lot to him. More than any other man's, to be honest. In the seven years that Kevin had known him, Oliver had become the closest thing he'd ever had to a father.

"Honor thy parents," Oliver said. "Sometimes, that can be one of the toughest scriptures in the entire Bible to abide by."

"Maybe I'll go see her this afternoon," Kevin said.

"I'm sure she'd appreciate that."

"She won't, but . . ." Kevin looked away, shrugged. "I don't want to talk about that right now."

Oliver nodded, but didn't push it further; he'd made his point. His cell phone rang—a ring tone with an old Isley Brothers song, "That Lady." He leaned back and dug into his jacket pocket to retrieve the phone.

"Who's that lady?" Kevin asked, and chuckled. Was Oliver dating again? As far as Kevin knew, he hadn't seen a woman since his wife had died.

"That's a private matter, brother," Oliver said with a sly grin.

"I need to take this call. I'll see you at the office tomorrow."

"Enjoy the rest of the weekend," Kevin said, as Oliver slipped away to answer the phone. Now that he'd mentioned going to visit his mother—which Oliver would question him about at work tomorrow—he knew he wasn't going to enjoy the rest of his weekend at all.

Even after all these years, the thought of his mother had the power to instantly make him miserable.

Chapter 12

Driving home, Kevin told Lauren that he was going to visit his mother that afternoon. Lauren cocked her head, eyebrows arched, and studied him intently.

"Are you sure you're in the mood?" she asked.

"No," he admitted. "But it's time that I go. It's been a while."

He'd lied to Oliver, told him it had been a month since he'd seen his mother—when in truth it had been close to three months.

Lauren touched his leg. "Want me to go with you?"

"Nah." He shook his head. "I'd hate to start your week on a sour note."

Lauren nodded, and appeared relieved. She tolerated his mom only because of him. Mom despised Lauren, or, as she called her, "that high-yella heifer who thinks she's better than us." Lauren, demonstrating the patience of Job and the compassion of Mother Teresa, tried to be nice to his mother, but their encounters wore her down. He didn't see any purpose in putting Lauren through that kind of stress today.

Besides, without Lauren's presence, he wouldn't have to mince words when he spoke to his mother, could be as direct as he needed to be without worrying that Lauren would think less of him afterward. She didn't understand his relationship with his mother. How could she, when she adored her own parents and they, in turn, treated her like a little princess?

They didn't speak much during the rest of the drive. Kevin pulled into the condo's underground garage and parked in front of the bank of elevators.

"I'm going to change clothes and go grocery shopping while you're gone," Lauren said. "What would you like for dinner?"

Food held no interest for him at the moment. "Whatever you feel like cooking is fine with me."

"When will you be home?"

He glanced at his watch; it was a quarter after one. "No later than five."

"Then dinner will be ready by five-thirty." Lauren kissed him quickly, opened her door. "Say hello to your mother for me."

"Sure."

He watched Lauren stroll to the elevator, the dress caressing her beautiful body, her long auburn hair swaying across her shoulders. He felt a sudden awakening of lust; he wanted to follow her inside, rip her dress away, bend her over, and give it to her from behind, rough and sweaty and raw. She'd never had sex like that with him. Sex with her had always been planned out, choreographed, conservative, *dull*.

If she'd only let him do things his way. Just once.

Kevin put the thought out of his mind.

There was no point dwelling on a fantasy that would never come true.

* * *

Walking away from Kevin's car, Lauren restrained the compulsion to dash to the elevator, and run like she would in her old high school track days.

But she had to hurry. She didn't have much time.

When she stepped into their condo, it was twenty past one, and she had to have dinner on the table by five-thirty.

That gave her only a few hours to take care of business.

She'd been counting on Kevin being away from home after church. On Sunday afternoons, he would often meet his friends for nine holes of golf, go. to a sports bar to catch a football game when the NFL was in season, or ride his motorcycle around town.

Or so he'd claim.

She had her own theories about where he would really go. It was time to begin testing them.

She kicked off her heels and removed a business card from her purse. Studying the number, she dialed it on her cell phone.

A man answered on the second ring. "Mosley Investigative Services."

"It's me, Lauren Richmond," she said. Although she was alone in their condo, she spoke in a whisper. "My husband is away for a few hours. How fast can you get here?"

"I'll be there within the hour."

Lauren glanced up at the loft, where Kevin kept his laptop computer.

"Perfect," she said.

Chapter 13

Kevin's mother lived in a three-story brick town house in Cabbagetown, an in-town Atlanta neighborhood on the rise. The streets were clean, the cars parked in front of the residences were shiny late models, and the landscaping was meticulously maintained. It better have been, or else he would have complained to the homeowners' association.

The deed for the town house was in his name. He had purchased the place for his mother three years ago. He paid the mortgage, the utilities, the insurance, the association fees, the maintenance—everything.

A Ford sedan was parked in the driveway. Kevin had bought the car, too. However, he had secretly hoped that the car would be gone, that his mother would be out running wild. Then he could have said, *I tried to visit her, but she wasn't home.*

But she was here. No easy way out this time.

He parked in front of the house, shut off the car, sighed heavily. After waiting in the car for a minute or two, he finally got out and shuffled down the walkway toward the front door.

A trail of old, wrapped newspapers cluttered the path, like a line of bread crumbs, their headlines announcing old news. Kevin bent and picked them up as he trudged forward. He dumped them on the porch beside the front door, near a potted plant that had wilted from lack of watering and sunlight. Lauren had bought the plant for his mother last year, he remembered. A peace offering of a sort.

His mother's neglect of the plant made it clear how she

viewed Lauren.

Kevin rang the doorbell.

A minute passed. No answer.

He thought of turning on his heels and leaving. *I rang the doorbell, but Mom didn't answer.*

But he knew better.

He turned the doorknob. The door wasn't locked; it opened.

Even when they had lived in one of Atlanta's roughest neighborhoods, Mom routinely neglected to lock the door. They hadn't owned anything worth stealing, really, and much of what they owned Mom had stolen from someone else, or one of her druggie boyfriends had. They lived on stolen goods.

He'd been happy to leave that sordid life behind and move in with his grandmother.

But this wasn't a shitty crib in the hood. This was an upscale town house, full of valuable items that he had bought. She needed to lock the doors, damn it.

He hadn't talked to his mother yet, and already he had something to argue with her about.

He stepped inside the shadowed foyer. It was humid, the heavy air redolent with the stench of spoiled food, garbage.

"Mom, it's Kevin," he said. "Where are you?"

He heard voices upstairs, then a thump. He mounted the staircase and ascended to the second floor.

The second floor had a living room, kitchen, sunroom, and dining area. Old papers, plastic bags, overflowing ashtrays, and fast-food wrappers were strewn everywhere, covering the nice contemporary furniture, sitting atop the coffee table and even the television. The television was on, tuned to a local gospel channel, a pastor hammering the pulpit, screaming about redemption.

As Kevin approached the TV to turn it off, he saw a couple of roaches scurrying into the shadows.

His stomach convulsed.

Roaches infesting a two-hundred-thousand-dollar town home. It was inexcusable.

"Where are you, Mom?" he called.

He heard water running, a toilet flushing. He took the steps to the third level, where the master bedroom was located. The door was cracked open.

He knocked. "Mom, it's me, Kevin." He pushed open the door.

The large room was full of shadows. His mother, Anita, was sitting up in the king-size poster bed, knotting a green house robe around her thin body. The bed-sheets were tangled, and a funky, male odor hit Kevin's nostrils that told him his mother wasn't here alone.

But was she ever? Mom always had a man around. Growing up with her, he recalled an endless procession of boyfriends, dudes who'd move into their place with only a garbage bag full of clothes and a mouthful of sweet talk. Mom would fall for them every time.

"Hey, baby," Mom said. She had a ragged, smoker's voice. She scratched her head. Her hair was a wild mess. "What you doing here?"

Although most days, Kevin wished that he had no blood connection whatsoever to this woman sitting in front of him, there was no denying that they were mother and son. He had her features, her soft brown complexion. She had once been an extremely attractive woman—before the drugs and the sorry men had ruined her. Mom was in her early fifties, but hard living had added fifteen or twenty years to her body.

"I came to see how you were doing," he said.

"Hmph." She reached for a pack of Newports on the nightstand, slid one out, lit it, took a pull. "You can't just be showing up here unannounced, boy. You needs to phone first. I got company."

"You always have company, and you never answer the phone."

"Who you talking to like that?" Her gaze sharpened like a knife. "What I do is my business."

Because what his mother did was "her business," and because "her business" had interfered with her desire to be a capable mother, Kevin's grandma had offered to take over raising him. He'd gone to live with her when he was thirteen. It had been the best thing that had ever happened to him.

Before she passed, Grandma had counseled him not to hate his mother, would say that his mother had a weakness for bad men and destructive behavior, the same way others had a weakness for alcohol or caffeine. Kevin understood the argument and thought that his grandma was probably right, but it didn't make him feel any better toward his mother.

He regretted that he'd ever been born to her. Being her son was a duty, an obligation. It sure as hell wasn't a pleasure.

"The door was unlocked," he said. "That's not safe. The house needs to be cleaned, too."

"Don't care 'bout locking doors—can't take none of this shit with me when I pass on." She blew smoke toward him. "You know I ain't never been no domestic woman, neither. Get somebody up in here to clean it."

"I already pay for everything, Mom. You want me to pay a housekeeper, too?"

"You gots the money. Anyway, ain't like I asked to live in this big-assed house. I was happy in my little apartment, till you had to come in and change everything, putting me up in this place 'cause you trying to impress your snooty-assed, bougie friends."

"That has nothing to do with it. I wanted to give you a better life."

"A better life? Nigga, please." She laughed, tapped cigarette ashes in a saucer sitting on the floor. "Just 'cause you went to college and got you a big-time lawyer job, you think you one of them now, don't you? Think 'cause you married that spoiled, high-yella heifer that you somebody special now? That what you think?"

Kevin kept quiet. This was an old argument She resented his making something of himself and enjoying a good life; she believed for some absurd reason that it was an indictment of her, evidence of her own failings as a mother. He was trying to help her, to share with her the fruits of his success, by doing what he felt was his responsibility— pulling her out of the gutter.

But she didn't appreciate it. She never had. His grandmother would have appreciated it. But she had been dead for five years.

Mom rose out of the bed on creaky knees. She shuffled toward him, pointing at him with her cigarette.

"Think you all that, don't ya?" she said. She looked him up and down with disdain. "Come up in here with ya fancy suit on and that shiny watch. Talking all proper and shit. Well, let me tell you—you ain't shit. You just like ya daddy. That nigga never was shit and never wasn't gonna be shit. And you just like him." She flicked cigarette ashes onto his suit jacket.

Kevin brushed the ashes away. He could handle the insults; again, they were nothing new. Everything with her was always the same. Coming to visit her was like stepping into a video that continuously looped.

Her charge that he was just like his daddy had long since failed to rattle him, too. He didn't know his father at all, and based on what he knew about the man, things were better that way. Some people were toxic and not worth having in your life—no matter how close the blood relation.

"Are you working anywhere yet?" he asked.

She blinked, and her expression softened. "I been applying for jobs. Nobody wanna hire an old black woman."

"Where'd you apply?"

"Aw, here and there," she said vaguely, and he knew that she hadn't applied for any jobs at all. In her youth, before her fall, Kevin recalled, she had worked as a hairstylist in a beauty shop, and his grandmother told him she had entertained dreams of opening a shop of her own. But she'd been a different woman then, living a different life.

"If you want help finding something—"

"Naw, naw." She waved him off. "I don't want you getting me a job, boy. You'd probably have me working somewhere for your uppity friends. I can take care of myself; you do enough for me."

He slid his hand into his pocket. "Need any money?"

"Didn't I just tell you that I can take care of myself?"

Kevin took his silver money clip out of his pocket. He peeled off three hundred dollars and handed it to her; on his way to visit her, he'd stopped by an ATM, knowing that he would have to give her money.

She snatched the cash out of his hand. As she was stashing it in her bra, the bathroom door across the room opened. A tall, gaunt black man stepped out, wearing a wife-beater T-shirt and wrinkled khakis, a belt trailing loosely from the waist like a tail. He had an unkempt Afro and dark eyes like hard candy.

"Who that?" the man asked in a guttural voice.

Kevin glanced at his mother.

"Rufus, this here my son," she said. She touched Kevin's arm and smiled. "He look just like me, don't he?"

Rufus sat heavily on the bed, as if he owned it. He lit a cigarette, too.

"You a hotshot lawyer, ain't that right?" Rufus said. "We need to talk, brotha—I got some shit on my record I wanna get dropped."

"Rufus ran into a little trouble with the law," Mom offered by way of explanation. "You know how the police always messin' with black folk."

"I practice corporate law, not criminal law," Kevin said.

"You gots to know somebody, though," Rufus said. "Help a brotha out."

"Maybe some other time," Kevin said. "I'm on my way out the door."

"So soon?" Mom asked in a false, saccharine voice. "You just got here."

"I'll send a housekeeper over this week," he said, backing up to the door. "And a pest control expert."

"They just God's creations, like you and me, baby."

"Right," he said. "Before I forget, Lauren said hello."

"High-yella heifer." Mom's face puckered sourly. "Remember what I said—you ain't one of them. Don't care what kind of job you got, how much money you got, where you live, who you marry. Don't forget where you came from. 'Cause they sure ain't gonna forget."

Kevin kissed his mother on the cheek and stepped out of the bedroom. He heard his mother and Rufus laughing as he descended the stairs.

He locked the door when he left.

Chapter 14

Marcus Mosley arrived at the condo within the hour, as he'd promised.

Although she'd spoken to Mosley on the telephone a few times, Lauren had never met him in person. She'd gotten the referral to his private-investigation company from a girlfriend who'd hired him to find out whether her boyfriend was cheating (he was). She was unprepared for meeting him in person.

He was gorgeous.

He was perhaps six one, athletically built, probably no older than twenty-seven or twenty-eight. He wore designer jeans, and a short-sleeve, button-down black shirt, the collar spread open to show a tempting lick of dark, curly chest hair. He passed the shoe test: He had on a pair of black, polished loafers (that probably were a size thirteen, she noted). His hair was cut in a neat Caesar, and he had a perfectly trimmed goatee.

And he had the most beautiful eyes she'd ever seen. They were gray, like autumn clouds.

Lauren's heart did a quick pitty-pat. She stood on the threshold of the doorway, staring at him, temporarily forgetting her place and situation.

He cleared his throat, breaking the silence.

"Pleasure to meet you, Mrs. Richmond," he said. He had a deep, authoritative voice with a gentle southern accent—the voice of a man sure of himself. He extended his hand, and she shook it. His hands were large and strong, his grip firm but dry.

"Nice to meet you, too. Please come in," she said, reluctantly letting go of his hand. "You came highly recommended."

"Is that so? That's great to hear." He came inside, a thick, black leather bag slung over his shoulder. "Hopefully you'll be another satisfied customer."

"Can I get you anything to drink? Water, soda, sweet tea?"

"Sweet tea would hit the spot. It's hot outside."

"You know that's why they call it Hotlanta." She had changed into shorts and a halter top, and as she walked to the kitchen, leaving him in the hallway, she swung her hips more energetically than was proper for a married woman home alone with a strange man.

But she could feel Mosley's admiring gaze on her, and she enjoyed it.

What had gotten into her? Why did she care whether this man liked her or not, and why had she been sizing him up as if he were a choice piece of male meat? This was a business transaction, not a date.

When she caught a whiff of his cologne, however— a bracing, masculine fragrance—her heart knocked faster.

She opened the refrigerator, grateful for the cold air that burst from inside. She needed something to douse the flames of her infatuation.

"Are you from here?" Mosley asked, leaning in the doorway.

"Yep—Savannah, exactly. I'm a genuine Georgia peach."

"I heard that," he said.

She wondered if he was flirting with her. The thought of such a handsome man finding her attractive . . . . well, she was accustomed to drawing attention from a lot of men, but it wasn't every day that you ran into a specimen like Mr. Mosley.

She took out the pitcher of freshly brewed sweet tea and poured some into a tall glass she filled with ice cubes. She returned to where Mosley waited in the hall.

"Thank you," he said. He took a long gulp; she watched his Adam's apple bob slowly, a sight that she found oddly arousing. "Delicious tea. Just like my mama's."

"Where are you from?"

"Mississippi. A small town called Coldwater. I moved here to go to college."

"Morehouse?"

He smiled. "Georgia Tech. I'm a computer geek."

You certainly don't look like one, she thought. *You look like you should be on the cover of* Essence.

"Aren't you kind of young to be a private investigator?" *And kind of hot, too?*

He shrugged. "What can I say? I watched too many Humphrey Bogart movies when I was a teenager. Being a detective seemed like an exciting career."

"But you went to a tech school?" She was getting all in his business, she knew.

"Most investigation these days requires you to be up on all of the latest technology," he said. He looked around. "Where's the computer, by the way?"

"His PC is in the loft. Follow me."

As she moved down the hallway, she could feel his eyes on her, drinking her in as deeply as he'd drunk that glass of tea.

"Nice place," he said. "I always wondered about the condos in this building. Quite upscale and spacious."

"It's all right. It's trendy, basically. My husband wanted to live here to be close to our jobs—and to impress his colleagues."

She had never spoken ill of Kevin in front of anyone, much less a man she didn't know. But something about Mosley inspired her trust, encouraged her to let her guard down.

Or perhaps she was just taken with him.

"Aren't you an attorney, too?" he asked. "I'd assume that an in-town condo would be good for both of your careers."

"I'm a country girl at heart," she said. "I'd be happiest somewhere with a lot of land, out in nature, away from all the noise and traffic and smog."

"Ain't that the truth? I'm planning to work my career here in the city, and then retire back in Mississippi."

"You sound like a man with a plan."

She mounted the stairs to the loft. She ascended slowly,

flexing her legs and hips, grateful for the Pilates workouts she'd performed religiously over the years. Her legs and her ass, firm and shapely, were her best features. She wanted to show them off.

Although she still wasn't quite sure *why* she wanted to impress this man.

"Nice view," he said softly, behind her.

She glanced over her shoulder, expecting to see him gazing appreciatively at her body.

But he wasn't looking at her. He was looking out the large picture window that offered a panoramic vista of downtown.

She felt like a fool. This man wasn't interested in her. He was there to do a job.

Hell, if anything, he probably felt sorry for her. She was paying him to spy on her husband, an act of desperation. And with her whining about how she disliked the condo, she probably sounded pathetic, too, like one of those spoiled bimbos on a TV talk show.

From here forward, she would be strictly business with Mr. Mosley.

"Here's the computer," she said, indicating the laptop on the glass desk.

Nodding, he set his briefcase on the floor and popped it open. It contained various electronic gadgets, and tools such as screwdrivers and wrenches.

"I'm going to install a device that'll record his keystrokes," he said. "Whenever he goes online, it'll secretly transmit the keystroke data to a secure Web address that only you and I will be able to access. It'll also decipher his keystrokes to make it easier for us to know exactly what he's typing, what he's doing."

"You're sure all of this will happen behind the scenes?" she asked. "He won't know what's going on?"

"Even the standard virus and security software won't detect what'll be happening. There's no way he'll have any clue, unless he's unusually savvy—and I don't think he is."

"Why do you say that?"

"Because he's stupid enough to fool around on a woman like you."

Mosley gave her a level gaze, the full effect of those lovely gray eyes. Heat warmed her cheeks, and a light perspiration coated her forehead.

"I. . . . I better let you get to work," she said. "I need to . . . . um . . . . start getting dinner ready."

"Sure." He smiled. "I should be done in half an hour or so."

She turned, stiffly, to walk away.

I knew I was right. This man is as attracted to me as I am to him.

But the voice of her conscience cut in, sternly.

I'm married. I'd be no better than Kevin if I fooled around with him.

She glanced over her shoulder. Mosley was still watching her, a soft, knowing smile on his face, as if he knew the dilemma that spun through her thoughts.

Walking away, she was so flustered she nearly fell down the stairs.

Chapter 15

Kevin parked in the driveway of a large, elegant brick house in Stone Mountain.

It was three o'clock. He'd promised Lauren that he'd be home for dinner by five. He didn't have much time, an hour or so at the most.

But ever since he'd left his mother's place, steel bands of tension clutched his chest, and his hands trembled. Like a post-traumatic seeing-his-mother disorder.

There was only one solution.

He hurried to the front door. The sprawling lawn was lush, green, perfectly maintained. Fragrant azaleas lined the walkway, and two stone lions stood guard on opposite sides of the faux-marble entrance steps. The subdivision was full of these McMansions, as they were called, just about all of them in this subdivision owned by black folk. The same upwardly mobile professionals that his mother despised.

You think you one of them now, don't you?

He pressed his fingers against his temple, massaged as if to wipe his mother's scathing voice out of his head. Then he drew himself up and pushed the doorbell. Melodic chimes rang within.

A woman opened the door.

"Hey you," she said.

Her name was Tammy. She was in her mid-thirties, a successful real estate agent, and had in fact sold Kevin the town house in which his mother lived. That was how he had first met her.

He came inside and kissed her quickly. "Thanks for making time to see me."

"I always have time for a tune-up." She smiled mischievously.

They'd progressed quickly from business associates to sex buddies. They never went to dinner, never went on dates. Their relationship was strictly sexual, an arrangement that fit both of their lifestyles and needs.

Right now, he needed her.

Tammy had a smooth caramel complexion, large brown eyes, and shoulder-length dark hair. She was only five feet tall, but she had curves for days. She wore a blue kimono-style robe that gave him a peek of her creamy flesh.

Kevin indicated his watch. "I have to leave by four."

"That's fine. I have to be at my fiancé's place soon."

"We're such busy people."

"Busy like bees." She shut the door behind him, grasped his belt, unstrapped it, and zipped his fly down. She cupped his rigid dick.

"You're always ready." She stroked him. "That's what I love about you. You should give Randall some lessons."

Randall was her fiancé. From what Kevin remembered, he was an older man, a rich businessman. Tammy had plenty of her own money, but marrying a wealthy man would sweeten the pot. Her wedding was in the fall.

"Maybe he needs Viagra," Kevin said.

"Tried it. He's one of the small percentage of men for whom it doesn't work. I suppose that means we'll have to maintain our arrangement."

"I'm happy to be of service." He kicked off his shoes and stepped out of his slacks. He stripped off his jacket, shirt, and tie, and tossed them to the floor.

"Let's hit the Jacuzzi," she said. "We can get freaky and clean simultaneously. Randall has a nose like a bloodhound, remember."

"Sounds good to me."

The Jacuzzi was located in a large chamber off the master

bathroom. A gigantic window along one wall gave a view of the swimming pool in the backyard.

The tub was full, the frothy water gurgling softly. Tammy peeled off her robe and bent over toward the lip of the Jacuzzi, thrusting her ass in the air.

Talk about a lovely sight. . . Kevin couldn't look away. He pressed his ready dick against her, and then gently slid his forefinger into her pussy.

"You're already wet," he said.

She glanced over her shoulder and winked at him. "All I have to do is think about you."

"You're right—we've gotta keep this arrangement going."

Tammy climbed into the water. She used a hairpin to tie her hair up.

"You know a sista can't get her hair wet," she said.

Nude, Kevin slid into the Jacuzzi. Tammy came into his arms. She reached down between them and grasped him.

"How's my little friend been doing?" she asked.

"He's being underfed at home."

"Aw, that's too bad. We'll have to fix that."

She guided him inside her. As he filled her up and she tightened around him, Kevin released a moan of pleasure . . . . of release.

Tammy was the only woman—other than his wife—with whom he had sex without a condom. She got tested regularly, and so did he. That was another condition of the arrangement. That, and her promise to stay on birth control. She didn't want a child any more than he did.

She began to grind against him, slowly and rhythmically. He gripped her gyrating hips and pulled her closer, pumping into her. Dipping his head to her neck, he licked away the droplets of water from her flesh.

"Don't give me a hickey now," she said.

But her voice came to him as if from the end of a long, dark tunnel. He heard, instead, his mother's scathing words:

You think you one of them now. . . .

Mom's angry, prematurely aged face flashed in his thoughts.

He moved his hands to Tammy's shoulders and pumped into her harder, faster.

Tammy began to cry out. She was always loud during sex.

You think you one of them. . . .

His fingers slid to Tammy's scalp, found the roots of her long hair. Tightened.

Think you one of them. . . . .

And before he realized what he was doing, before he became fully conscious of the rage that was rising in him, he had gripped fistfuls of Tammy's hair in his hands and plunged her head down, underneath the surface of the churning water. He held her there, ignoring her struggles.

Mama, I hate you, I hate you, you motherfucking bitch, I wish you were dead!

Pain stabbed his stomach. Shocked, he loosened his grip on Tammy.

What was I doing to her?

She exploded out of the water.

"What the fuck is wrong with you, Kevin?" Her wet hair matted her face, and she angrily flung it out of her eyes. "Were you trying to kill me or what?"

Kevin's stomach ached. Had she punched him? He couldn't have blamed her—he deserved to be hit for what he'd done. What the hell had he been thinking?

Gasping, he climbed out of the tub.

"I. . . I lost control," he said. "I'm sorry . . . . I didn't mean it."

"Well, I'm *not* sorry for punching you in the stomach. You were holding me under the water!"

"I'm so sorry, Tammy. Really. I don't know what came over me. I'd gone to see my mom before I came over here and. . . . "

His voice trailed off, and he shook his head.

"Oh, your mama," Tammy said, and her lips curled derisively. He'd told her a little about his strained relationship with his mother. "You know what? You got serious issues, Kevin. Issues with women—and it's because of *her.*"

Kevin didn't know what to say. But he suspected that she was right.

"I enjoy fucking you," Tammy said, "but it's sad, really. You got a pretty wife at home, but you still come see me, and who knows how many other women. You need to think about why you do that. You need to look at your mama, and why you treat every woman you meet like shit 'cause of her."

"Look, stay out of my business, all right? If I want a shrink I'll go see one."

"Maybe you better. Go get your head right."

"Whatever. I'm outta here."

He grabbed a towel from the rack beside the Jacuzzi and began to dry off. Tammy got out of the tub, fussing over her hair.

"I *told* you I can't get my hair wet." She glared at him. "Now I'm going to be late getting to Randall's. Thanks to your psychotic-episode-having ass."

"I'll make it up to you," he said.

"Please. Not until you start getting counseling. You'll have to show me you passed a mental health exam before I see you again."

"Okay, fine, whatever." He put on his boxers and went downstairs to get the rest of his clothes. He left the house without saying good-bye.

He screeched out of the driveway and roared down the tree-lined street. When he veered around the corner, he almost hit a man who was walking his dog. The guy glared at him and shouted an obscenity.

"Fuck you, too," Kevin muttered.

Tammy's words rang in his thoughts. Her psychology bullshit about his mom. Maybe she was right. Maybe he did treat women the way he did because of her.

But so what? He enjoyed his life. He loved being Kevin Richmond, and he loved having sex with as many fine ladies as he could score. He was a professional playa. A damn All-Star in the game of fuckin' females.

Even if a doctor told him tomorrow that if he ever used his dick again, he would drop dead on the spot, he was going to die up in some pussy.

He was a grown-ass man. He wasn't going to change.

Chapter 16

Lauren was preparing dinner and trying to ignore the gorgeous man in the loft, lest she do something that she would regret, when he called her upstairs.

Oh Lord, here we go again. She walked upstairs on shaky legs.

Mosley was hunched in front of the computer. "I finished the installation, but found something strange."

"What is it?"

"Had you hired another detective before me?"

She shook her head. "Why do you ask?"

"Because there was another keystroke recorder hooked up to the laptop." He showed her a small, metallic gadget, the size of a thumbnail.

"I don't know anything about that. I know Kevin takes the computer to the firm sometimes."

"Maybe someone else was spying on him," Mosley said. He chuckled evilly, and then shrugged. "Anyway, I cleared it out. You're all set here." He pushed away from the desk and stood, stretching. She noticed that a tattoo of a rose adorned one of his sculpted arms.

He took note of her attention. "I got this in memory of my mother," Mosley said, and ran his finger along the tattoo. He smiled, and the beauty of his smile struck Lauren—his whole face had brightened at the mention of his mother. It was a stark contrast to the anger that contorted Kevin's face whenever the subject of his mother arose.

That's not fair, Lauren. Don't compare these men. They're

nothing alike. For starters, one of them is your husband.

Lauren realized she was studying Mosley too intently, and caught herself. "Well, okay, thank you. You work fast."

"It was a simple installation," he said. He handed her a clipboard with a slip of paper attached to it. "Here's your invoice. Please review it and sign the bottom. I accept various forms of payment—cash, check, all major credit cards . . . dinner."

She looked up at him. He was smiling. "Dinner?"

"I'd like to take you out," he said. "Somewhere country folk like us can kick back, relax, and enjoy a down-home meal."

She blushed fiercely. "Mr. Mosley—"

"Call me Marcus."

"*Marcus,* you know perfectly well that I'm a married woman."

"Not happily married. If you were, I wouldn't be here, would I?"

She paused. "I don't know for sure that my husband is cheating. For all I know, he could just be surfing Internet porn sites, which wouldn't be right, but it's not exactly infidelity."

"What does your intuition tell you?"

"It doesn't matter," she said. "Even if he *is* cheating, that doesn't give me a license to do the same thing. Two wrongs don't make a right. Someone here needs to take the high road."

"Having dinner with me wouldn't qualify as cheating—technically," he said. "It's only a meal."

She had to chuckle. "You don't want to get into semantics with me, honey. I'm an attorney, remember? Do we need to debate the specifics of when infidelity begins?"

"All right, you win. It probably would be cheating." He raised his hands in mock surrender, grinned. "I respect your morals. But answer me this—if you weren't married, would you have agreed to dinner?"

She laughed again. "Aren't you persistent?"

"It's a simple question. Yes or no."

She knew she should refuse to answer the question. She couldn't figure out why she was even having this conversation with him. She should have ended this transaction and been in the kitchen, preparing dinner for her husband.

But Mosley—Marcus—was so charming, so fine . . .

"Yes," she said.

"Aha, that's all I need to know." He seemed pleased with her answer, as if he had proven a point. He turned away and began to put his tools in his briefcase.

"I'll go get your check," she said.

He nodded—and winked.

I've gotten myself into something, and I don't know where it's going, she thought, returning downstairs to get her checkbook out of her purse. She felt giddy, and more than a bit naughty.

She hadn't felt that way in a long time. Not since she had made up her mind to get married, and had tamed down her ways. It wasn't proper for a married woman to be flirtatious with anyone other than her husband. Period.

But she couldn't restrain a giggle.

It felt good to be desired by such a handsome man. Kevin was handsome, of course, and he told her all the time that he loved her, and he definitely wanted her sexually. But something was missing: She suspected that she wasn't the only recipient of Kevin's affections.

Getting married to Kevin was the equivalent of getting a two-carat diamond engagement ring and discovering that it contained a huge black speck in the center, a glaring imperfection.

But she had taken a vow in front of her family, friends, and God. A solemn promise to be faithful. And that was what she intended to do, no matter how charming Marcus might be.

She was standing at the counter, writing a check to Mosley's company out of her separate bank account, when he came up behind her and put his hands around her waist.

"I know you want me just as much as I want you," he whispered, close to her ear.

She should have screamed, should have smacked him and demanded that he get the hell out of her home before she called the police and accused him of assault.

But she did none of those things.

She turned around and gazed into his eyes.

Marcus kissed her on the lips. She let him. It was a soft, tender kiss. A kiss for the sake of a kiss, not because he wanted to get her into the bedroom.

She couldn't remember the last time a man had kissed her like that.

When their lips parted, her chest was rising and falling rapidly. Warm tingles spread throughout her body.

"That was nice," he said.

"Yes. But we shouldn't have gone there."

"It was only a kiss."

"And only a kiss turns into only dinner, and only dinner turns into only sex . . . . "

"One step at a time, sweetheart. Live in the moment."

"That's a very Zen statement." She reached behind her and retrieved her checkbook. She tore the check along the perforated edges and handed it to him.

Marcus ripped the check in half. "Dinner."

"I thought we were living in the moment."

He only smiled. He picked up his briefcase off the floor and went to the door.

"We'll talk soon," he said. "About the business you hired me for. . . . and other, more personal matters."

He flashed her another brilliant smile, and then let himself out, whistling a tune that she recognized as "Sexual Healing," by Marvin Gaye.

What a fine, fine man.

She was both relieved and sad to see him go. She could still feel his lips on hers, the ghost of the kiss.

What have I gotten myself into? she wondered.

Chapter 17

Lauren was acting strange.

Kevin had arrived home at five, after spending time driving around the city, trying to get his mind in order again. The drive did him good, gave him clarity on things, and when he got home, he felt almost normal.

Until he noticed Lauren.

She bustled around the kitchen finishing preparations for dinner, and she was listening to the radio. She wasn't listening to the local gospel station, as she was prone to do on Sundays after church. She was listening to V-103, the R&B/hip-hop station, and singing along with some hot new female singer who'd made a song about how a man had to go "downtown" if he wanted to be with her.

It was weird behavior for Lauren. But it was a catchy tune, with an addictive hook. Even devout Christian folk like Lauren sometimes enjoyed secular music, he figured. Look at Kirk Franklin—the guy had sold millions of records partly because he sampled popular R&B party songs.

"How'd the visit with your mother go?" she asked cheerfully.

"Not well. I don't want to talk about it."

She shrugged. "Okay. Well, dinner will be ready in fifteen minutes. Salmon with dill sauce. Your favorite."

"Cool," he said. But her blasé reaction to his statement about his visit with his mother puzzled him. Ordinarily, she would have probed further, tried to get him to reveal exactly what had happened, and then offered her sympathies and support.

But today, she acted like she didn't give a damn.

Perhaps she no longer cared. Perhaps she had tired of the subject of his mom. He couldn't blame her for that. Mom had been a bitch to Lauren from the beginning and didn't deserve his wife's energy anymore.

Still, it was odd.

Kevin showered—though he had been in the Jacuzzi with Tammy, he thought it wise to clean up again—and changed into Sean John shorts and a polo shirt. By the time he was done, Lauren was setting their meal on the table.

Kevin got a bottle of Chardonnay from the wine cooler near the wet bar. He popped the cork and poured himself a glass.

"I'd like wine, too," Lauren said.

"But it's Sunday."

His wife never consumed alcoholic beverages on Sunday. It was one of her oddities—she spoke of keeping the Lord's day holy and all that. She'd sip wine (never more than a single glass, of course) from Monday through Saturday. But Sundays were dry days. Her family had observed the practice for years, which had raised eyebrows when Kevin, Lauren, and her parents had gone out to dinner one Sunday evening and Kevin, ignorant of their ways, had ordered a Heineken.

"I know it's Sunday, honey," she said. "And I'd like wine with my dinner. My parents aren't here to rebuke me, are they?"

He fetched another glass and poured wine for her, but the pistons of his mind were working.

What's going on here? She's having wine with dinner? Next thing you know, maybe she'll actually want *to have sex with me instead of doing it out of her sense of wifely duty.*

When thoughts of sex entered his mind, that was when it hit him.

Lauren is having an affair.

He noted the rosy glow in her cheeks. It wasn't due to makeup, because she wasn't wearing any. She had glowed like that when they'd first begun dating, when she was spinning in a whirlwind of infatuation. The glow of burgeoning attraction, young love. To a man like Kevin, who made it his business to study women, it was obvious.

Goddammit, she's cheating on me.
He was surprised by the sudden anger that burned in his stomach, like a hot coal. The nerve of her to cheat on him. On *him!*

At the table, they bowed their heads, said grace, and began eating.

"So, what've you been doing this afternoon?" he asked. "Other than cooking this wonderful meal."

"Oh, you know, the usual after-church things," she said. She didn't meet his eyes as she cut a small piece of salmon. "Studying Scripture, calling my family, doing a little cleaning."

And fucking somebody, he thought. The fact that she didn't meet his eyes as she spoke about her activities was proof that his suspicions were dead-on.

"How're your folks?" he asked.

"They're doing fine. Daddy was out—he was preaching a sermon in Valdosta. Mama was gossiping about everyone in the family. The usual stuff. She invited us to come visit next weekend. I told her we'd have to check our schedules and get back to her."

"Yeah, I've got a busy week ahead of me," he said, though he had no idea what he had on his schedule that week. He was so consumed with the notion of Lauren cheating on him that he couldn't think of anything else. He began eating, but it was without pleasure; he ate with the indifference of a machine that needed fuel to function.

Turnabout is fair play, he thought. It was one of Oliver's favorite sayings. Oliver, forever lecturing him about the wily ways of women, and how it was best to treat them well because if you didn't, they would get you back—where and when it hurt the most.

Could he have been jumping to conclusions? He had no concrete evidence that Lauren had done anything other than what she'd told him she'd been doing. Her infidelity could be his imagination, a case of him projecting his own actions onto her as a way to make himself feel better.

But that wasn't what his gut told him.

Nevertheless, he decided to rein himself in and play it cool. *What's done in the dark will soon come to light.* That was one of his grandma's much-loved proverbs. He would go about his business, as usual, but would keep a circumspect eye on Lauren, certain that the truth would eventually surface.

For one thing was clear: He didn't know her as well as he thought he did.

Chapter 18

Later that evening, while Lauren was in their bedroom reading a Christian romance novel—her good-girl facade didn't faze him one bit—Kevin went to his loft.

After such a roller coaster of a day, he'd almost forgotten about Black Venus. He relished the thought of meeting her, with an almost savage glee.

Wanna cheat on me, Lauren? Go ahead. You can't outdo me, baby.

He logged on to the Sexcapades Web site. He had three messages: Two of them were from women he had never communicated with before. After a quick check of their profiles, he deleted the e-mails without reading them.

The last message, the only one he was interested in reading, was from Black Venus.

Dear Supershaft,

I hope you've enjoyed your Sunday. As promised, I am writing you (I'm a woman of my word). I would like to discuss the possibility of a meeting. A rendezvous. Very soon. Are you game?

If so, take the lead, my Nubian prince, and tell me what you have in mind. In the meantime, for your viewing pleasure, I've attached another photo.
I look forward to your timely reply.
Black Venus

His fingers tingling, he downloaded the attached file and opened it.

"Damn," he said.

He looked around to make sure that he was still alone, and then he bent back toward the screen.

It was a full-body shot of Black Venus—from the rear. As in the other photo, she was posed in front of a cloudy white background, her face set straight head, preserving her anonymity. Her long dark hair flowed past her shoulders. She wore no bra; her hands cupped her ample breasts, juicy glimpses of them visible from behind. She had a narrow waist, a black leather thong splitting her perfectly shaped ass into luscious twin globes. Black stilettos set off her long, sculpted legs.

"You're torturing me, girl," he whispered.

He'd developed a huge hard-on. She was so beautiful it bordered on supernatural.

He wiped his lips. Although he was more eager to meet her than he'd been to meet anyone in ages, he did not immediately reply to her message. He wanted to carefully consider where he would propose to meet her. Black Venus was not an ordinary Internet hookup.

She was something special.

* * *

The bait had been set.

Eve had e-mailed Kevin earlier that Sunday, including yet another photo of herself, to further whet his appetite.

She wanted to put the ball in his court and let him set the conditions of the meeting.

And let him think that he was in control.

Eve had learned that the easiest way to manipulate a man was to lead him into thinking that you were malleable to his will, his desires. A wise woman, however, understood just how to play a man, knew just which strings to pluck and which buttons to push, to influence him to do whatever you wished.

Kevin was no different. In fact, his voracious sexual appetite made him more readily influenced than most men. He was like a panting dog, searching frenziedly for a female to mount, and his unbridled lust made him especially vulnerable to a woman like her.

A woman with revenge on her mind.

Eve checked her e-mail account late that night, before retiring to bed. Kevin had not yet replied, but according to the message status, he had read her e-mail that evening.

"Pondering our rendezvous, are you, my dear?" Eve said. "Thinking of something special?"

She expected to receive a response from him within twenty-four hours. He would be unable to bear waiting any longer than that.

She shut down the computer. With her dogs, Snow and Storm, accompanying her, she walked through the house and descended to the basement.

It was time to feed her prisoner.

Chapter 19

On Tuesday afternoon, Marcus called Lauren on her cell phone.

"Lauren," he said, in his deep, syrupy voice. "Is this an all right time for us to chat?"

Although Lauren was in serious work mode, sitting in her office at Thompson & Roberts with legal briefs stacked on her desk, his voice instantly pulled her back to that past Sunday. That forbidden, tender kiss in the kitchen. Those gorgeous gray eyes.

"I can talk now," she said. She put her hand against her chest to slow her racing heartbeat, and then she got up from her desk to close the door. She didn't want her colleagues to overhear her conversation.

"Your husband has been active," Marcus said. "He's been visiting a Web site called—I'm really serious— Sexcapades."

Revulsion twisted her stomach. "Is that a porn site?"

"It's a dating Web site—well, sort of. After figuring out that was where he was surfing, I visited it myself. It was something else. They offer an opportunity for their members to arrange . . . . uh, discreet sexual encounters with one another."

Lauren felt as if she had been kicked in the face. She'd been right about Kevin. He was cheating.

"I mean, these folks are freaky," Marcus continued. "They've got people on there who want to be whipped with chains, folks who just wanna suck toes, men who want women to dress up like their mamas—"

"I get the idea," she said, cutting him off.

"Sorry." He laughed self-consciously.

She was almost afraid to ask the next question, but she had to: "What's Kevin been doing on there?"

"He's arranged to meet another member, a woman who goes by the name of Black Venus. I couldn't find out much of anything about her. He's planning to meet her this weekend. Saturday night."

Like a date, she thought. She felt ill.

Suspecting Kevin of cheating was one thing. But getting confirmation, and then hearing the gory details on what he was planning, was another matter altogether.

"Where are .they going?" Lauren asked.

"They're meeting at the Ritz-Carlton, in Buckhead," Marcus said. "Seven o'clock. He told her, and I quote, 'I'll be the fine brother in the lobby, wearing a gray Armani suit and carrying a brown Prada duffel bag.'"

Lauren knew that bag. She had bought it for Kevin last Christmas.

Now he was taking it with him while he went out to cheat on her.

The fuckin' nerve of him!

Her head felt as if it might explode, she was so angry. Tears pushed hard at her eyes. She was about three seconds away from a breakdown . . .

Then she saw one of the partners stroll past in the corridor outside her office. She gritted her teeth, drew in deep breaths. She couldn't afford to lose control of herself. Not here at work. She had to keep it together.

She forced herself to focus on the details of the situation. Kevin was planning a rendezvous with a woman for this coming Saturday night. How the heck was he scheming to get out of the house with a plausible story?

"Are you there?" Marcus asked.

"Hold on a minute," she said.

The answer came to her: On Sunday, she had mentioned to Kevin about going to visit her parents in Savannah this weekend. He was going to beg off and encourage her to go on her own, like he did at least half the time. He didn't like her parents at all, though he tried to front as if he did.

He was thinking that he would have the entire weekend to himself, to do all the dirt he wanted.

Not this time. I've got your number.

The beginning of a plan was forming in her mind. A means to get even with Kevin's lying, cheating ass—in more ways than one.

"Okay, I'm back," Lauren said. "So, Marcus, do you have plans for Saturday?"

Chapter 20

On Thursday, Kevin and Oliver went to lunch at Mary Mac's Tea Room, an old-fashioned, southern-style restaurant on Ponce de Leon, not far from the office in which they worked. Over glasses of sweet tea and platters of fried chicken, macaroni and cheese, collards, and corn bread, they discussed firm business, then matters pertinent to the men's ministry at Rebirth.

Kevin's week had been going well. On Monday, he'd sent his Saturday night rendezvous plans to Black Venus, and she had responded with her approval within hours—and with one more digital treat: a shot of her from the front this time, but from the neck down. Kneeling on a chaise, she was completely nude. One of her long fingers caressed a chocolate nipple; the other poked inside her clean-shaven pussy.

Sitting at his desk, Kevin had promptly yanked down his boxers and masturbated.

Saturday night couldn't get there soon enough.

He was hoping that he would get through lunch with Oliver without a probe into his personal life, but as they were finishing their food, Oliver took a sip of sweet tea, leveled that penetrating gaze of his at Kevin, and then asked:

"How is your mother doing?"

Kevin's shoulders sagged. "She's the same."

"Did you visit her this past weekend, like you said you would?"

What are you, my father? Kevin almost shouted. *None of your goddamn business.*

But he couldn't say that. Because Oliver *was* the closest thing he had to a father.

"I did," he said. "The place was a mess. I called a housekeeping service to visit once a week, clean the house from top to bottom. She won't do it. She's too busy with her men and her drugs."

Although Kevin hadn't wanted to discuss his mother, he now felt an aching need to talk about her. Since his grandmother's death, he didn't have anyone else to talk to about his mom. Mom had been so nasty to Lauren that Lauren hated bringing her up. Oliver's was the only ear he could bend.

"Dealing with her is such a pain in the ass," Kevin said. "I do everything for her, and she doesn't appreciate it at all. You know what she said? She said I moved her into that town house, bought her a car, and give her money because I'm trying to impress my friends, as if I'm embarrassed that she's my mother and feel the need to dress her up, if you will, make her more presentable."

Oliver's bright eyes seemed to see right into his heart. "Is that how you feel?"

"I don't see how I could be trying to impress anyone. I never take my friends around to her. You haven't met her, either, remember."

"A true statement," Oliver said. "But do you boast to your friends about how you provide for your mother? Do you tell your friends about the nice town house, the furniture, the car?"

"I don't tell anyone about those things," he said. He paused. "Well, I've told you. And. . . . maybe a few other people, I admit. But only if they ask about where my mother lives. I don't brag about it."

"I think you're a wonderful provider for your mother," Oliver said. "But you might find it helpful to examine your relationship with her. I think your feelings toward her can shed light on your attitude toward women in general."

"You think I have issues with women?" Kevin shook his

head. "Funny, I heard the same thing earlier this week. Do I have a sign on my forehead that says 'analyze me'?"

"No, but you're a man—a black man. The majority of black men have issues with women, to a degree." Oliver smiled. "I'm not excluding myself from that group."

"What kind of issues do brothers have with women? Educate me, Counselor."

"How much time do you have?" Oliver asked. He looked around the dining room, which was populated with many other black men enjoying business lunches. "I'd presume that most of the brothers in this restaurant were raised in households headed by a single mother— or grandmother. Strong, independent sisters who did whatever was necessary to bring home the bacon and keep the family together."

Kevin was nodding; Oliver was speaking the truth. "How is that a bad thing?"

"In one sense, it's not a bad thing at all. These hardworking women are raising families, keeping the kids clothed and fed, and sending them to college. That's a blessing. But sometimes, they go too far and do too much for their kids—especially the boys."

"They spoil them," Kevin said.

Oliver snapped his fingers. "Exactly. The girls in the house catch hell, have to cook and clean and be little mamas. But the boys? They get to sleep late, don't have to cook, don't wash their own clothes or even clean their rooms. The women coddle the boys, which hurts the kids in the long run. These boys grow up into men who expect women to wait on them, hand and foot. They view women as their personal assistants, who should be willing to do whatever a man asks for to keep him happy."

Kevin sipped tea, thinking about his grandmother. She'd cooked, she cleaned, she did his laundry. She'd let him sleep in late—Sundays being the exception. And in regard to Sunday mornings, once he'd hit the age of sixteen or so, she no longer forced him to go to church with her. He was free to stay home and sleep in, which he normally did.

Life with Grandma had been easy, carefree. Although she had also taken care of his two cousins—both of them girls, who worked as hard as Grandma did around the house—Kevin had never been expected to contribute anything.

"I agree with you," Kevin said. "But you have to realize that it's a rough world out there for brothers. There's nothing as hard as walking a mile in a black man's shoes. I think these women nurture the boys because they know that once the boys are released into the world, their lives as men are going to be difficult."

"Point taken," Oliver said. "But why not prepare the boys for the harsh realities that they are going to face? Why not teach the boys how to work *with* girls, instead of expecting the females to shoulder all of the burdens? Why not show the boys how to view girls as equals, instead of slaves existing solely to be at their beck and call? This kind of home training would go a long way toward reducing the rate of single-mother households, and would make the brothers more responsible—especially in regard to their sexual proclivities." Oliver gave him a pointed look.

Kevin winced. Well, his sex life was none of Oliver's business. He didn't have to explain what he did to Oliver, or anybody else.

He enjoyed Oliver's company, but he was ready to terminate this conversation.

Kevin glanced at his watch. "I need to get back to the office. I've got a conference call in an hour and need to do some prep work."

"I must've gotten too deep for a lunchtime chat." Oliver signaled the waitress to bring the check. "Blame the amateur psychologist in me."

"There's nothing wrong with a friendly debate." He shrugged. "Keeps the brain cells sharp, right?"

"Right. But as your mentor—and friend—I have to warn you that playing with a woman's heart is like playing with fire. I speak from experience, because I've been burned a few times in my day. Be careful, my brother."

Oliver's face was solemn, and Kevin could not shake the sense that Oliver had a foreboding of the future, a presentiment of disaster heading toward Kevin. Goose bumps pimpled Kevin's flesh, and Oliver's words reverberated in the lower chambers of his mind for the rest of the day.

Be careful, my brother.

Chapter 21

Saturday morning, Kevin saw Lauren off as she went to visit her parents in Savannah.

"Are you sure you don't want to come with me?" Lauren asked. She zipped up her leather overnight bag, which, in typical female fashion, she had packed with enough clothes for several days, even though she'd be returning tomorrow. She brushed a strand of hair out of her eyes, smiled. "My family always enjoys seeing you."

That's a lie, and you know it, Kevin thought. *Your folks think I'm a heathen and wish you'd never met me.*

But he only smiled back. "I have a pile of work I need to take care of, baby. Give them my love."

"You're going to work all weekend? No wonder the firm loves you."

"They love those billable hours. I'll take a few breaks here and there, maybe ride the bike for a little while if the weather holds."

She wrinkled her nose. "I don't know why you keep that crotch rocket. I hate that thing—it's far too dangerous."

"Keep your cell phone on, in case I crash and wind up in the emergency room."

"Don't joke about that. It's not funny."

They had similar conversations every time Kevin spoke of riding his motorcycle, a souped-up Kawasaki. What Lauren would never know was that this weekend, he didn't intend to ride the bike at all.

If things went as planned tonight, in fact, a gorgeous woman who went by the alias of Black Venus was going to be riding *him.*

"You worry too much. It'll be fine. I might be so tired once I finish working that I'll be too tired to ride out anyway."

Carrying Lauren's bag, he accompanied her to the parking garage. He placed her luggage in the trunk of her BMW, gave her a hug, and kissed her quickly on the lips.

"Drive safely," he said. "Call me when you get there."

"Will do. I love you."

"Love you, too."

Lauren climbed in the sedan and rolled out of the garage. When she turned into the flow of traffic and veered out of sight, he had to restrain the sudden impulse to leap in the air and click his heels together like an exuberant cartoon character.

He was alone for the weekend. A bachelor again.

Giddy, he went back upstairs to the condo. In the master bedroom, he slid off his wedding band and buried it deep in a bottom drawer.

It was only nine-thirty in the morning. He had plenty of time before he was scheduled to meet Black Venus at the Ritz. A glorious summer day lay ahead, full of possibilities.

He'd lied about having work to do. He was on the verge of making partner and had a considerable workload, but he'd worked extra-long hours all week to ensure that he would have the weekend to do as he pleased.

He took the stairs to the loft. At the desk, he unlocked a large drawer and fished out his Sidekick, an upgrade from his little black book. He was about to scan it for potential daytime hookups when he found the card that Valerie, the hottie from church, had given him.

Remembering how well she had drawn him inside her mouth gave him a delicious shiver.

He clicked on his cell phone—he kept a separate prepaid phone, to use exclusively for talking to other women—and called her.

"Hello," she said. She sounded out of breath, and music played in the background.

"It's Kevin," he said. "From church."

"Hey!" He could hear the smile in her voice. "Let me turn down the music so I can hear you better—I was in the middle of my workout."

She lowered the volume, and then came back on the phone. "So, what're you up to, baby?"

"Thinking that maybe you need a workout partner this morning."

She laughed. So did he.

He had a busy day ahead of him.

Better take his vitamins.

Chapter 22

After Lauren left home, she drove not toward Savannah, where Kevin believed she was headed, but to her law firm ten minutes away. The firm offices were located in an office plaza on Peachtree Street, within walking distance of numerous cafes and restaurants that she frequented for lunch during the workweek.

Lauren parked in the underground parking garage, and sat silently in the car. A Yolanda Adams song played on the radio—a song about granting forgiveness to someone who had done you wrong.

Kevin had done her wrong, and he was preparing to do even more dirt behind her back.

But she wasn't the least bit prepared to forgive him, even though it was the Christian thing to do. She was nowhere near ready for that.

She cut off the radio and left the car.

She met her girlfriend, Charmaine, at Gladys Knight's Chicken 'n' Waffles. Charmaine was a soror, one of her line sisters. They had been tight ever since.

"Morning, girl," Charmaine said, as they exchanged a sisterly hug. The hostess showed them to one of the booths. Their waiter, a well-built brother who couldn't have been any older than twenty-one, materialized almost instantly at their table.

"Good morning, ladies." His gaze flickered from Lauren to Charmaine—and settled mostly on Charmaine.

Lauren was accustomed to that reaction when she and Charmaine went out together in public. Charmaine was tall and statuesque, like her—but unlike Lauren these days, she had no qualms about showing as much flesh as possible. Although Lauren wore a conservative white sundress, Charmaine had on a tight pink halter top that barely contained her considerable cleavage, and high-cut green shorts that displayed her long, shapely legs. That was Charmaine for you. She liked to be the center of attention.

Lauren didn't mind. . . . though there was a time in her past when she and Charmaine had been a lot alike. Perhaps that explained why they were such close friends.

"What can I get you to drink?" he asked.

"Orange juice for me, please," Lauren said.

"What's your name, Chocolate?" Charmaine asked him. She batted her eyelashes.

The waiter grinned, showing so many of his straight white teeth he could've lit up a nightclub.

"Malik," he said.

"I'll have sweet tea, Malik," Charmaine said in a husky, bedroom voice.

"Coming right up." Blushing, Malik hurried to retrieve their beverages. Charmaine admired the view of the waiter from behind, turned to Lauren, and winked.

"He's way too young for you, girl," Lauren said. "I thought I smelled Similac on his breath."

"I like 'em young and virile," Charmaine said. "I need a man who can keep up with me. Most of them can't."

Only thirty, Charmaine had been married twice, and divorced twice. She claimed both her ex-husbands had bored her. That might have been true, but Lauren knew that both of the men had also cheated on her.

Cheating husbands. It was yet another thing that she and Charmaine had in common.

The waiter delivered their drinks.

"You have such big, strong-looking hands," Charmaine told the young man. "Do you work out?"

"Five times a week." He grinned so hard it looked painful. "I go to Morehouse, do a little modeling on the side, so I need to keep it tight. I must say—you look like you know all about that."

"Get on out of here, boy, I'd hurt you," she said, and waved him away with a laugh. The waiter drifted away, desire in his eyes.

"You're something else," Lauren said.

"Hey, a sista has needs," Charmaine said. "You *do* remember that, don't you?"

Lauren didn't want to go there with her this morning. So she changed the subject.

"Kevin thinks I'm on my way to Savannah right now," she said. "I've never tried anything like this with him. I'm kind of anxious."

"About him finding out that you're still here? Please, girl, who's the one doing the dirt? It's not you. All you're doing is getting to the bottom of things."

"I've always been honest with him, to a fault." Tears welled in her eyes, and she dabbed at them with a napkin. She sniffled. "I thought our marriage was something special."

"I know." Charmaine patted her hand. "You gave him your best, Lauren. He just doesn't appreciate it. You know what I say—once a dog, always a dog."

"I thought he'd changed. He told me he had before we got married."

Charmaine tilted forward in the booth. "Let me tell you something, girl—*men don't ever change.* Not for the better, anyway. If they change, it's normally for the worst. Like he used to put his dirty drawers in the hamper, and he changes and starts leaving them nasty suckers on the floor for you to pick up."

"But I changed my ways," Lauren said. "Why can't he? It's not fair."

"No, it's not fair. But that's the way it is. Women are always changing to accommodate the men in their lives. The men keep on doing the same shit."

"I'm not going to stand for it," Lauren said. Anger arose in her, replacing her sadness. "I'm not going to sit back and play sweet little wifey while he sleeps with every whore in Atlanta."

"You shouldn't," Charmaine said. "You should get you some get-back. Revenge is a meal best served cold."

Lauren's cell phone rang. Anxiety flashed in her. What if it was Kevin? He would hear that she wasn't in her car. . . . .

She glanced at the number on the display, and her heart continued to race, but for a different reason. It was Marcus. She'd hired him to tail Kevin all day Saturday; he must've been calling with an update.

"Morning, Lauren," he said, with that sexy, soulful voice of his. "I'm on the job this morning, just like you asked me to be. And guess what? Your husband is on the move."

"Already?" Lauren looked at her watch. It was only a few minutes past ten.

"At first, I thought he might be going to work, but he passed right by the office," Marcus said.

An ulcer seemed to burn in Lauren's stomach. "I thought his meeting wasn't going to happen until this evening."

"He might be going to see someone else," Marcus said. "Or it could be a normal errand. What does he like to do on Saturday mornings?"

"He's supposed to be going to the office," she said. She looked at Charmaine, who was casting flirtatious glances toward the waiter. Although Charmaine had referred her to Marcus, she felt a bit of embarrassment about having a discussion regarding her personal life with this man, who, as fine and nice as he was, was a relative stranger to her.

"I'll keep an eye on him, see where he ends up," Marcus said. "My gut tells me that he's into something, though. Brothers like him are always on the prowl."

"Are you speaking from experience?" she asked, her tone sharp.

Marcus sighed. "My papa was a rolling stone. He fathered something like five or six kids outside of his and my mama's marriage. Broke her heart."

God, I know how that must feel. A pang shot through Lauren's chest. It felt like her own heart was breaking.

"Sorry, I was out of line," she said.

"It's cool, girl. I'll call you later with an update."

Lauren ended the call and tucked away her phone in her purse.

"Let me guess," Charmaine said. "K.-Dog is hunting for his next meal."

"I don't know." Lauren shook her head.

"You *know*, right here." Charmaine tapped her heart. "A woman's intuition is never wrong. You've gotta listen to it—and when the truth finally comes to light, you've gotta do whatever's necessary."

Charmaine was right. She usually was, in marital matters. Two painful divorces had taught her all of the hard lessons.

She was going to let the truth come to light.

In the end, the truth always did.

Chapter 23

Dressed in workout gear—Nikes, baggy shorts, and a muscle shirt—Kevin drove to a quiet park in Marietta. He parked under the boughs of an elm tree, next to a gold Toyota Camry.

As soon as he cut the ignition, Valerie climbed out of the Toyota and went to her trunk.

Looking at her, Kevin whistled lowly. Valerie wore white Spandex and a matching tank top that appeared to have been shrink-wrapped to her body. Her nipples, hard as buttons, pressed against the fabric.

He met her at the trunk of her car.

"All I can say is, my, my, my," he said. He slid his hand to her butt and squeezed.

Valerie removed a leather bag from the trunk. She smiled with false modesty. "I don't know what you mean, mister. I'm here for an innocent workout."

"That so? And where are you exercising?"

"In the woods." She handed the bag to him, nodded toward the forest beyond the parking lot and tennis and basketball courts. "Òff the trails out there."

"Okay." Sex in the great outdoors; a little kinky; he liked that. He peeked inside the bag. "What's in here?"

"Something we can use—but you've gotta catch me first."

"Holdup—"

Laughing, she took off running on the paved trail.

"Wait up!" He chased after her.

Kevin considered himself to be in good shape. He hit the weights four times a week, ran on the indoor track at the

114

health club, and followed a healthful diet. For a man of thirty-two, he was in better condition than most guys ten years younger than him.

But Valerie was a phenomenal runner. She had to have been a track and field athlete in college; she ran with elegant, powerful strides.

Still, Kevin ran as hard as he could, the bag bouncing against his ribs, his shoes slapping across the pavement The woods around them thickened, and insects swarmed through the humid air, buzzing across his face. Ahead, Valerie was a white blur, steadily pulling farther ahead.

Does this woman think I'm Carl Lewis?

She rounded a bend, around a gigantic oak tree. He thought he saw her dart off the path. Where was she going?

As he neared the big oak, he left the trail and plunged into the woods, too.

He found Valerie in a small clearing. She leaned against a tree, arms crossed, grinning. She wasn't even sweating.

"About time," she said.

"Damn, girl, you trying to kill me?" He bent over, gasping. He dropped the bag onto the grass.

"A brisk morning run is good for the body." She unzipped the bag and removed a folded cotton blanket. She spread it on the grass.

Then she rose, and began to take off her clothes.

"Just like a morning fuck," she said.

"Now you're talking my language." He began to strip out of his gear.

* * *

Concealed in a thicket of trees and shrubs, Marcus aimed his high-powered Canon digital camera at the two lovers and snapped one incriminating photo after another.

Although investigations of domestic problems were the bread and butter of his business, he despised men like Kevin. Men who had the love of a good woman and took it for granted. Men just like his own father.

Kevin didn't deserve Lauren. She was too good for him, and even she realized it, too.

If she didn't, she surely would after he showed these pictures to her.

Then she would be open to the advances of a real man . . .

* * *

Remembering that Valerie had hooked him up with some oral love in the stockroom of the church bookstore, Kevin decided to repay the favor.

As she lay on the blanket, nude, he knelt in front of her. He parted her legs and slid his hands underneath her ass.

Then, lifting her pelvis, he bent and kissed the outer folds of her pussy. Feather light kisses.

"Oooooh," she said. Eyes closed, she clenched fist-fills of the blanket in her hands.

He began to pleasure her with his tongue. Licking her up and down, as if he were eating an ice cream cone.

Valerie cried out, squirmed, trembled.

He pushed his tongue into her, slow and deep, then flicked it, flicked it, flicked it.

"Oh. . . . oh. . . . oh!" she cried.

Her warm juices flooded his mouth. As she began to thrash and convulse, he continued to lick and kiss. When the orgasm hit her, she released a cry that echoed in the woods like the sound of a wild animal. She spasmed, twitched. . . . and then dropped to the blanket, panting, sweat glistening on her lovely body.

Kevin unwrapped a condom and rolled it on. Then he rose on all fours and looked down at her.

"That was just a warm-up," he said.

She grinned at him. "Can I catch my breath first?"

"Put your legs around my waist," he said. "And your arms around my neck."

After a moment, she did as he said. As she held on to him, he picked her up off the blanket. He carried her to a nearby pine tree and pressed her back against the thick trunk, for support, and he gripped her ass to keep her from sliding down.

She quickly got the idea. Unwrapping her arms from his neck, she reached up and grasped a sturdy, low-hanging branch.

As she held on to the tree, her legs twined around his waist, he began to plunge into her. Her pussy was tight, contracting around his dick like a warm, moist mitten; she probably worked it with Kegel exercises or Ben Wa balls. He ground into her slowly at first, finding his rhythm, and then gradually picked up speed and intensity.

Valerie's head was thrown back, lips parted with ecstasy. As she shook and moaned, rattling the branch she was gripping, pinecones began to tumble out of the tree and rain to the ground. One of them bounced onto Kevin's head.

Still, he kept thrusting, hammering into her as if trying to nail her against the tree.

"Ain't . . . . no. . . . body gave it. . . . to you. . . . like this!" he shouted as he jammed into her.

Her legs tightened around him, pulled him in deeper.

"Nobody . . . . nobody!" she cried.

Pinecones and needles dropped onto them. Insects swarmed around their sweaty bodies. Kevin was oblivious of everything but the delicious sensations surging in his dick and rippling through his body.

"Oh, shit!"

The orgasm hit him so hard he almost fell down. His knees buckling, he plopped on his butt on the soft grass. He was breathing hard, and sweat poured from his brow.

Dangling from the tree branch, Valerie gently lowered herself to the ground. She came to him, sat beside him on the grass.

"Now it's time for a cooldown," she said.

Kevin ripped off the used condom and tossed it into the grass. His dick was already growing hard again.

"Not yet," he said.

Chapter 24

About an hour later, Kevin and Valerie headed back to their cars.

"So, what're you doing the rest of the day?" she asked.

"Enjoying my temporary bachelorhood."

"Hmph. I don't even want to ask what you mean by that."

He cracked a smile; though sex with Valerie had been incredible, he was already salivating at the thought of meeting Black Venus that night.

"Nope, you don't," he said.

They arrived at their cars. Valerie popped open her trunk, placed her bag inside. She cocked her head, studied him.

"What?" he asked.

"Do you ever feel guilty about it?"

"About what?"

"You know. Being with other women. Do you ever feel guilty about it?"

He shrugged. He wasn't in the mood to be analyzed again.

"I have needs," he said simply and honestly. "My wife refuses to meet them. Why're you asking? Are you trying to give me a guilt trip?"

She smirked. "Please, I ain't mad at you. One woman's loss is another's gain." She stepped into the circle of his arms, pressed her lips against his, drew his tongue into her mouth, and sucked gently. He kneaded her firm hips, remembering how wonderful it had felt to hold on to her booty and thrust with all his might. His dick stiffened; it had gotten such a vigorous workout that morning that it ached.

"I need to bounce," he said. "You're teasing Mr. Big here. He needs to recuperate."

She placed her hand on his crotch. "I hope I get to see him again soon."

"You most definitely will. You going to church tomorrow?"

"Of course." She smiled knowingly. "Should I attend the ten-thirty service?"

* * *

Kevin was back home, taking a much-needed nap, when his cell phone chirped—his main phone, not the cell he kept for his extracurricular women.

Lauren believed that he was working. He sat up, grabbed the phone off the nightstand, cleared his throat, and then pressed the button to accept the call.

"It's me," Lauren said. She sounded as if she was still driving. "Calling to let you know I made it to Savannah. I'm about to pull into my parents' driveway."

"Great. How was the drive?"

"It was fine. No traffic. Have you gotten a lot of work done?"

"Yep, been very productive so far."

"I won't keep you, then. I'll call you later this evening."

"I'm hanging with the crew tonight," he said quickly. "Someone put together a card game, so—"

"I know, when the boys are playing cards, no talking to the wives on the phone is allowed," she finished for him. "You don't want to be teased as a henpecked punk."

"Something like that."

"I'll call you tomorrow, then."

"Appreciate it, love. Tell your parents I said hello."

"Bye, honey," she said.

Kevin replaced the phone on the nightstand. He stared at the phone, a frown creeping across his face.

He had lied to Lauren, of course, about the boys' night-out card game. Although he did play cards with some frat brothers a couple of times a month, there was no game scheduled for tonight. He had used the card-game story many times as an excuse for why he'd be unable to talk on the phone on some nights.

But why did he now suspect that Lauren was lying to *him* about something?

It was crazy to think such a thing of her—the woman was honest to a fault. But he couldn't ignore the suspicion in the pit of his stomach.

Earlier in the week, he had wondered if she was seeing another man. He decided to take that hypothesis a step further.

What if she had gone to visit her lover this weekends— and not her parents?

He couldn't imagine Lauren, Miss Innocent, doing such a thing, but his imagination was running away with him. Lauren had been acting strange lately, and there had to be a reason why.

There was one simple way to test his theory.

He picked up the landline phone, punched the button to view the address book, and located the number for Lauren's parents. He called.

After five minutes of forced friendliness with Lauren's mother, he hung up.

Lauren wasn't at her parents' house. She had told her folks that neither she nor Kevin could visit that weekend, due to other obligations.

She had lied to him.

Kevin paced through the condo, tapping the phone against his thigh.

Where was Lauren?

And what the hell was she up to?

Chapter 25

"Jesus," Lauren said, examining the photos that Marcus had taken earlier that day. "I knew Kevin was fooling around, but this is . . ." She shook her head, struggling to hold in the tears that wanted to gush out of her. "So *shameless*. He doesn't have an ounce of guilt about what he's doing. Not one ounce."

It was late in the afternoon. She and Marcus were on the patio of a Mexican restaurant on busy Ponce de Leon. A basket of tortilla chips and a bowl of salsa sat on the table between them, untouched. Although it was steamy outdoors, in the low nineties, Marcus hadn't sipped his Corona, and Lauren hadn't drunk her ice water, either. She didn't have an appetite for anything, and Marcus probably hadn't drunk or eaten out of respect for her.

At least some men in the world had feelings.

Marcus had snapped a dozen black-and-white photographs of Kevin's erotic rendezvous that morning. Kevin had met up with the woman at a park in Marietta, and they'd had sex in the woods, like wild animals. Afterward, they'd been groping and necking in the parking lot.

Shameless.

Lauren recognized the woman, too. She was positive that she'd seen her at church, working in the bookstore. She was striking, Lauren admitted, and had a great body. But Lauren didn't think the woman was any prettier than she was.

Then why did Kevin want to be with her?

She knew the answer even as she asked the question: sex. Lauren would never have sex outdoors in the sweltering, bug-infested woods. She would have done something like that in her youth—had, in fact—but she was a married woman now, and that kind of conduct wasn't proper for a Christian wife.

"I'm so sorry," Marcus said. "I hate to be the bearer of bad news."

"You're only doing your job." Tears were pushing at her eyes again, and this time she didn't have the fortitude to hold them back. She picked up her purse. "Excuse me."

She staggered to the ladies' room. She locked herself in a stall, slammed down the toilet lid, plopped down on it, and wept.

I gave this man everything, and this is what I get? Photos of him fucking a whore in the woods?

She snatched a fistful of toilet tissue from the nearby roll and blotted her eyes.

She and Kevin had been living a storybook lifestyle— hot careers, a beautiful condo, luxury cars, an exciting social calendar, fabulous vacations. They were the envy of their family and friends, the quintessential buppie couple.

But none of it meant anything if she couldn't trust Kevin to honor the basic vows of their marriage. She wasn't one of those pitiful women who could look the other way as their husbands cheated, so long as the men were paying the bills and keeping their wives draped in jewelry and fine clothes. She could buy *her own* jewelry and clothes. She needed Kevin to give her what she couldn't buy for herself: his heart. Completely.

By cheating on her, he was robbing her.

The bitter realization brought a fresh wave of tears to her eyes.

A black woman—Lauren could tell from the pedicured toes she glimpsed underneath the stall door— knocked on the door.

"Hey, are you okay in there?"

"I'm fine, thanks," Lauren said thickly. She had to pull herself together; she was in a public restroom, she reminded herself. This wasn't the place to have a nervous breakdown.

"Whatever he did, he ain't worth it, girl," the stranger said, her voice full of sisterly understanding.

The wisecrack made Lauren smile through her tears.

She used another handful of tissue to wipe her cheeks. Her makeup smeared the paper. She must look like a hot mess.

But the woman was right. Kevin wasn't worth it. She had given him too much power over her heart.

She was an independent woman. Her parents had raised her to take care of herself, whether she had a man or not. She was better than this. Stronger than this.

She rose off the toilet seat, dumped the soiled tissues in the bowl, and hit the flush lever. She left the stall and approached the mirror above the sink.

She was right—her makeup was a mess. Her eyes were bloodshot from crying, her hair tousled.

I have a handsome, sexy man sitting outside waiting for me, and here I am with teary eyes and disheveled hair, looking like crap.

A flicker of the youthful, carefree Lauren—the one she had tried to stamp out with heavy churching and Bible reading and prayer—pried at the edges of her thoughts.

Lauren decided not to hold back anymore. She'd played good, innocent wifey for all this time, and what had it gotten her?

Nothing but heartache.

No more, damn it.

She snapped open her purse, dug out her Visine, makeup compact, and lipstick, and set about fixing herself up.

Ten minutes later, Lauren strolled out of the ladies' room, swinging her hips, head held high and proud. As she strutted through the dining room, men stopped what they were doing and gawked. One admirer spilled salsa on his shirt.

She smiled to herself.

Marcus was taking a swig of Corona when she neared the table. He set down the bottle quickly, as if guilty.

"Go ahead and drink your beer, honey," she said. She settled into her chair. "I'm going to have a drink, too."

With a wave of her hand that was pure diva attitude, she summoned over the Latino waitress.

"I'd like a margarita, frozen, with a double shot of tequila," she said. "Top shelf, too, not the cheap stuff."

As the waitress hurried away to retrieve the order, Marcus gaped at her. "Are you okay, Lauren?"

She popped a tortilla chip in her mouth and crunched on it with gusto. "I'm doing fine. I've just rediscovered my priorities."

"Oh." He fidgeted with his beer bottle, looking unsure. "Meaning?"

"I'm going to take care of Lauren's needs." She slid her hand across the table and grasped his. She brushed her finger across his knuckles. "Do you have any plans for later tonight?"

"I thought you wanted me to follow your husband at the Ritz, be there when he meets this woman from the Internet—"

"That's not necessary." She smiled sourly. "He told me earlier that he's going to be at a card game with his boys."

Marcus scowled. "You don't believe that."

"He's lying through his teeth, obviously." She indicated the envelope that contained the incriminating photos. "I know where he'll be, and it'll only be more of the same. I've seen enough."

"In that case, then, I'm free tonight."

The waitress delivered the margarita. Lauren flicked her tongue across the salt-encrusted rim of the glass, keeping her gaze on Marcus all the while. A cute blush bloomed in his cheeks.

She realized that, like most men, Marcus was accustomed to being the predator, not the prey. She took a mischievous— almost malicious—delight in flipping the script on him.

She couldn't wait to do the same thing to Kevin.

Chapter 26

Ever since his conversation with Lauren's mother, Kevin had been trying to figure out what kind of game Lauren was running on him.

At home, he searched through her dresser drawers, purses, jackets, and other clothes, looking for a scrap of evidence to support his theory that she was out with another man.

He logged on to the laptop she used at home, looked in her Outlook folders for a record of e-mails she'd sent, rummaging for anything revealing—a photo of a man, a love letter, a phone number.

He didn't find a damn thing. Not one thing.

Desperate, he took his search outside their condo and drove by her job. Not finding her car in the underground garage, he drove past the house of Charmaine, her best girlfriend, in Decatur.

No luck. Charmaine's Lexus coupe was parked in the driveway, but Lauren's BMW was not.

Now what?

He was hungry by now. Heading back into the city, he stopped at a cafe in Buckhead to grab a quick bite and to rethink his strategy. He sat on the patio and started eating a chicken Caesar salad, washing it down with tea.

He worried that he was overlooking something obvious, something simple.

Midway through his salad, he hit upon the idea of cruising past Lauren's favorite restaurants. Perhaps, thinking she was free from suspicion, she would be foolish enough to visit one of those places with her man.

The mere thought of seeing Lauren with another man made his jaws clench. He didn't know what he would do if he found her out with a guy. He'd probably wind up in jail, because there would likely be a murder.

He quickly finished his meal and hopped back in his Jaguar.

Although Lauren had enjoyed a privileged childhood, she had surprisingly mundane tastes when it came to food. A bar-and-grill that served good hot wings, a smoky barbecue joint with slammin' ribs, a hole-in-the-wall Mexican spot with spicy salsa and tasty margaritas . . . Lauren preferred no-frills dining. When they went to an expensive restaurant, it was usually because Kevin wanted them to go.

A couple of her favorites—a Mexican place and a sports bar— were on Ponce de Leon. Kevin drove onto that road first. He was driving on the busy thoroughfare, feeling a bit like a detective—Columbo or someone— when he rolled past the Mexican restaurant Lauren liked, El Azteca, and saw her sitting on the patio with a young black man.

He nearly slammed on the brakes.

Goddammit, I was right. I don't believe this shit!

Rage seized him; his hands gripped the steering wheel almost tightly enough to bend it out of shape, as if it were no more than a loop of wire.

He swung a vicious left at the next intersection and jammed to a stop in front of a bank, parking illegally.

Right then, he didn't give a damn. He had *seen* his -wife cheating on him, firsthand, and he was going to kill the man, and then do something to her. He didn't know what, yet, but it would be something horrible.

He banged open the door.

From where he'd parked, he could see Lauren and the soon-to-be-dead guy across the street, drinking and eating as if they didn't have a care in the world. They were laughing; Lauren brushed her fingers across the guy's arm, suggestively.

The bitch!

Kevin gnashed his teeth. So much white-hot fury consumed him that he felt that if he opened his mouth, he would spit flames.

His cell phone rang.

Who the fuck is calling me right now?

Turning away from the restaurant, he snatched his phone from the holster on his hip and answered without checking the number. "What?"

"Are you okay, Brother Kevin?"

It was Oliver. His baritone had the immediate effect of anchoring Kevin back to reality.

"Oliver . . . sorry, man. I didn't know it was you calling." Kevin cast a glance across the street, where Lauren and the guy continued to chatter and flirt. "I'm in the middle of something right now. Can I call you back?"

"You sound upset, my brother. What's going on?"

Kevin expelled a sigh. He was in no mood to let Oliver play psychologist.

"Listen, Oliver—"

"I was calling to discuss the agenda for the men's ministry meeting tomorrow," Oliver said. "But it appears that I may have called at a bad time."

Kevin didn't say anything. He squeezed the phone hard enough to leave a red imprint on his palm.

"It's always a bad idea to act in anger," Oliver said sagely. "Whatever the matter may be, a cool head always prevails."

"Thanks for the words of wisdom. But I really do have to go."

"Call me back as soon as you can."

Kevin stuffed the phone back in his hip holster. He wanted to charge across the street and tear shit up . . . but Oliver's call had given him pause.

Maybe he shouldn't confront Lauren and her man right now.

Maybe he should take a step back, cool off, and take time to plot his next move. Something much better than a beat-down.

He looked at Lauren and the guy one last time, felt a reawakening of his fury, and then, before he acted on it, he got back in the car.

He was sweating profusely. He wiped his face dry with a handkerchief.

He knew the truth about Lauren. That was the good thing, as

angry as it made him. She couldn't make a fool of him anymore.

But he could continue to do whatever he wanted, and she would have no idea. She was still in the dark about his secret life.

In other words, he had the upper hand.

The dashboard clock read a quarter to five. Suddenly, he was more eager than ever to meet Black Venus that night at the Ritz.

He grinned savagely.

Living well wasn't the best revenge, as some people believed.

Fucking well was the best revenge.

* * *

Eve was preparing for her date with Kevin.

She dressed very conservatively, in an unadorned, long blue dress that left no thigh exposed, and black pumps. She tied her hair up in a no-nonsense, old lady bun, and put on glasses (nonprescription) that had chunky black frames. She wore light makeup and clear lip gloss.

Full-length mirrors covered the outer doors of her walk-in closet. She surveyed herself in the glass.

She looked like the stereotypical librarian, on the path to becoming an old, unsexed maid.

She grinned.

Kevin had seen enough in her photos to know that underneath the plain dress, she possessed a body that could make grown men worship at her feet. He would get a kick out of her downplaying her considerable assets. It would excite a man like him.

She wanted to please him. At the beginning.

Her dogs, Snow and Storm, flanked her in the mirror. They wagged their tongues approvingly.

She'd fed the dogs earlier. She would feed the other, basement-kept dog before she left the house.

She had a wonderful evening ahead of her, and she didn't want to have to hurry to return home.

Chapter 27

At seven-fifteen, Kevin entered the lobby of the Ritz-Carlton in Buckhead. He and Black Venus had agreed to meet there at seven.

He'd come fifteen minutes late, on purpose.

A man in charge always made a woman wait. Besides, making her experience a little anxiety about whether he would show up would get her blood pumping, stoke the flames of lust.

As he'd promised her, Kevin wore a gray Armani suit and carried a brown Prada bag; the bag contained a change of clothes, and basic toiletries. If this escapade turned out anything like he thought it would, he would be spending the night there.

Kevin looked around the elegantly appointed lobby. He'd visited the hotel a couple of times before, once on business, once with Lauren to celebrate New Year's Eve, and the establishment was no less impressive on a third viewing. The Georgian and Regency antique furniture . . . the crystal chandeliers . . . the eighteenth-century English paintings and sculptures. . . . the shining marble tables . . . the opulent decor impressed upon Kevin how *special* this particular rendezvous was to him. Black Venus was not an ordinary woman.

He hoped.

Silver-haired white folks, their haughty bearing reflecting their well-heeled backgrounds, milled about in the lobby. A dark-haired Persian couple was at the registration counter, checking in. A knot of Japanese businessmen emerged from the gleaming elevator, chatting in their native language.

Kevin didn't see a woman who matched the description of Black Venus.

What if she got tired of waiting for me and left? he wondered. A dull panic stirred in him. He might have pushed the game-playing too far. If Black Venus was as gorgeous as she appeared in her photos, she might not wait around for a man—any man. Because she didn't have to.

Relax, Kevin. Check in first, and then look around before you jump to conclusions.

He checked in at the front desk. At the rate he was paying for the room, Black Venus had better show up, damn it, or else *he* was going to call someone else to meet him there.

Pocketing the room key card, he saw the entrance for the Lobby Lounge. He headed there.

When he stepped into the doorway, he saw her.

She sat at the bar, sipping a glass of white wine. Her hair was pulled back into a bun, and she had on a pair of glasses with thick black frames. She wore a long blue dress that showed virtually no skin, and sensible black pumps.

Kevin's heart clutched.

Although she was dressed in a way to deemphasize her looks, she was still gorgeous, easily the most attractive woman in the room. The men—rich white guys, most of them, their faces flushed red from alcohol— couldn't keep their eyes off her.

One of them sat next to her, too, chatting nonstop. She was barely paying attention to him.

Squaring his shoulders, Kevin made his approach.

"Excuse me." He cleared his throat. "Sorry I'm late, baby."

The woman turned around in her seat. Although she wore glasses, the lenses didn't detract from her striking honey-brown eyes. Her lips—luscious and glistening with light gloss—parted into a dazzling smile.

"Well, hello there," she said. She had a low, throaty voice with a hint of a Georgia accent.

The portly man who'd been talking her ear off took one look

at Kevin, and then slid away like a dog with its tail between its legs. Kevin took the empty seat and placed his bag on the floor between them.

The woman shifted in the stool to face Kevin.

"Would you like a drink?" she asked. "Chardonnay?"

"That would be great."

She signaled the bartender, who zipped over as if he were her personal assistant. The bartender quickly poured another glass of wine.

"To a fabulous night," she said, and raised her glass for a toast.

"To a fabulous night," he repeated, thinking: *I know that's right. I'm gonna blow her back out.*

They clinked their glasses together, and drank.

"So what's your name?" he asked.

A smile played along the edges of her lips. "You don't like Black Venus?"

"I like it just fine. But I figured you probably don't sign your checks with that name."

"My name is Eve. And yours? Or is it really . . . Supershaft?" She flicked her gaze downward to his crotch.

He laughed. "It's Kevin."

"You looked great in your photo, Kevin. I must say, you look even better in person."

"You didn't see my face in the picture."

"True, and you didn't see mine. I don't think our faces are very important for what we have planned. Would you agree?"

"Preach on, sista." He nodded, taking in her body. "You've concealed the assets well with that old-fashioned dress, and those thick glasses and your bun hairstyle. I actually find it sexy."

"How would you know whether this is my normal attire or not? I might be an old-fashioned kindergarten teacher for all you know."

"Are you?"

Eve grinned. "I'll never tell."

"Funny." He sipped his Chardonnay. He was digging this

woman—a lot. In spite of her looks, she was easygoing, relaxed, friendly. And she had a naughtiness about her that came to the surface, librarian getup or not.

"Would you like to have dinner?" he asked. "Their restaurant here, the Dining Room, is top-notch. We might be able to squeeze in without a reservation."

She shook her head. "The only thing I was planning on eating is sitting right here in front of me."

She slid her hand to his groin and squeezed.

Kevin's Freak-o-meter shot off the charts. *This woman is something else!*

"All righty, then," he said, and sucked in a great breath. Cool perspiration formed like dew on his forehead. "I think we'd better go upstairs."

Chapter 28

Kevin had reserved an executive suite. It was the size of an apartment, with a separate parlor and bedroom, a king-size bed, and a bay window that featured a view of the Atlanta skyline.

"Very nice," Eve said. Surveying the suite, she walked inside, her long dress swishing around her legs. "A simple girl like me could get used to this kind of luxury."

"A simple girl like you, huh?" Kevin placed their bags—she had brought a wheeled piece of luggage— near the closet. "You don't seem all that simple to me. You seem pretty damn sophisticated."

She smiled, shrugged. "Good home training, I suppose."

Per Kevin's request, an ice bucket containing a bottle of premium champagne stood on a table in the parlor. He checked the label, nodded with approval.

"Have you ever done this before?" he asked.

"Done what before?"

"Arranged a meeting with a man you've never seen in person."

"How do you know I've never seen you in person?" Mystique sparkled in her eyes.

He sat on the bed, chuckled. "I would remember meeting you. Believe that."

"So you say." She sat next to him. Her fragrance, a soft spicy scent, teased his nose.

"Regarding whether I've ever done this before— a lady never discusses her prior . . . adventures."

"Adventures. Nice word."

"Doesn't it seem apropos?" She fingered his silk tie and loosened the knot. "That's precisely what this is. An adventure. A game. Of an erotic nature."

"And we're players."

"Exactly." She slid his tie from around his neck, slung it over her shoulder. "But before we go any further, would you mind doing something for me?"

"What?"

"Don't take this the wrong way, dear. But. . . . would you please shower?"

He frowned. "Do I stink?"

"Of course not. It's an idiosyncrasy of mine. I always ask a man to take a fresh shower before I become intimate with him. There's something so sexy about a man who's just stepped out of the shower."

"Now that you put it that way." He smiled, rose. "I'll be back shortly."

"Wonderful. I'll prepare the room and the champagne— and myself."

"I can't wait." He headed to the bathroom.

Eve's shower request didn't really surprise him. Some women had peculiar tastes when it came to sex. One woman he'd been with would have sex with him only if he wore a Kangol while they were in the midst of the act. She said seeing him in the hat made her horny, and she would show up for their trysts with caps of different colors for him to wear. He'd decided that she had a secret fantasy to sleep with LL Cool J.

As Kevin lathered soap over his body, he thought about Lauren. Where was she? What was she doing? He almost never thought about his wife while he was with another woman, but since he'd seen her with that dude earlier that day, she kept popping into his mind.

It was an ego thing. He considered himself as a virile, desirable man, capable of pleasing virtually any woman he encountered. Lauren had seemed happy with him and their lives. It was inconceivable that she would seek out another man for satisfaction. No man could ever satisfy her the way he could.

He wondered if she let her boyfriend go downtown on her. Or if she went downtown on *him*.

He tightened his grip on the bar of soap.

He had to let go of these thoughts, at least for tonight. His worries would prevent him from maintaining a hard-on, and he didn't want to risk ruining his rendezvous with Eve.

A woman like Eve required his full concentration.

* * *

Done showering, Kevin returned to the bedroom. He wore one of the fluffy hotel bathrobes.

Eve had shut off the lamps. She'd lit several candles, arranging them in a circle around the room. The candles cast dancing, golden light, and shadows dwelled everywhere.

He didn't see Eve.

"Eve, where are you?"

"Here." She rose from a darkened corner of the parlor and came into the light.

She had let her hair down; it fanned out around her head like a halo. She'd taken off her glasses, too.

He drew in a deep breath.

And she'd taken off the dress.

She wore a black leather teddy that exposed a lot of skin, and black stilettos. Her body, if it could be believed, looked even better in person than it had in her phenomenal photos.

"Damn," he said. "I'll say it again—there's no way in hell I've ever met you before. You're unforgettable."

"Thank you." She lifted the champagne flutes, which she had filled with bubbly, from a nearby table. She offered one to him.

"Bottoms up," she said.

They clicked their glasses together, and sipped. The champagne percolated deliciously in his stomach. He drank all of it and set the glass on a table.

Eve finished her drink, looked him up and down, and licked her lips.

Then she grabbed the belt of his bathrobe and tugged him toward her.

"I like a take-charge kind of girl," he said.

She untied his bathrobe and peeled it away from his body. His dick stuck out in front of him like an exclamation point.

"Nine inches," she said in a hushed tone. She put her hand on him and stroked softly. "I thought you might've been lying about that."

"I don't lie," he said. "Now it's time for you to eat."

Smiling, she sank to her knees. Pressing her nose against his flat stomach, she inhaled deeply.

"You smell so good," she said. "Are you ready?"

"Doesn't it look like it, girl?"

She brought him toward her lips—and nipped at him with her teeth. Pain stung him.

"What the fuck was that?" He pulled away from her. "You don't bite a man's dick! Are you out of your damn mind?"

She grabbed his arm, and, with surprising strength, swung him around and threw him. He fell onto the bed. He tried to sit up, and it was like trying to move while submerged in the deep end of the swimming pool. His muscles suddenly felt sluggish.

She put something in my drink, he thought. *Drugged me . . .*

Eve planted her heel against his chest and forced him back onto the mattress.

As he lay there, stunned and slowly growing numb, she climbed on top of him, dipped her head to his abdomen, and clamped her teeth on the soft flesh of his stomach.

His muscles might have been failing him, but his nerves were working. The bite hurt like hell. He yelped in pain.

She jerked her head upright and gave him a savage glare. "Shut up! Stop acting like a fuckin' bitch!"

Madness gleamed in her eyes. Blood dribbled down her chin. *His* blood.

The sickening realization energized him. He grabbed her arms, tried to shove her off him.

Roaring like a tiger, she latched her nails into his flesh and pulled him with her. They tumbled onto the floor together, like wrestlers.

Kevin, unable to fight the increasing effects of the drug, struggled, but couldn't get her off him. Eve quickly regained the upper hand, straddling him on the floor.

"You said you like it kinky!" she shrieked in his face. "Said you wanted a walk on the wild side! Get with the program, you punk-ass bitch!"

She bit him on the neck, hard. Kevin cried out. He grabbed fistfuls of her hair in his hands. He pulled, trying to rip her hair out by the roots.

She screamed, tore her hair out of his grip. She clamped both of her hands around his throat and began to squeeze.

He gagged. Her choking him, combined with the drug, made his vision veer crazily.

I'm going to die, he thought, with certainty. *This crazy bitch is going to kill me.*

Choking him, she leaned closer, her lips near his.

"Erotic asphyxiation," she whispered. "Turns me on to administer it, just like drugging a man does. Wanted to give you the double whammy, Kevin Richmond. You deserve it and everything to follow for what you did to me."

How does she know my full name, and what the hell is she talking about? he wondered vaguely. And just as vaguely, he felt himself inside her, erect and throbbing in spite of his terror. She was tight and warm around him, and she moved her hips rhythmically, milking him—even as she tightened her choke hold.

The world was turning gray.

Then an orgasm buckled through him, the strongest climax of his life, like a bolt of lightning blasting away the darkness. Eve threw back her head and screeched, like a wolf baying at a full moon.

Her lunatic eyes, shining in the candlelight, were the last things Kevin saw before he blacked out.

Chapter 29

When Kevin awoke, he was lying in bed, a lamp burning nearby.

Which bed, he didn't know. Groggy, he looked around, bunking slowly. The room was high ceilinged, opulently decorated . . .

The Ritz. I'm at the Ritz-Carlton.

His mouth was cotton-dry; he swallowed. Swallowing made his windpipe hurt—it felt as if he'd eaten broken glass. Several points on his body were tender and sore, too.

He pulled away the bedsheet that covered him. He was wearing the hotel bathrobe. He parted the folds to examine himself. Angry red bite marks marred his flesh, as if a wild animal had savaged him.

That crazy bitch, Eve.

The memory of his experience with her felt surreal, like a fever dream. He would have doubted that it had ever happened—if not for his wounds.

There were no signs of the psycho woman. The candles were gone; her luggage was gone. She had left.

Wondering how long he had been out, he peered at the digital clock on the nightstand. It read a quarter past one in the morning. He had been unconscious for several hours.

What kind of drug had she put in his champagne that would knock him out like that?

And why?

He thought about his wallet. Maybe she'd set him up, stolen his credit cards and his money and was even now on a spending spree at a twenty-four-hour Wal-Mart, charging his accounts to the max.

He remembered leaving his suit in the bathroom, when he'd undressed to shower. He sat up and swung out of bed, still feeling sluggish, as if he had a helluva hangover.

That was when he saw the blood on the floor.

Chapter 30

The blood was pooled on the hardwood floor, near the bed. It *was* blood, unmistakably; almost dry, it was a dark rust color, and gave off a familiar, coppery odor.

Whose blood was it? His? Although Eve had drawn blood when she had bitten him, he hadn't bled so profusely that he would've spilled *this* much blood.

Maybe it's Eve's blood, a voice whispered to him. *Maybe you killed her, Kevin.*

"No," he said, aloud. Although, after her ferocious attack on him, he had perhaps been furious enough to kill her in a blind rage, he had never actually gotten his hands on her. He remembered pulling her hair, to try to get her off him.

But drawing blood, and this much of it?

It made no sense.

But whomever it belonged to, he had to clean it up. Immediately. He was in a hotel, and if the staff found out about this, they would want an explanation—and he didn't have one.

See, there was this fine-ass woman in my room. We had sex—the craziest sex I've ever had in my life. But she drugged me, too, man, and when I woke up, I found all this blood on the floor. I know, it's a nutty story, right? But I swear, I didn't do anything wrong. . . . .

Yeah, right. It sounded like bullshit even to him.

Feeling a growing panic, Kevin stumbled into the bathroom—and almost stepped on a shard of glass. The champagne bottle lay on the marble floor, just past the doorway, the bottle's blunt end shattered to jagged edges that were splattered with a dried substance.

More blood. As if the bottle had been used like a billy club.

What the hell's going on?

He looked inside the bathroom. He'd left his suit hanging on a hook behind the door. It was gone.

Being careful to avoid stepping on glass fragments, he crossed the bedroom and went to the closet. His suit hung inside. He fished inside the inner jacket pocket.

His wallet was there. He opened it—none of his cash or credit cards were missing. Eve hadn't robbed him.

He reached inside the jacket again, to verify that he still had his cell phone.

There was a cell phone in his pocket. But it didn't belong to him. He'd brought the phone he used for his extramarital activities, a basic, prepaid Motorola model.

This phone was a Samsung, smaller than his.

Did it belong to Eve? Why would she have left her phone in his pocket?

He had no idea.

He had no idea about any of this stuff: the blood on the floor, the busted champagne bottle, the cell phone. It was as if he'd been dropped into a real-life *CSI* episode.

That's precisely what this is. An adventure. A game. Of an erotic nature.

Eve had spoken those words to him before he'd left to take a shower. Before the night had taken a sharp turn into bizarre, frightening territory.

She had to be behind this.

He flipped open the phone and turned it on.

There was a new text message awaiting him. He pressed the key to read it.

It consisted of a single word: CONFESS.

What? Confess to what?

The message had arrived an hour ago. It had been sent from a familiar number—the number of *his* prepaid cell phone.

Someone—it had to have been Eve—had swapped his phone

with this one, and now she was using it to communicate with him.

But why?

He'd never been so confused in his life.

As he stood there, staring at the phone and thinking that he needed to get started cleaning the blood off the floor, someone knocked on the door.

Chapter 31

Kevin stood near the closet, paralyzed with fear.

The visitor knocked again, harder.

"Who is it?" Kevin asked, his voice cracking on the last word.

"Hotel security," a gruff voice announced. "Are you in there, Mr. Richmond? We've received a call about a disturbance in your room."

Shit, shit, shit!

Looking around, frantic, Kevin grabbed the bedsheet, snatched it off the bed, and used it to cover the bloodstain. Then he closed the door to the bathroom, to hide the broken bottle and glass shards.

Another knock, sharper.

"Mr. Richmond, I'm coming in."

Kevin threw another look around to make sure nothing else was out of place, and then rushed to the door, cinching the bathrobe tight as he ran.

A tall, hyper muscular black man dressed in a navy-blue security uniform waited outside. His eyes were narrowed with suspicion.

"What's up?" Kevin asked. "There's no disturbance in here. I was sleeping, man."

The guard tried to look over Kevin's shoulder. "Someone reported hearing a woman screaming, sir."

"What?" Kevin gave the best false laugh that he could summon. "That's crazy, man. There's no one in here but me."

"Someone reported seeing you enter the room with a woman."

"And? She left hours ago."

"You mind if I come inside, have a look?"

Kevin faltered, thought of telling the guy that he needed a warrant to do a search, and then wondered if the law applied to a hotel room, which, technically, wasn't his property.

Not waiting for an answer, the guard shouldered past him and walked inside. Kevin hurried to head him off before he reached the other side of the bed, where the piled sheet concealed the blood.

"Who called in a report?" Kevin asked.

"It doesn't matter," the guard answered. "You a wild sleeper? Why are the sheets on the floor over there?"

Kevin's face grew hot. "Look, obviously I'm in here alone. I think you're finished here."

"Not yet. Step aside, sir." The guard nudged Kevin out of the way so he could come around the bed. He lifted the bedsheet off the floor. "Is this what I think it is?"

"It's, ah. . . . fruit punch." Kevin was slowly backpedaling toward the closet. He reached inside, grabbed his suit and his shoes.

"Fruit punch, my ass." The guard stepped to the bathroom door and pushed it open. "What the hell . . . "

Kevin didn't hear the rest of his sentence, because he ran out of the room.

"Get back here!" the guard shouted.

Kevin sprinted to the stairwell at the end of the corridor, his suit flapping in his arms, like wings. He took the descending steps two and three at a time, reached the floor below, and banged through the door and stumbled into the hall.

In an alcove off the main corridor, he threw on his suit and shoes, dropping the bathrobe to the floor.

He'd kept the mystery cell phone, figuring that it might be important later. Important for *what,* he had no idea.

Fully dressed, he marched quickly to a stairwell at the opposite end of the hall and took it to the lobby level. Instead of entering the main lobby, he took the service exit, to a maintenance area. He walked through a laundry room, steamy yet vacant at this late hour, and found a door that opened into a shipping and loading dock behind the hotel.

He returned to the front of the hotel, trying to act as if nothing was wrong, and gave his card to the valet. While the valet went to retrieve his car, he stood in front of a pillar, hiding from security that might be searching for him inside.

When the valet finally returned with his car, he was so frazzled that he forgot to tip the guy. He screeched out of the parking lot and onto Peachtree Street, driving toward his condo.

He had to figure out what was going on, and soon.

His freedom might depend on it.

Chapter 32

Scanning the road warily for cops as he drove, Kevin finally arrived home. He parked in the underground garage.

Lauren's parking spot was empty.

She must've still been out with her boyfriend, under the pretense of visiting her parents. Lying ass.

Kevin set aside his anger. He had more important matters to deal with than his unfaithful wife. Like avoiding a prison sentence.

Although it was late, nearing 2:00 a.m., he was amped on adrenaline. He took the stairwell to their fourth-floor condo. With the police presumably searching for him, he didn't want to risk getting stuck in an elevator.

He opened the door to the condo and quick-stepped to the side of the doorway.

You think someone's gonna shoot at you, man?

He didn't know what to expect anymore. He decided it was wisest to be prepared for the worst.

The interior was dark. He reached inside and thumbed the wall switch, turning on the ceiling lamp in the entry hall.

At a glance, nothing appeared to be out of place. The closet door was partly open; the Nikes he'd worn to visit Valerie at the park that morning peeked out from inside, grass bristling from the laces, as he'd left them.

He rushed inside—leaving the door open in case he needed to make a quick exit—and swept through the rooms, turning on lights in each. Family room, living room, dining room, bathrooms, guest bedroom, study, master bedroom.

In the master, he dug into the nightstand drawer on his side of the bed and retrieved the .38 Smith & Wesson revolver from its wooden storage case. The gun was already loaded.

Aiming the muzzle at the ceiling, he climbed to the loft.

The loft was empty, too.

His home was safe.

He returned to the front door and closed it. Engaged the chain and dead-bolt locks.

Leaning against the door, he let the gun drop to his side. He closed his eyes and sighed.

He felt as though he had awakened from a bad dream. Maybe he had. Maybe he had never gone to the Ritz, had stayed home and fallen asleep on the couch.

He wished he had kept his ass at home. He wished he had never communicated with Black Venus, Eve, whatever she called herself. None of this would ever have happened.

If you messed around with freaks, sooner or later you would run into one who was truly crazy. It was like natural law.

You deserve it, and everything to follow, for what you did to me . . .

What had the woman been talking about? He'd never met her in his life.

Perhaps she had mistaken him for someone else. Yet she had known his name, hadn't she?

He massaged his temples. He had to gather his thoughts.

He shuffled to the kitchen, dumped his gun on the counter, and opened the refrigerator. He took out a can of Red Bull and popped the tab. He took a long gulp.

The super caffeinated beverage was going to set his synapses sizzling more than they already were, and that was exactly what he wanted. He didn't plan on going to bed for a while.

Before he sat at the table, he switched on the small television mounted next to a bank of cabinets. He flipped through the local stations.

There were no news bulletins about a black man fleeing a crime scene at the Ritz-Carlton. But he took little comfort from that; a luxury hotel chain like the Ritz, with its own private security staff, might have joined forces with the Atlanta PD and secretly launched an investigation. He could imagine a crime scene tech in the room, like one of those guys in *CSI*, taking samples of the blood, examining the broken, blood-spattered champagne bottle . . . and using it to construct an airtight case against him.

He gnawed on his thumbnail, ruining a recent manicure.

He had to think this through. He went to the refrigerator, grabbed the pen and pad of paper that were pinned to the door with one of Lauren's sorority magnets. Sitting at the kitchen table, he crossed out the *Grocery List* heading and wrote, *What I Know So Far.*

1. *Black Venus/Eve claims she had a prior relationship with me.*

2. *She put a drug in my drink, in order to gain control.*

3. *I was unconscious for at least five hours.*

4. *There was blood on the floor, glass fragments, and a broken champagne bottle with blood on it.*

5. *Someone swapped my cell phone with a new one, sent a text message that said, "Confess."*

Kevin took the cell phone out of his pocket and placed it on the table, beside the notepad. The phone was on, but no more messages had come in.

He added two more points.

6. *A hotel security guard said he had heard of a disturbance in the room and he came inside to investigate.*

7. *The guard saw me flee the scene.*

The memory of that frantic run to freedom kicked up his heart rate.

He flipped to the next page of the notepad, and scribbled another header: *Questions.*

1. Who is Black Venus/Eve?

2. Why does she think we had a prior relation ship?

3. Whose blood was on the floor? Who got in a fight and broke the bottle?

4. Who gave me the cell phone, and who told me to "confess"?

5. What am I being told to confess to doing?

Kevin studied the questions. He couldn't fathom answers to any of them. He didn't know anything about Black Venus/Eve—he didn't have so much as a phone number for her. The rest of the questions were equally perplexing.

He examined the cell phone. He retrieved the text message. *Confess.*

On a whim, he typed in a response: *Who are you?*

He sent the message and waited, hoping that the recipient, whoever it was, was awake at five past two in the morning.

Several minutes passed with no reply.

He went upstairs to the loft. He turned on the laptop and logged on to the Sexcapades Web site.

He had a couple of messages, from new women. Nothing from Black Venus.

He did a search on Black Venus, to study her profile again in the vain hope that it would provide a clue.

He received the system message *Member Profile Does Not Exist.*

"I don't believe this shit," Kevin muttered.

Black Venus had deleted her profile from the system. He had no means to get in touch with her.

She'd exited his life as mysteriously as she'd entered it.

Chapter 33

A knock at the door drew Kevin out of an uneasy slumber.

He'd fallen asleep in the loft, curled up on the rubber exercise mat, still wearing his Armani suit. Nightmares had tortured him: visions of himself murdering Eve by swinging a champagne bottle at her head, and then disposing of the body in the hotel's garbage chute . . .

The images disturbed him. He hadn't really killed Eve. Had he?

The knocking at the door tethered him back in the here and now. The clock beside his computer read 8:13. Who would be visiting him this early on a Sunday, and unannounced at that?

The police . . .

Cold sweat broke out on his forehead.

He didn't want to answer the door. But he didn't see an alternative. If the cops had a warrant, they could enter, and forcibly.

He went to the door and peered out of the fish-eye lens.

The visitor was a middle-aged black man in a gray suit. It was no one that Kevin recognized.

"Mr. Richmond?" the man asked in a hard-edged voice. "You home? Open up—I'm from the Atlanta Police Department."

Kevin's knees turned mushy. He looked behind him. He was on the fourth floor. Short of jumping out the window, there was nowhere to run this time.

He put his lips near the door. "What do you want?"

"Open the door, sir, and we'll discuss it."

Kevin tried to smooth down his rumpled suit—he was sure

that he looked as bad as he felt—and then he unlocked the door and cracked it open.

"Let me see your badge first," Kevin said.

The cop flashed a gleaming, official-looking badge: DETECTIVE ROBERT GARRETT, HOMICIDE DIVISION.

Kevin's heart whammed. "Homicide?"

"Let me in, Mr. Richmond, and I'll tell you what this is all about."

Kevin let the cop inside. Perhaps in his mid-forties, Garrett was about three inches shorter than Kevin, but he was wider, built like a fullback. He had sharp brown eyes and a face like a slab of granite. He smelled of cigarette smoke.

"Apologize for dropping in so early, but I wanted to catch you before you went to church," the cop said.

"Oh, yeah, okay."

The cop sized him up with a quick look. "From the looks of it, though, you ain't gonna be sitting in the front pews this morning. Long night?"

"I'm a lawyer. I was working. Now, what's this all about?"

"Why don't we have a seat in the kitchen?"

"Fine." Kevin led the way. He noticed the revolver that he'd left sitting on the counter. "Before you ask, I have a permit for that."

"I know you do," the cop said, sitting at the table. "Wasn't gonna ask."

Kevin sat. He flipped over the list he'd been working on last night, so the detective couldn't read what he'd written.

"Where's the wife?" Garrett asked.

"She's visiting her parents. How'd you know I was married?"

"I do my research," Garrett said absently. "Anyway, there's a big engagement photo of you two out there in the hall. She's a beautiful woman. You're a lucky brother."

"What are you here for, Detective?"

"Yeah, I'd say you're a *very* lucky brother." Garrett looked around the kitchen, nodding appreciatively. "But you know how life is—everything we have can be taken away, just like that." He snapped his fingers.

Kevin tried not to flinch. It was clear: The detective was

toying with him, trying to lead Kevin to believe that the cops had something on him. But what?

Garrett took out a pocket notebook and a pen. "Where were you last night, Mr. Richmond? The truth."

Kevin considered refusing to answer without an attorney present, but that seemed like the recourse of a guilty man. He hadn't done anything wrong. By talking directly with the cop, maybe he could defuse this situation before it went any further.

"I spent some time at a hotel," Kevin said.

"Which hotel?"

"The Ritz-Carlton, in Buckhead."

"Nice place. Never been in there, but pass by it all the time. What were you there for?"

"I was meeting a friend."

"A female friend?"

Kevin blew out a tight breath. "Yeah."

"When the wife's away, the doggie will play, huh?"

"It wasn't like that."

"Why don't you tell me what it was like, then? Since witnesses spotted you going upstairs to your room with your female friend."

Kevin's face reddened. "Do you really need me to go into all the details?"

"Yes, I do. I want to see how closely our stories match. 'Cause according to our story, you met this mystery woman, took her to your room, and you got rough with each other. Very rough. We've got blood on the floor and a busted champagne bottle. You ran out when a hotel rent-a-cop stopped by to investigate the noises."

Kevin's heart pounded. *I should've refused to say anything without an attorney present,* he realized. *I've fucked myself.*

Garrett put down his notepad and gave Kevin a cold gaze.

"So what's your side of the story, Richmond? You know what it's looking like to me? It's looking like foul play. It's looking like a murder."

"Murder?" Kevin shot to his feet, knocking over his chair. "That's bullshit!"

Garrett showed no emotion; he was as cool as an Arctic breeze. "Where'd you hide her body, Richmond?"

They're going to charge me with murder. Jesus.

"I'm not saying another damn thing without my attorney present," Kevin said.

Garrett waved his hand. "There's no need to get a lawyer involved. All you have to do is ... *confess.*"

Something about the way the detective said the word, and the strange gleam in his eyes, gave Kevin pause.

Confess.

It was the same message he'd received on the cell phone.

"What's going on here?" Kevin asked.

"What's going on is that you're the prime suspect in what appears to be a case of foul play." Garrett tucked his notebook in his pocket and stood. "I can't book you—yet. But I have a high success rate in my investigations, brother. I'm like one of them pit bulls that locks its jaws on you and just doesn't let go."

Garrett placed a business card on the table. "Call me when you're ready to start telling the truth."

The detective let himself out.

Kevin sank back onto the chair. He studied the detective's card. He wanted to tear it up, forget that he'd ever had this encounter. There was no way it was going to resolve in his favor.

He was going to go to prison.

You just like ya daddy.

His dad had spent most of his adult life in and out of jail, for various offenses. Now it seemed Kevin was going to carry on the family tradition.

No, there has to be a way out of this. I'm innocent.

A high-pitched beeping sounded from the loft.

He ran through the condo. The beeping was coming from the cell phone, which he'd left sitting on the computer desk last night.

It was a signal that he'd received a new text message. Like before, it came from his prepaid cell phone. *Look in the past. The truth will set you free.*

Chapter 34

For the first time in years, Lauren awoke in another man's bed.

She lay in a tangle of sheets in Marcus' king-size sleigh bed, sunshine piercing the blinds and painting warm bands on her bare leg. The rest of her body was bare, too; she had gone to sleep in the nude, something she'd never done as a married woman.

I've been a naughty girl.

As she thought about last night, a smile slid across her face. Her inner freak, long buried, had been unleashed again. It was all thanks to Kevin; because of his infidelity, she believed she had the right to indulge her own secret desires. She didn't feel any guilt at all about what she'd done.

However, she did wonder what had happened between Kevin and his Internet psycho chick last night. (In her opinion, any woman who would correspond with a man online and then agree to meet him at a hotel must be crazy.) She hoped that he'd had a horrible time, that the mystery woman had turned out to be four hundred pounds with warts and a mustache.

Damn him.

Anyway, forget about him. She had another man on her plate, so to speak.

Marcus had left the bed. She heard him in the kitchen moving pans and dishes, and she smelled the aroma of sizzling bacon, and brewing coffee.

He was preparing breakfast. That was when you knew for sure that you had rocked a man's world: when he rose the next morning and cooked for you.

She still had her charms. The thought made her warm, contented.

She rose out of bed and sashayed to the bathroom. Marcus's town house was much cleaner and more stylishly furnished than one would expect of a hardworking bachelor. According to him, his mother helped him around the house, and Lauren was inclined to believe him. He was an honest, decent man, a rare find these days.

She did her business on the toilet, and then brushed her teeth. Since she'd packed luggage as part of her plan to deceive Kevin into thinking that she was leaving to visit her family, she had all of her toiletries and clothes.

Although she hadn't needed those clothes last night.

She smiled again.

Shortly after she returned to the bedroom, Marcus entered, carrying a tray of food and beverages. He wore a pair of white lounge pants and no top, his glorious muscles flexing as he transported the food to the bed.

"Breakfast is served," he said, setting the tray down on the mattress.

He'd prepared a platter of scrambled eggs, bacon, toast, and sliced fruit. He'd included mugs of steaming coffee (with cream and sugar on the side, bless him) and tall tumblers of orange juice.

"Thank you, you're such a sweetheart," she said. She sat up, not bothering to cover her breasts, thrilling to how Marcus could barely keep his eyes off them. Yes, her charms were fully intact.

Trying to conceal a growing erection, Marcus settled beside her on the bed and added cream to his coffee. "I want to thank *you* for a great evening. Did you enjoy yourself?"

"I absolutely did." She tasted a slice of bacon. It was crispy, just how she liked it.

"Then maybe we can do this again, soon." His gaze was eager.

"Hmmm." She fed him a forkful of fruit, used a napkin to catch the juices that dribbled down his cheek. "I honestly hadn't considered that, Marcus. While we've been together, I've been living in the present, enjoying your company. I haven't paid any thought to what might happen tomorrow."

"Your husband doesn't deserve you, Lauren. You're too good for him."

"You think so?"

"I know so." He nodded firmly.

"I might believe you." She sipped the orange juice. "But a woman should never believe a man who has a gorgeous set of ta-tas staring him in the face."

"I'm serious," he said. Then his gaze strayed to her breasts again, and he grinned. "But damn, I have to admit I can't keep my eyes off you."

"Know what I think?" Lauren asked. "I think you need some milk with your coffee."

"But I have cream—"

She put her hand over his mouth and nudged the tray away with her foot. She rose in front of him on her knees. She took her fingers away from his lips, cupped the back of his head, and guided his mouth to one of her nipples.

He sucked hungrily, like a nursing baby.

She reached between them and freed his dick from his pants. She eased down on it, loving the sensation of him entering her, filling her up. Marcus released a sigh of pleasure and raised his head.

"You're something else," he murmured, eyes dreamy. "I really, really want to see you again, Lauren."

He was so sincere and nice, almost naively so. And such a *fine* specimen of a man, too.

But she wasn't prepared to start planning a future with him. As a married woman, she had responsibilities— such as scheming what she was going to do about Kevin. Marcus was a great guy, and she was grateful for how his company had brought her old nature out of the cave . . . but he was for fun.

"For now, focus on today," she said. "Later, we'll discuss tomorrow."

He opened his mouth to talk about it further, but then she

began to grind against him, squeezing him inside her with all the considerable skill she'd developed in her youth, and whatever words he'd planned to speak quickly turned into moans and exclamations of pleasure.

Yep, she still had her charms.

Chapter 35

Look in the past. The truth will set you free.

Kevin had sent a message last night, asking about the identity of the message sender, and the person, whoever it was, hadn't bothered to answer. This was a one-way conversation, and none of it made any damn sense.

Kevin paced through the condo, gripping the cell phone. The visit from the detective, and his not-so-subtle threats, had shaken him to the marrow; the new message had given him a headache.

What was going on?

He wanted to assume that Black Venus was behind all of this, that she had made him the unwitting participant in some sort of sick game. But what if she really had been murdered or mortally wounded, her body dragged out of the room by her attacker? What if the attacker had left evidence behind to frame Kevin for the crime?

Look in the past. ... .

What if the message sender really was a friend with knowledge of Kevin's predicament, and was attempting to steer Kevin out of trouble?

He decided that, the messages notwithstanding, the scene at the hotel was a setup. It only made sense.

Someone wanted him to take a fall.

But who? He practiced corporate law, not criminal law (though white-collar crime, ironically, was on the rise), and didn't interact with felons. He didn't have any known enemies in his profession.

No one in his professional life could be responsible.

How about his personal life? He barely spoke to his family members. When his grandmother, the glue holding the family together, had died, his aunts and uncles and cousins had scattered like dust to the wind; he hadn't seen or spoken to any of them since Grandma's funeral. And his mother, her brain blasted by drugs, hardly possessed the mental acuity to engineer a setup of anything other than her next hit, and she had no motive, either.

A family member couldn't be responsible.

Friends? He was tight with Oliver, a few frat brothers, and that was about it. All of them liked him and wouldn't try to pull something like this.

How about women?

Ah, then, the possibilities grew.

What if one of his ex-lovers had decided to get revenge on him? He'd been with countless women over the years, leaving a trail of broken hearts in his wake. Hell hath no fury like a woman scorned.

The idea that an ex-lover was responsible *felt* right to him, deep in his gut. The woman probably had help from someone; he could figure out the details later. For the time being, he needed to figure out who was behind it

So, a woman was the likeliest answer. But which woman?

There had been so many, it could be akin to finding the proverbial needle in the haystack.

To narrow down the possibilities, he figured it had to be someone that he'd recently been with. He couldn't imagine a woman from ten years ago suddenly resolving to exact revenge.

He went to the loft and logged on to the computer.

On the hard drive, he had a folder titled "Motorcycle Pics." That title was only to mislead Lauren if she ever happened to get on to his laptop.

The folder contained photos of women he'd met via the Internet. He had a photo of every woman he'd met from a dating site in the past three years, since he refused to rendezvous with a woman who wouldn't supply a picture—Eve being the notable exception to that rule.

Over seventy women were represented. Black, white, Asian, Latino, all of them in various poses, in various stages of dress: at home with a dog; a night on the town with a posse of girlfriends ("That's me in the red dress"); sunbathing at a beach; grinning for a glamour shot; lying nude on the bed . . .

There were too many to choose from. He had to shorten the list further.

Out of all these women, which of them had resisted ending their short-lived affair with him?

And to cut it down more, say that he'd met the woman within the past six months, meaning that whatever emotional wounds she believed Kevin had inflicted on her might still be fairly fresh.

To aid his recollection, Kevin pulled up Microsoft Outlook under the primary e-mail addresses he used for his dalliances. He sorted the messages by date received, bent toward the screen, and studied the e-mails.

He arrived at three possible suspects.

He still had their personal data stored in his Sidekick. Full names, phone numbers, addresses. Enough for him to begin an investigation.

He headed to the bathroom to take a quick shower.

It was time to find out what the hell was going on.

Chapter 36

As Kevin was taking the elevator down to the parking garage, his primary cell phone rang. It was Oliver.

"Brother Kevin, what happened to you? I didn't see you at church. Did you forget about the men's ministry meeting this morning?"

"Damn!" Kevin said. "I forgot—I didn't plan on coming to church today. You wouldn't believe the shit I've been going through lately, Oliver."

"I have an open mind. Why don't you fill me in?"

Kevin was tempted to tell him. He wanted to unload his burden on someone. Someone cool and levelheaded. Someone who would reassure him that he wasn't losing his mind. Someone like Oliver.

But this situation was too personal to share with anyone, especially someone like Oliver. He worked with the man, after all. Although Oliver knew how to keep his mouth shut, if Kevin told him that he was the main suspect in a criminal investigation, Oliver would be forced to tell the firm's partners—and then Kevin's career would be on the line.

He couldn't risk it.

"I'm sorry, I can't go into it right now," Kevin said.

"I'm sorry for missing the meeting. It won't happen again."

Oliver chuckled. "Don't make a promise you can't keep, brother. That'll get you in more trouble than you're already in."

"Tell me about it. I'm up to my neck in it as it is."

"Trouble at home? Or with the law?"

"With the law? Why would you say that?"

Oliver cleared his throat. "I'm only fishing for information, son."

The elevator reached the garage. Kevin rushed outside, brushing past the sliding doors.

"Oliver, man, I just can't talk about it. I've gotta run." He ended the call.

But Oliver's question disturbed him. Why would he ask if Kevin was in trouble with the law? Did he know something?

Had the cops already approached the firm's partners and made inquiries about him?

Dread seeped into his chest, like sludge.

He ran to his car, his shoes clapping across the concrete floor. He pressed the button on the key chain to deactivate the locks. He was about to throw open the door when he noticed the rear left tire.

It was flat. Not merely flat, but slashed; a gaping hole yawned in the meat of the rubber, as if a knife had been plunged deep inside.

Whoever was behind all of this madness had struck again.

Chapter 37

"I don't believe this. Damn it!"

As Kevin stood there, glaring at the tire as if doing so would cause it to magically inflate, his cell phone rang again.

"Good morning," Lauren said. "How are you?"

Hearing her voice made his jaws clench. "I'm fine. You?"

"Wonderful. Just had one of Mama's old-fashioned country breakfasts—eggs, smothered potatoes, grits, country ham, peach preserves, buttermilk biscuits."

Oh, give me a motherfucking break! Kevin wanted to scream. *You aren't at your mama's house and you know it!* "Sounds delicious. Tell her I said hello."

"I certainly will. She wishes you were here."

I wish I were there, too. So I could put my foot in your boyfriend's ass.

"Maybe next time," he said.

"I should be home by this afternoon," she said.

"Okay. See you then." He hung up.

He had to give it to Lauren—she was one hell of a liar. Giving him details about an "old-fashioned country breakfast," and all that bullshit. He was amazed that she had it in her to be so duplicitous.

But it didn't matter at the moment. His present problem was this flat tire.

He had an alternate means of transportation—the motorcycle. But he wasn't in the mood to power up the bike and zip through Atlanta's insane traffic. He was distracted, and riding a motorcycle in Atlanta while preoccupied with other thoughts was a prescription for a fatal accident.

He had to fix the tire. There was a full-size spare in the trunk.

He pressed the button to pop the trunk's lid. He raised it.

He couldn't believe what he saw inside.

Chapter 38

After concluding her conversation with Kevin—she couldn't recall the last time she'd lied so convincingly— Lauren placed her cell in her purse and turned to Marcus. Lying beside her on the bed, he gazed at her with adoring eyes.

He looks like he's in love with me, she thought, and felt an uncomfortable pinch in her chest.

"I've gotta go," Lauren said.

Marcus gently brushed a strand of hair away from her eyes. "No, you don't. He thinks you're driving home from Savannah. That's what—a four-hour drive? You can hang out here for a while longer, baby."

"I have a few things I need to do before I go home."

"Such as?"

She frowned. "Why do you want to know?"

"I thought maybe I could go with you."

He was showing some clinginess, and she didn't like that. She didn't like that at all.

"Thanks, but I'm sure you're a busy man. You run your own business, you must have some work to do. Why waste your time accompanying me on some boring errands?"

"I just want to spend more time with you before you become Mrs. Kevin Richmond again."

"That's sweet. But we've spent an entire evening together— and it was wonderful, I agree. But now I have to go."

He sat up in bed. A scowl creased his face.

"So it's like that, ain't it?" he said. His Mississippi accent suddenly got thicker.

"Like what?"

"You ain't taking me seriously. You only wanted a little fling with the young country boy. Now that you got what you wanted, you wanna kick me to the curb."

"Don't be ridiculous, Marcus. What did you think this was?"

"I thought we might get into a real relationship." His eyes were hurt. "But I see now, you used me to get back at your no-good husband. I wasn't nothing but a tool to you—and now you're done with me."

"That's not true," she said, but she knew it was.

"Whatever." Marcus climbed out of the bed and strode, naked, across the room to the chest of drawers. He pulled open a drawer and dressed in shorts, and a T-shirt that had the words *Southern Gentleman* emblazoned across the front.

Then he turned on the television that sat in the corner and settled on the edge of the bed, focusing his attention on the screen, as if she didn't exist.

Lauren felt like shit. She rose out of the bed and started to get dressed.

"You're a nice guy, Marcus," she said softly. "You deserve a woman who can give herself to you completely. I simply can't do that—I'm married."

"To an asshole." He threw an angry glare over his shoulder.

"You're right, he's an asshole. But he's still my husband, and I'm still his wife."

"But do you wanna be?" He shifted on the bed to face her.

Lauren faltered. He'd asked her the question that she'd been asking herself since she had found out what Kevin had been doing behind her back.

"Do you?" Marcus asked again. He came around the bed, took her hand. He massaged his thumb across her palm, a delicious sensation.

"I don't know," she said.

"I can take care of him," Marcus said, in a whisper.

Lauren pulled back. "What do you mean, 'take care of him'?"

"You know what I mean, girl. I don't think I need to come right out and say it."

Lauren felt as if she had been punched in the stomach. Was he talking about killing Kevin?

Marcus's lips were drawn into a solemn line.

Yes, that was exactly what he was talking about.

"We're *not* going to have this conversation," she said. She began to put items in her overnight bag.

"I'd do it for us," he said. "With him outta the picture, we could be together."

"Marcus, please, stop it."

"I could make it look like an accident, or a suicide—"

"Stop it!" She slapped him full across the cheek, the smack loud in the room.

Marcus touched his cheek. "Damn, you didn't have to hit me."

"Are you insane? You're talking about killing my husband!"

"He deserves it."

Shaking her head, Lauren went into the bathroom, swept her toiletries into her bag. Marcus followed on her heels.

"You know you agree with me," he said. "I saw the look that crossed your face when I showed you those pictures of him with that woman at the park. You wanted to kill him."

"That was then," she said. "Don't ever say anything to me again about hurting Kevin. It has nothing to do with you. I've come up with a much better way to deal with him—my way."

"Like what?"

She brushed past him on her way out of the bathroom and went to the door. "Like getting back at him where it'll hurt him the most—in the bedroom."

As Marcus gaped at her, she walked out.

Chapter 39

Someone had been in Kevin's trunk. That was the only way to explain what he saw inside.

Unlike many people, Kevin kept his trunk clean of clutter, storing only a roadside emergency kit, a rain slicker, and an extra pair of shoes. Back in the day, when he'd driven cars that broke down on the road on the regular, he'd learned the hard way to be prepared if he was stranded.

All of those items were still in the trunk.

But in the midst of it all lay a large Buck knife, used for hunting deer. The sharp edge was crusted with blood and dark hair, as though the blade had been used to scalp someone.

The stench of blood rose out of the trunk and permeated the humid summer air.

Nausea whirled through Kevin. He stepped away from the car, bent over, and vomited.

Pulling in ragged breaths, he covered his mouth with a handkerchief. He swung around in a circle in the garage, to see if anyone was around who might have seen him.

No one. The garage was empty.

Although he dreaded looking again, he turned back to the car. He had seen something else, too.

There it was: a manila folder, wedged underneath the blood-spattered knife handle.

Someone had planted the folder, too. For some unknowable reason.

Kevin reached toward it. . . . and then hesitated. His gut instinct, which he had been following lately since logic had been failing to guide him through this insanity, told him mat looking inside the folder was going to open a door that he might later regret opening. Like Pandora's box.

It's too late, he thought. *I'm in too deep in this shit. I've gotta follow it through.*

Using the handkerchief to cover his fingers, he pulled the folder out of the trunk. It spilled to the pavement, flapping open.

He knelt to take a closer look.

It contained a photo that Kevin hadn't seen in years. A black-and-white picture cut out of the yearbook from Benjamin Banneker Middle School. Kevin, all of thirteen years old, wore an Izod polo shirt, the collar flipped up (it was cool back then), and he had a high-top fade. His face was hard, unsmiling.

He was posed with his two best friends from that time period: Andre Green and Jason Simmons, also eighth graders. They were polo shirts, collars turned up like his, and had similar hairstyles.

The three of them leaned against a set of lockers, arms crossed. Jason had a mischievous smile—he was the prankster of the group. Andre, like Kevin, had a don't-fuck-with-me expression. He'd been the muscle.

Not surprisingly, Kevin had been the leading ladies' man of their trio, the one who got the girls for all of them, like an adolescent pimp. The three of them, with their respective talents, had formed a little school gang, would shake down the other kids for lunch money, pick fights, and fuck around with girls.

Those had been the days, man.

But an alteration to the photo drew him back to the present.

Large *X's,* written with a red marker, had been drawn across the faces of his old friends.

Whoever had left the photo for him had done this. Why?

Tension wormed through Kevin's shoulders.

This photo was from a long time ago—almost twenty years. He'd lost touch with Andre and Jason soon after eighth grade, when he moved to live with his grandmother on the other side of the city and she put him in a different school system for high school. He had no idea what had happened to any of those kids, where they had wound up or what they were doing now.

As he examined the red *X* marks slashed across their faces, a terrible thought came to him: Andre and Jason had been murdered.

Perhaps the blood on the knife belonged to one of them.

A car turned into the garage and rolled toward him. Kevin quickly threw the photo inside the trunk and slammed the lid shut.

The car—a Mercedes owned by someone who lived down the hallway from him—veered into its pre-assigned slot, and the guy, a deeply tanned white man, who, Kevin suspected was gay, got out and bopped toward the elevator. He waved cheerfully at Kevin.

Kevin waved back at him.

Seeing the neighbor reminded Kevin that the garage was under surveillance. Security cameras were strategically mounted in various areas. He couldn't risk being recorded on tape while handling a knife drenched in someone's blood The homicide detective would use the evidence to throw his ass *under* the jail.

He had to dispose of the knife elsewhere, or at least conceal it for the time being.

As he rode the elevator back to the fourth floor, he realized that just as the security cameras could record him in an incriminating act, the cameras also could have captured the person responsible for planting the knife in his trunk.

Hope blossomed in him.

Back in the condo, he grabbed a dark-colored towel and a trash bag. He took them with him back to the garage.

After looking around to ensure that none of his neighbors were in the vicinity, he opened the trunk again. He quickly wrapped the knife in the towel and stuffed both of them in the trash bag. He took the trash bag back to his condo and stored it deep in the guest room closet.

Just as it could be evidence used against him, it could be evidence that could be used *for* him, if he ever went to trial.

Then he took the elevator to the lobby. The head security guard, Cliff, a black man with a thick Afro, sat behind the circular desk, reading a Bible.

"Hey, Cliff," Kevin said. He reached across the desk to shake the man's hand. "How's it going, brother?"

"Just studying the Word, Kevin." Cliff tapped the book. "When the job keeps me from making it to church, you know I got to get my Scriptures in somehow."

"I hear ya," Kevin said. "Listen, I have a favor to ask you. Last night or early this morning—after two a.m.— someone slashed a tire on my car."

"That so?" Cliff leaned forward, eyes alert. He swept his gaze across the bank of screens in front of him as if to catch the perpetrator in the act. "I wasn't on shift then. I'll write up a report."

"Actually, I don't want you to do that, Cliff. It's not necessary. All I want you to do is review the tape and see if you can identify who did it."

Cliff nodded. "Slashing a tire . . . . sounds like something a woman would do. A jealous lady hot under the collar." Curiosity sparkled in his eyes.

"It does." Kevin didn't share more; although he had once thought one of his Internet lady friends was responsible for what was going on, in light of the old yearbook photo he'd seen, that theory no longer worked for him. "Can you help me out?"

"It'll take me a little time to run through the tapes," Cliff said. He glanced at his watch. "That's about nine hours' worth of activity. But it's not as though things are jumping here." He set the Bible on the counter and turned to the screens. "I'll see what I can do."

"I appreciate it, man." Kevin passed him a business card that had his cell phone number on it. "As soon as you find something, give me a ring."

Kevin left the lobby and returned to the garage.

A hunch about his old friends percolated in his mind, and he wanted to look into it, immediately.

He replaced the flat tire with the full-size spare and got on the road.

He was going to visit his mother.

Chapter 40

Kevin's mother wasn't home. Her car was missing from the parking space beside the town house.

Kevin was about to pull away when he remembered her boyfriend, Rufus. In the past, on the infrequent occasions when Mom had access to cars, she was known for letting her boyfriends drive them. Some of the men had been so shameless that Kevin had heard of them using his mom's cars to go on dates with other women.

Mom sure knew how to pick 'em.

Just because the car was missing didn't mean that she wasn't home.

The front door was unlocked, as he expected.

"Mom?" he called, stepping inside the dark foyer.

No response.

He climbed the stairs, thankful for the lemony fragrance in the air; the housekeeping service had cleaned the house from top to bottom.

When he reached the living room, though, he saw that Mom and her man already had been busy taking the home back to its former squalid state; KFC buckets littered the coffee table and sofa, and empty bottles of malt liquor beer and overflowing ashtrays covered the table, like objets d'art.

Grim-faced, Kevin stalked toward the bedroom. "Mom, you in here?"

"Ya mama ain't here, boy."

Frowning, Kevin squinted. The musty bedroom was swathed in shadows, A large dark form shifted on the bed, like an awakening beast.

"Rufus?"

Rufus farted, sat up. "She went to church."

"Church?"

"Yeah, nigga, *church*. Think ya mama some kinda heathen? She got a song for the Lord."

"Which church did she go to?"

"Do I look like 411, ma'fucka?" Rufus made a wild motion with his arm, grabbed a pamphlet on the cluttered nightstand, and flung it to the floor. "She brings them in here, gives 'em to me. I don't give a damn about that shit, though. God don't give a fuck 'bout a nigga like me."

Kevin could tell that Rufus was suddenly in a talkative mood, and he didn't have the time or the desire to indulge the man. He walked into the room, nose wrinkling from the sour odor, and bent to the floor.

It was a program from a church called Taylor Temple, in southwest Atlanta. Typical of a smaller church, they held one service on Sunday, at eleven. Kevin glanced at his watch; it was a quarter to noon. He could catch his mother on her way out of the church.

"Thanks for this," Kevin said.

Rufus waved his hand. "I know you a big-shot lawyer and all, but God don't give a fuck about you, neither. He's cursed the black man. Every last one of us." He nodded, sagely, brushed cigarette ash off his chest.

"I don't know about that," Kevin said, although, with the whirlwind of events he'd been through lately, he certainly felt targeted for destruction. But God had nothing to do with it.

"You a damn fool. Got all them degrees and don't know shit."

"Watch it, old head. I'm not going to be disrespected in *my* house."

"Your house? Fuck you, nigga."

That did it—red came over Kevin's face, as if he'd slipped on a crimson hood. All of the rage ... all of the frustration that had been seething in him since yesterday—it all came to a head. He grabbed Rufus's arm and flung the thin guy out of bed as though Rufus weighed no more than a paper Halloween skeleton.

"Get the fuck out of my house!" Kevin shouted. He tossed Rufus's smoky clothes to the floor.

Bent double, Rufus spat at him. "Fuck you and your mama."

Kevin kicked the man in the ass as if he was trying to kick a field goal. Rufus yelped and crashed to the floor.

Kevin hauled him to his feet and shoved him toward the staircase. "Don't ever let me see you up in here again!"

Cursing under his breath, Rufus staggered down the stairs. Kevin heard the front door slam.

He went downstairs. Rufus shuffled down the sidewalk, stuffing his shirt in his baggy pants. He turned and gave Kevin the finger.

"Oh no, you didn't." Kevin started to go after him. Rufus took off running like a frightened cat. He rounded the corner and vanished.

There was nothing like taking out the trash, Kevin thought. Growing up, he'd always longed for the opportunity to throw out one of his mom's sorry boyfriends. But he'd been too small, too weak, to mount a challenge. It felt good to get rid of Rufus.

But knowing his mom, she would bring Rufus back into her house tomorrow. She was as addicted to worthless men as she was to weed and alcohol.

Shaking his head at the thought, Kevin left the house, locking the door behind him. He got in his car, checked his watch.

Time to meet his mom at church.

Chapter 41

Just south of downtown, Taylor Temple was located in a small, old brick building with a fresh coat of white paint; it sat on an island of recently blacktopped asphalt Kevin noticed his mother's Ford parked near the front door.

So she really was going to church. It was hard for him to believe. The mother he knew despised church and everything about it; Grandma had forced her to attend, as a young girl, and when Mom left high school—and home—at sixteen, her church days abruptly ended, too.

What had brought her back?

Kevin parked in the corner of the lot and slipped inside through the heavy, creaking doors.

"Morning, brother." A gray-haired usher nodded at him and motioned him toward the rear pew.

Kevin quickly took a seat.

The pastor—a surprisingly young man, probably Kevin's age—was smacking the pulpit with his fist, in the midst of a fiery sermon.

"And the Lord said, you *cannot go back* to your wicked ways! Go back, and you might be cut off—wandering in the desert of ignorance for forty years! You wanna know what it feels like to be without the Lord's comfort for forty years? I don't think you do, brothers and sisters!"

Cries of "Amen!" burst from the congregation.

Kevin looked around for his mother. He spotted her near the front. She wore a bright orange hat and was fanning herself. Just like his Grandma had done.

He felt as if a time machine had transported him into the past.

He listened to the rest of the sermon—he was catching the tail end of it—marveling at how peaceful he felt here. This church was the exact opposite of everything he was accustomed to at Rebirth—it was small, modestly furnished, with a congregation composed of working-class people and senior citizens. But noting the shining attentiveness on the faces of everyone in the congregation, he sensed a genuine love for the Word there—not the love for money and status that permeated the atmosphere at Rebirth.

He was still marveling at the difference when the service concluded and people began to file out in the daylight. As he waited beside his pew, saying good-bye to those who passed him and wished him a blessed week, his mother slowly made her way down the aisle. She was talking to the pastor, who mingled with the congregation as if they were members of his own family. He appeared to be counseling Mom on some matter.

Was he really seeing this? Mom, the superbitch herself, talking to a pastor, of all people?

He barely recognized her, too. She wore a bright orange dress that matched her hat, white panty hose, and white heels. Artful makeup had cleared years away from her complexion. She actually looked attractive, a more mature version of the pretty woman Kevin had seen in her old pictures.

He wondered if he was dreaming.

When Mom saw him, she gave a cry of surprise.

"Kevin? I can't believe you're here, praise the Lord."

Beside her, the pastor was grinning and nodding. "Your son?"

"I am." Kevin shook the pastor's hand. "Nice to meet you."

"Your mother speaks so highly of you," the pastor said. "She said you take good care of her."

"She did?" Kevin looked at his mother, stunned. The last time he'd talked to his mother, she'd virtually spat on everything he'd done for her.

Mom laughed into her hand, self-conscious.

"It was nice chatting with you, Pastor," Mom said. "See you next Sunday."

Kevin nodded at the young reverend, and he and his mother went outside.

"What was that all about?" he asked.

But Mom brushed aside the question with a question of her own: "Did you enjoy the service?"

"It was cool. I haven't been to a church like this in a long time."

"Since Mama passed."

"Yeah."

"Are you going to start attending? Bring your wife?"

"Mom, I don't know. Honestly, I didn't come here to talk about that."

"Then why you come?"

Kevin walked to his car and opened the passenger door. "Hop in, Mom."

Chapter 42

Sitting inside the car, the air conditioner blowing cool air from the vents, Mom studied the yearbook photo of Kevin's old friends.

"Ooh, yes, I remember these boys. They was some bad-assed kids, like you." Mom covered her mouth, seeming to realize that they were in close proximity to the church. She put her index finger on the picture. "This here was Selma Green's child . . . and this other boy, his grandma raised him, Mrs. Simmons."

"They stayed in the neighborhood after I moved in with Grandma, right?"

Mom pursed her lips. "They sure did. Selma lived down the street from us. Mrs. Simmons was right around the corner. Them boys kept their rusty asses up in the house till way after they dropped out of school, from what I recall."

"They both dropped out of school?"

"Yep. Sorry niggas. You woulda done the same thing, if you'd stayed around. You damn kids all act alike."

Mom's carefully cultivated church lady persona was melting away. She was beginning to sound like the spiteful, mean-ass woman he remembered.

He actually found it reassuring. Mom hadn't changed. She probably had an ulterior motive for going to church— as far as he knew, she was trying to fuck the pastor—and that was it. Grown folks didn't change. They just played different roles from time to time, as it suited them. The underlying personality, though, was permanent, virtually cast in concrete.

179

"Okay, Mom, this is important," he said. "I need to know—where are Andre and Jason now?"

Mom gave the photo to him, shrugged. "Hell if I know. Probably in jail or dead, one or the other."

"Who would know for sure?"

"How the fuck would I know, boy? Why's it matter to you, anyway? You wanna hook up with them hoodlums again?"

Kevin pressed back in his seat. He massaged his temples. Talking to his mom had the predictable effect of giving him a headache.

"I just need to know, okay?" he said. "It's important."

"Why was them red Xs written over they faces?"

"I don't know. Someone gave the photo to me."

"Who?"

"I don't know, Mom. That's what I'm trying to find out"

"What kinda shit are you mixed up in?" She gave him a hard, probing look.

"Forget it." Kevin turned the key in the ignition. "I need to get going."

She started to open her door, then turned. "You better not be pulling me into some kinda shit, boy."

"I wouldn't do that, Mom." *You have enough shit of your own to deal with,* he wanted to say.

"Better not." She opened the door and climbed out.

He rolled down the window. "By the way, I stopped by your house and took out the trash."

"Why you do that? Rufus can do that for me."

"He *was* the trash," Kevin said, and drove out of the parking lot, leaving his mom there, glaring at him.

Chapter 43

After leaving the church, Kevin drove to his old neighborhood.

For many people, going back to their childhood home inspired a sense of nostalgia, warm memories of times gone by.

Returning to the block made Kevin, who hadn't been there in several years, slightly ill.

Although gentrification had transformed many in-town Atlanta neighborhoods into oases of cosmopolitan charm, this area had been left behind—and had plummeted straight to hell. Rusted cars with cracked windshields and flat tires lined the narrow, pothole-ridden street, like an auto show for the damned. Small tract houses hugged the road, their windows boarded and busted, their tiny yards overrun with weeds and trash, like crumbling monuments to some forgotten age.

A platoon of young black men milled around, too, the street soldiers. They held brown paper bags bulging with malt liquor, or they were smoking—weed or cigarettes. Blunt shapes—guns, undoubtedly—swelled underneath their long, baggy shirts.

They glared at Kevin as he drove by, as if daring him to stop or look at them a moment too long. In his shiny Jaguar, he was far too conspicuous, a desirable target for a cocky young head wanting to make a rep.

He sped up, cruising to the end of the block.

Selma lived down the street front us . . .

Kevin slowed as he neared a house that he thought belonged

to Selma Green. When he saw the broken windows, and two hard-faced young men standing guard on the sagging porch, he picked up his speed.

He didn't know what had happened to Selma Green and her son, Andre, but her home had become a crack house.

At the end of the block, he made a left turn. The road on the right was blocked off by a Dumpster overflowing with garbage.

Mrs. Simmons was right around the corner . . .

A wild-haired woman, freakishly thin yet with a pregnant belly, skittered across the road. She wore ragged jeans, a dirty pink blouse, and flip-flops that exposed ashy feet.

She stopped in the middle of the street, preventing Kevin from driving farther. Her eyes were excited, hungry.

Kevin tapped his horn.

She smiled, showing several missing teeth, and approached his window. He looked around to make sure no one was coming up on him from behind, and then lowered his window a couple of inches.

"Want me to suck your dick?" she asked. "Gimme ten dollars."

She was a crackhead. And pregnant. It was sad.

"No, thanks, sister. I'm looking for Mrs. Simmons's house."

Disappointment washed over her face.

"She around the corner," she said. The woman twitched, scratched her arms with her overgrown, dirt-encrusted nails. "The green house with the high-ass fence."

Kevin slid her a twenty-dollar bill. "Go to rehab, sister. Do it for your baby, please."

"I will, God bless you." The money disappeared in her bra. She cast her gaze inside the car, fishing for something else of interest, and then she settled on Kevin again. She licked her lips, a gesture that was intended to be erotic, but verged on frightening, coming from her—Kevin felt as if this desperate woman could devour him whole.

"I suck a *good* dick, baby. I could hook you up if you give me another twenty . . ."

Shaking his head sadly, Kevin pulled away.

He located the house on the next block. Painted forest green, with black shutters, it sat far back from the road; a tall, chain-link fence surrounded the property. The lawn was trimmed, and boxes of brightly colored flowers flourished underneath the windows and flanked the porch.

But the houses on either side of this one needed to be condemned.

He parked in front of the house, got out, quickly locked the doors.

A BEWARE OF DOGS sign hung on the front gate. Kevin paused, looked around; he didn't see a canine come loping toward him out of the shadows. He pushed the gate open.

When he reached the porch, an enormous dog popped up in a front window with the suddenness of a jack-in-the-box. It snarled and snapped.

Kevin hesitated.

An elderly black woman, still wearing her ultra white "mother of the church" dress, came to the heavily fortified screen door. But she didn't open it.

"Yes?" she asked through the thick glass, her voice muffled. Kevin would have bet that the glass was bulletproof.

"Are you Mrs. Simmons?"

"I am. How may I help you?"

"I used to go to school with your grandson, Jason. My name is Kevin Richmond."

Recognition came into her eyes. But she still didn't invite him inside. Behind her, her dog barked savagely.

"I have reason to believe that he's in danger," Kevin said. He added: "I'm an attorney."

That did the trick. Finally, Mrs. Simmons opened the door.

"It's about time someone came by who cares," she said.

"What do you mean?" he asked, moving closer, but pausing, due to the vicious dog snarling somewhere behind her.

"My grandbaby . . ." She wiped her eyes, sniffled. "He's been missing now for two weeks."

Chapter 44

The crazy bitch had put him in a cage. Like he was a fuckin' dog.

Jason Simmons had no idea how long he had been imprisoned. It seemed like weeks had passed; months, even. Stripped naked, he had no watch with which to mark the passing of time, and the cage in which he was kept was completely dark. The only items inside with him were a coarse blanket, a bed of pine straw, a couple of metallic bowls, and a large femur bone.

A fuckin' *bone*.

You behaved like a dog. Now you'll see how it feels to be treated like a dog.

The only times Jason got any glimpse of the outside world was when the crazy bitch fed him or refreshed his water. She would open a door in the room that contained his cage, weak electric light filtering inside from behind her, and she would dump a heap of food into one of the bowls, and a few cups of cool water in the other, the bowls were bolted to the wall of the cage, like bird feeders. Once, he'd tried to rip them free, to use them as weapons to knock her crazy ass senseless, and he'd failed. He didn't have the strength for such a feat

His diet of dog food was largely to blame. The bitch was feeding him Purina or some shit. He'd tasted a kibble once, as a stupid kid playing around, and the salty, crunchy food she fed him was just the same.

What was even crazier was that he was so hungry he'd begin to salivate when he heard her approaching the door at meal times.

He was a grown man, hungering for dog food.

I'm going to kill that bitch.

Jason sat in the corner of the cage, atop his bed of pine straw, the blanket wrapped around him. In the midst of his rage, he wondered, as he'd wondered endlessly, *why?*

Why was she doing this to him?

He'd met her at a nightclub in Decatur. He was married, but he liked to fool around, you know, keep the spice in his life. He saw her sitting at the bar, looking distant and unapproachable in a tight black dress that had the fellas drooling—and he knew right then that he had to have her. She was a challenge.

He approached her. A few drinks later, she asked him if he wanted to come to her place. Of course he said yeah.

She was gorgeous, and clearly a freak, but something about it still seemed a little strange to him. She seemed too classy to be taking home some dude she met at a club. A little voice in the back of his mind told him that something was wrong. But he ignored it—the call of his dick was louder.

They went to her house—a mansion, really, out in Lithonia. In the massive bedroom, both of them nude and getting ready to fuck, she gave him a drink, a flute of champagne, and the next thing he knew, he started to get weak.

He realized that she had drugged him.

As he flailed about, she snatched a dark leather hood over his head. Then she began to beat his ass with a bullwhip.

He was grateful when he finally passed out.

But when he awakened, hours later, that was when the nightmare really began.

Nevertheless, he still wrestled with the question *why?*

She seemed to believe that he had done something terrible to her, years ago. What he'd supposedly done, she would never say—*you know, I don't need to explain it,* she answered, when he asked. To Jason, it was further evidence of her madness. He'd never met the woman in his life.

Had he?

He didn't know anymore. Maybe he'd met her and done something fucked up—he'd broken many hearts in his day—

but maybe he hadn't. His logical thought processes, his ability to follow a line of reasoning, had broken down like an old car. Hunger and sensory deprivation could do that to you. He knew because he'd been in prison once and had spent four days in solitary. Those had been the worst days of his life.

Until now.

Approaching footsteps drew Jason out of his thoughts.

Time to eat.

Saliva streamed out of the corners of his mouth. He hated to think of himself, salivating at the promise of a bowl of foul-tasting dog food, but he couldn't help it. He shook with hunger and thirst.

He scrabbled toward the door on all fours, his overgrown nails clicking against the floor.

The door opened.

Revealed as no more than a gorgeous silhouette, the woman came inside the chamber that contained the cage. Her two, hulking dogs flanked her, like guards. She carried a bowl of food and a pitcher of water.

"Come eat, doggie," she said sweetly.

He grunted and lowered his head toward the bowl, aching for the vittles soon to come.

Using a scoop with an extended handle, she dumped the kibble into his bowl.

He buried his face in the food and ate.

He heard her pouring water into his bowl, and he couldn't wait to drink, too.

Then he felt something stab his neck.

Startled, he looked up.

The crazy bitch had jammed a syringe into him.

"What the fuck?" he asked, through a mouthful of dog food.

"Our time here is coming to an end, doggie," she whispered. "Before I release you back into the world, we have business we must discuss, and I have something I need to do."

He crashed onto his side on the cold floor. He tried to move, but couldn't, not one finger. Whatever she had pumped into his blood had immobilized him.

But he was still wide-awake.

She opened the gate of the cage. She came inside, knelt next to him.

Although it was shadowy, he saw that she was wearing a robe, and nothing underneath. Through the folds in the fabric, he got a glimpse of her clean-shaven pussy.

Did his dick start to get hard? It felt like it did. He was more terrified than he'd ever been in his life and his dick still wanted to get wet. That was fucked up.

The woman caressed his head. "I'm going to tell you why I've done this to you."

I know why, because you're outta your ma'fuckin' mind, bitch!

But he couldn't speak. Saliva drooled from his lips.

She began to talk. Stroking his hair, she spoke to him for about five minutes, in low, even tones.

When she finished, even if he'd had the capacity to speak, he wouldn't have known what to say. All he could think was: *I'm fucked. She's going to kill me. And I might deserve it.*

The woman looked at him for a moment, as if ensuring that her confession of her motives had sunk in.

"Now for the next item on our agenda," she said. She rose, and left.

Her dogs stood guard while she was gone. It didn't matter, though. Jason's entire body was numb and useless.

A bright white light suddenly came on overhead. It seared his eyeballs, and he cried out. He tried to shut his eyes against the glare, but lacked enough muscle control to do so. He continued to blink, involuntarily.

Maybe that was a good thing. He didn't want to miss what was going to happen next.

She returned a moment later. She had changed into green scrubs that surgeons wore in a hospital. She was pushing a wheeled cart. He caught a glint of a silver tray on top. Metal instruments clinked on it.

What the fuck is she about to do to me?

He strained to get up, to fight her, but his muscles didn't obey. He lay there, powerless.

From a shelf in the tray, she took a swab of cotton, doused it with an antiseptic-smelling solution.

She wiped down his groin.

No, she ain't doing what I think she's gonna do. ... .

Done cleaning him, she picked up an object from the tray.

A scalpel.

No, no, no!

"To make sure that a dog like you doesn't ruin any more lives, I have to do the responsible thing," she said softly, almost sadly.

She bent closer to him. She flipped up a paper mask, to cover her mouth, so her next words came out muffled— but they were as clear to Jason as a knife in the gut.

"I have to neuter you."

And Jason, who had thought his nightmare couldn't get any worse, found his voice, and began to scream.

Chapter 45

Kevin sat in Mrs. Simmons's small but comfortable living room, drinking a glass of sweet tea, while she told him what had happened to his old childhood friend, Jason.

She'd locked her dog, a Rottweiler named Prince, in one of the bedrooms. She didn't allow the dog to meet visitors, she said, wanting to keep him distrustful of strangers. Never could be too careful in her neighborhood.

"Growing up, Jason got into his share of trouble," Mrs. Simmons said. "Like a lot of boys. He got hooked up with the wrong crowd."

He didn't get hooked up *with the wrong crowd,* Kevin thought, remembering how wild Jason had been. *He was a key part of the wrong crowd.*

But he said nothing. He'd let her keep her comforting illusions about her grandson.

"After he dropped out of high school, he spent some time in prison," Mrs. Simmons said.

"For what?" Kevin asked.

But Mrs. Simmons was going to reveal her grandson's past at her own pace. "That was a terrible time for the family— terrible. To think of our baby locked up with those evil men. He never deserved to go to jail. But he spent five long years in there." She studied him. "You ever been to jail?"

Kevin shook his head. "I was fortunate." He was about to say, *My grandma kept me out of trouble,* but he thought Mrs. Simmons might take it as an indictment of her own job as Jason's grandmother, so he kept quiet.

"Pray to God that you never go," she said. "But as bad as it was for my baby, it helped him turn his life around. He got saved while he was in prison. He earned his GED. When he was finally released, he got a job, met a young lady and settled down to raise a family. He's become an upstanding Christian man."

Mrs. Simmons rose and waddled to a small glass table. She picked up a framed photograph and gave it to Kevin.

The picture depicted an attractive family: a handsome man Kevin recognized as Jason, a pretty woman, and a boy with a head full of hair. Jason had the same mischievous smile that Kevin remembered from the old yearbook photo.

"Beautiful, ain't they?" she asked.

"They sure are," Kevin said. He handed the picture back to her. "So when did he go missing?"

"About two weeks ago," she said. "He'd come here to stay with me for a few days. That dumb wife of his—" She stopped, cleared her throat. "He and his wife were having some problems. I think. . . . well, I think 'cause of her he'd started messing with that stuff again."

Kevin knew what she meant by *that stuff*: drugs. The weary way Mrs. Simmons said it, and Kevin knowing how the legal system worked, a drug-related offense had probably landed Jason in prison in the first place.

"That's the only way to make sense out of how he was acting when he came to stay with me," she said.

"How was he acting?"

"Like he'd lost his ever-loving mind. Crazy talk about someone trying to frame him for something he didn't do. He said some cop was following him around, promising that they was gonna send him back to prison. But my baby swore up and down that he didn't do anything."

Kevin's heart had begun to race. Jason's predicament sounded a lot like his own.

"Then, one Sunday morning, I went into his room to wake him up for church, and he was gone." She dabbed at her eyes with a handkerchief. "I ain't seen or heard from him since."

"You think he ran away because he was worried about the police?"

"I don't know." Mrs. Simmons blew her nose, crying softly. She looked up at him, her eyes desperate. "Can't you help me?"

"I'm sure gonna try," he said. "Can you show me the room Jason was staying in here, please?"

She wiped her eyes dry, rose off the couch, and motioned him to follow.

Although Mrs. Simmons's house appeared tiny from the outside, as she led Kevin down the hallway, the house seemed larger, as if it had magically expanded somehow, like a home in a fairy tale. As they passed one of the bedroom doors, he heard the dog scratch angrily at the door.

"Knock off that racket, boy," Mrs. Simmons snapped, and the dog quieted.

She opened a door at the end of the hall.

"This is my baby's room. He moved right back in here, like he always would when he needed a place to lay his head. So long as I have this house this room'll be his."

"I just want to look around, see if I find any clues," Kevin said.

"I'll give you a few minutes," she said.

Kevin walked inside the bedroom. It was a smallish room, afternoon light filtering through the heavy, gauzy curtains. A full-size bed stood in the center, the white bedspread pulled so tight you could have bounced a dime on top of it. Every surface was fastidiously neat. Kevin was willing to bet that Mrs. Simmons cleaned this room, even when Jason had lived there as a grown man.

He didn't have any idea what he was looking for, so he nosed around, checking out the dresser, opening the closet—it was full of old clothes, circa 1990— sweeping a quick look across the nightstand, glancing in the wastebasket beside the bed . . .

He stopped. He bent to examine the trash.

A business card, torn into several pieces, lay inside, atop a wad of napkins. Kevin retrieved the shreds of the card, placed them on the oak nightstand, and fitted them together.

The Last Affair

Detective Robert Garrett
Atlanta Police Department
Homicide Division

Garrett was the same cop who had visited Kevin at home that morning, flinging around his ridiculous allegations of foul play in regard to Black Venus, demanding that Kevin confess where he'd buried the woman's body, promising him that the cops were going to nail him.

He'd scared the shit out of Kevin. Apparently, he'd frightened Jason, too—so much that the guy had gone on the run.

Mrs. Simmons knocked on the door. "Did you find anything?"

"I'm not sure." Kevin stood. "This crime that the cops were after Jason about—did he tell you what it was?"

Mrs. Simmons lowered her eyes. "They thought he'd killed somebody."

"Who?"

"A woman. But my baby had nothing to do with it. He said he was innocent."

"Did he spend time with this woman he supposedly killed? Maybe . . . have an affair?"

Mrs. Simmons's face turned red. But she nodded. "I think he may have. He didn't say, but I know him and Pamela—that's Jason's wife—was having problems at home. She made him go outside the house. You know how you men are."

Kevin ignored the insult. His nerves were jangling. Jason's situation was exactly like his. This couldn't possibly be coincidence.

But what struck him as highly coincidental was Detective Robert Garrett's involvement. Atlanta was a city of hundreds of thousands of people, and lots of homicides. Why would Garrett, of all the homicide detectives employed by the Atlanta PD, be investigating Kevin, too?

Perhaps all of the cases were related, and Garrett was the lead detective, charged with pulling everything together and nailing all of them.

But wouldn't Garrett have said something about that when he confronted Kevin? He'd made no mention of working on a related case.

Of course, the cop could have been deliberately hiding the big picture from Kevin, as one of his strategies to get a confession out of Kevin. Cops told you only what they wanted you to know, after all.

But that just didn't feel right to Kevin.

"Did Jason say anything about the cop, this detective, that sticks out in your mind?" Kevin asked.

"No," she said. "But I think they lying about my baby. I called them after he went missing, and they wasn't helpful at all. When I told them about that policeman who'd been harassing my baby, they said they didn't even know who I was talking about. Damn police. I threw his card in the trash."

An electric charge leaped through Kevin. "Did you call the number on the card?"

She nodded. "A man answered and hung up on me, wouldn't say nothing. So I called the main number for the police, and they said they'd never heard of that cop— ain't no detective by that name on the force, they said. But you know they was just lying. Black folk can't trust the police."

"No," Kevin said. He began to shake. "I think they might have been telling the truth."

"What you mean?"

But Kevin was heading toward the front door. "Thanks so much for your time, Mrs. Simmons. When I find out more about Jason, I'll get in touch."

Chapter 46

Kevin left the old neighborhood and drove to a safer area, where he could sit in his car without fear of being jacked or hounded by a crack addict. Parked under a tree in the corner of a gas station parking lot, the air conditioner blowing but unable to cool the flow of his adrenaline, he used his cell phone to call information and get the main number of the Atlanta Police Department.

Before he made a conclusion about what was happening, he had to check this out for himself.

When the operator answered, he asked to be connected to Detective Robert Garrett in the Homicide Division.

"Hmm. We have no detective with that name, sir," the operator responded. "We have a Robert Gary in Homicide."

"No, it's *Garrett"* Kevin said, fingering the card.

"We don't have a Robert Garrett, sir. Would you like to be connected to Detective Gary?"

"No, that's okay." Kevin hung up.

Son of a bitch.

If there was no Detective Garrett, there was no murder.

And no murder case.

It had all been a setup, as he'd suspected. But not even a genuine setup. A ruse.

He thought about the hotel security guard who'd burst into the room last night.

He had probably been a phony, too.

Like paid actors, following a movie script.

But why? They had made his life a living hell, had driven him almost insane with worry and fear for his future.

Maybe that was the whole point.

His elation at uncovering the truth about the detective had vanished, and given way to a deeper fear, and more disturbing questions.

What had really happened to Jason Simmons? Had he gone on the run?

Or had something worse happened?

Anyone who went through the trouble of staging such an elaborate, disturbing game had to have an ultimate objective in mind. No one would do all of this merely to play a sick joke.

Black Venus, Eve, the psycho woman, had to be the one behind it all, pulling the strings. Kevin was certain she was the one that Jason had met. Had she drugged him, too?

Most important of all: Why was she doing all of this to them?

Troubled, Kevin shifted the car into gear and began driving home, where he could think clearly.

When he pulled into the parking garage, he saw Lauren's BMW parked in her designated space next to his.

So his cheating wife had finally left her boyfriend's arms and come home, huh?

Although he had a lot on his mind, he relished the prospect of seeing his wife, secretly knowing the dirt she was slinging behind his back. *Let the games begin.*

Before confronting Lauren, Kevin dropped by the lobby to talk to the security guard, Cliff.

"Any luck with the surveillance tapes?" Kevin asked.

"Still working on it," Cliff said. "I should have an answer for you by this evening, if nothing else comes up to distract me. You sure you don't want to file a police report? You'll need that to collect on any insurance, you know."

"I don't care about insurance, and I don't want to get the cops involved," Kevin said, thinking about the phony detective. "I'll handle it myself. Just call me as soon as you find something."

"Will do."

Chapter 47

When Kevin entered the condo, he heard the shower running in the master bathroom.

He smirked.

Taking a shower after doing the nasty with another man. That was as good a sign as any of fooling around. He knew all about that trick.

In the bedroom, Lauren's overnight bag sat on the bed; her clothes spilled out, scattered across the bedspread.

Kevin grabbed her pajama bottoms and pressed them to his face. Sniffing for the scent of another man.

He didn't pick it up, though. The clothes smelled of the laundry detergent she used—a fresh, springlike fragrance.

That didn't mean she wasn't guilty.

It meant only that she hadn't bothered to wear any clothes when she was with that motherfucker.

He imagined Lauren with the brother from the Mexican restaurant, nude, her legs flailing in the air as he pumped into her.

A ball of tension inflated in his chest. He clenched and unclenched his fingers.

He couldn't stew like this. He had to do something.

He had to get her back for what she'd done.

He stripped out of his clothes, leaving them in a pile on the floor. He strolled into the bathroom, swinging his considerable length in front of him like a rope.

Lauren continued to shower, glorying in the stream of water. A fine mist filled the air; she didn't appear to notice that he had entered.

He opened the shower stall door, and without waiting for her response, stepped inside with her.

Lauren would always refuse to shower or bathe with him. She said it was a filthy thing to do, to mingle your dirt and bacteria. Another of her wacky beliefs about what constituted proper intimate behavior.

"Welcome home," he said.

She flung her hair away from her face—surprisingly, she was getting her hair wet; she usually wore a shower cap to protect her precious mane—and said something that stopped him cold.

"I was hoping you'd join me," she said in a husky voice.

"Huh?"

She grabbed his arm and pulled him underneath the warm water. She slid her hand to his growing erection and stroked it.

"I missed this," she said.

And then, while Kevin stood there in the jet spray, stunned, Lauren knelt to the shower stall floor and took him in her mouth. Completely.

Kevin rocked backward on his heels. He had to splay his hands against the walls of the stall to keep from falling down.

Lauren was going to town on him, sucking him with fervor.

It felt incredible, but this wasn't right, this didn't make any damn sense. He pulled out of her mouth.

"What the hell's the matter with you?" he asked her.

"Gimme that dick." She groped for him. "It belongs to me—you're my husband, your body is all mine. *Mine.*"

Lauren had lost her damn mind. Or become possessed, like that crazy girl in *The Exorcist.*

Kevin shoved open the door and stumbled out of the shower, feet slapping wetly on the marble floor.

"Are you high on something?" he asked. "What's gotten into you?"

"I want to fuck my husband." In the jet of water, Lauren rose, ran her hand across her nipples, slid her fingers to her pussy, and moved them in a circle inside.

"What?"

197

She came out of the shower. Both of their bodies were dripping water. Kevin started to grab a towel, but she pushed him out of the bathroom and into the bedroom. He fell onto the bed, on his back, atop her clothes and the sheets.

"We're getting the sheets wet," he said.

"Spread 'em," she ordered. Kneeling on the carpet, she yanked his legs open. She wrapped her lips around his dick and took him all the way in.

"But, Lauren, what's going on . . . ?" Kevin's words sputtered into silence as ecstasy crashed through his body. Jesus. He'd had hundreds, maybe thousands of blow jobs over the years, but none quite like this. Lauren was *devouring* him.

It felt so amazing that he couldn't summon the words to ask her why she was suddenly so interested in oral sex. Couldn't even form the question in his mind.

Within a few minutes, the waves of an orgasm rose in him. He started to pull out, not wanting to come in her mouth.

But Lauren kept him locked in. She propped his legs over her shoulders and dragged him closer, bobbing her head faster and faster.

Gripping the sheets, yelling, he came so hard that he shook the bed down to its foundation.

Lauren consumed his fluids, greedily, sucking him until he was dry. He lay there, legs hanging over the bed limply, gasping.

"What . . . was . . . that . . . all . . . about?" he asked.

"Shut the hell up." She climbed onto the bed. "I'm not through with you yet."

He started to rise. She planted her hand on his chest and pushed him back onto the bed.

Then she scaled his body like a ladder, ending with her pussy hanging just above his mouth.

"Eat it," she said.

She cupped the back of his head and pulled it up, pressing his lips into her.

Kevin was shocked, but he obeyed. He worked her with his lips and tongue. Her juices ran down his chin and cheeks.

Lauren rolled sideways onto the bed, twisting her legs around his neck, to keep him in place. She squirmed and shrieked.

I can't believe she's letting me do this. Is this a joke?

He licked her up and down, like a lollipop. She gripped his head, screaming now.

"Yes, baby. Yes, yes, yes!"

Before, during sex, Lauren had been as quiet as the proverbial mouse. This woman was like a porno star.

She climaxed with a scream, digging her nails into his scalp.

Kevin licked her a final time, and then came up for air.

"So you liked that, huh?" he asked. "I told you you would."

Lauren smiled, mischievously.

"Where'd you learn how to give head like that?" he asked. "That was incredible, baby. I mean, mind-blowing. Damn." He shivered with pleasure, and his dick began to harden again.

"He's back," Lauren said, eyeing his growing length with shining eyes. "Good, 'cause I'm not finished with him."

She flipped onto her stomach and rose on all fours, arching her back and thrusting her glorious ass high in the air.

"Dive in," she said, glancing at him over her shoulder. "Gimme some of that backdoor love."

"Are you serious?" Lauren—*Lauren, his sweet, innocent wife*—was asking for anal?

She shook her booty at him. "Don't you want it?"

"But it's gonna hurt, baby—"

"Do it!"

Kevin mounted her. He guided his dick deep inside her ass, slid into the tight chamber, pushed, and began to thrust.

"Harder!" she demanded.

He obliged. He gripped onto her breasts, tightening his hold as he rammed into her. The bed shook, squeaked.

Lauren let out small cries of pain, pleasure. She looked at him over her shoulder as he pounded into her. Their gazes locked.

A tear trickled down her cheek.

She knows, Kevin suddenly realized. *She knows all about the other women. She knows everything.*

The realization forced him to pull out of her. He backed away from the bed.

"You know," he whispered.

Lauren rolled over to face him, her legs spread wide, exposing her glistening pussy.

"What do you care if I know about you fucking those sluts?" she asked. "So long as I'm meeting *your needs* here at home, you asshole?"

Feeling as if a mallet had slammed onto his head, Kevin looked down. Then he bent, gathered his clothes off the floor.

"It's always been all about you, hasn't it?" she asked. "What *you* want. *Your* needs. *Your* desires."

"No," he said weakly.

"The way we just fucked." She laughed, but it was a harsh sound. "I could've done that for you every night. But I didn't—because I knew in my heart that you still would've cheated on me."

"How . . . . how long have you known?"

"In my heart? Since the very beginning. But I recently got proof."

"Proof?"

She dug in her overnight bag, withdrew a folder, and flung a bunch of photos at his feet.

He glanced at the pictures. Someone had photographed his tryst at the park yesterday with Valerie.

Shame burned his face. "Lauren, I can explain—"

"Save it for divorce court, sweetheart."

"What?"

"Let me spell it for you. D. I.V.O.R.C.E. Don't tell me you don't understand all about court, Counselor."

"But I *saw you* cheating on me, too! I saw you at that Mexican joint you love yesterday, all hugged up with some guy!"

Lauren blinked; he'd clearly surprised her. Then she shrugged. "He was the detective I'd hired to give me the evidence of what you were doing."

"Bullshit. I know you didn't go to your mother's, Lauren—I called her. You spent the night with that dude."

"You can't prove it. And anything I *might've* done pales in comparison to what you've been doing behind my back. How was the rendezvous at the Ritz with Black Venus?"

"How . . . how did you know about that?"

"Kevin . . ." She shook her head sadly. "Do you think you married a fool? What's done in the dark will always come to light. Always."

Kevin sank into a chair.

"You played yourself," she said.

She started to get dressed. Then she went to the closet and returned with a suitcase.

"Where are you going?" he asked. He added, derisively: "To your mother's again?"

"This place makes me ill," she said. "It reeks of *you*. I don't want to spend another night there."

"You're going to spend the night with him?"

"Wouldn't you like to know?" She walked to the door. "You'll be hearing from my attorney in the next few days."

He got up to stop her. "Listen, please, don't go, baby. I'm going through some shit you wouldn't believe . . . please. I need you right now."

"Whatever it is, I'm sure you deserve it," she said. "I couldn't care less about what you need—it's been all about your needs ever since we got married."

"Lauren, baby. Come on." He took her by the arm.

She snatched her arm out of his grasp and marched to the door.

And slammed it in his face.

Chapter 48

Speeding away from the condo, Lauren wept. She wept for what could've been with Kevin—and she wept for what, now, never would be.

Three years of her life. Thrown away.

All because her husband couldn't keep his dick in his pants.

Wiping her eyes with a Kleenex, she guided the sedan onto the highway. She was going to her mother's house. For real this time.

She needed to get away from Kevin and the life they'd built together. Staying in Atlanta would be like being suffocated. In her mission to make partner, she'd accumulated plenty of unused vacation days at the firm; it was time to put them to use.

Her cell phone beeped. It was Kevin, calling again.

She didn't answer.

A couple of minutes later, her cell rang again. It was Marcus. Again.

She turned her phone off.

She was taking a vacation from men. All of them were the same. The cliché was true: They cared only about sex. The words "I love you" were a lie that they used to coax sex out of women, to put women at their mercy.

She'd had enough.

She might even stay in Savannah, open her own practice, buy a house in the country with a nice flower garden. The thought made her smile through her tears.

An India Arie song came on the radio. India was her girl—

she loved her songs about independence, self-confidence, loving yourself, and not giving a damn about what a man thought of you.

Cruising down the highway with the music on full blast, Lauren put the bright lights of Atlanta behind her, and she didn't look back.

* * *

Marcus paced through his house, hitting the REDIAL button on his phone over and over and over.

Lauren refused to answer. The tenth time, when the voice mail automatically picked up, he realized that she had turned her phone off.

He felt as if one of his limbs had been severed.

Lauren had dumped him. For that no-good, lying husband of hers.

It wasn't fair. Kevin didn't deserve her.

No one deserved her, but him.

He hurled the telephone across the bedroom. It smashed into the wall and clattered to the floor.

He stormed into his home office and opened his file cabinet. He pulled out a folder.

It contained photos of Lauren. Pictures he'd taken of her, without her knowledge. Snapshots of her out shopping, walking to her car, strutting into her office . . .

She was so beautiful. Gazing at her in those pictures made his heart kick.

Then he opened another file. It contained shots of Kevin, with that ho from the park.

You don't deserve Lauren. She should be mine.

High on angry adrenaline, Marcus rushed back into his bedroom. He opened the closet and knelt.

A small oak gun cabinet stood against the back wall. He opened it and took out two firearms: a Beretta nine millimeter and a .22 pistol.

Lauren had declined his offer to take care of Kevin. Devotion to her worthless husband had blinded her to the fact that Kevin would never treat her the way she deserved to be treated, like a queen.

He checked that the weapons were loaded—they were—and grabbed his leather holsters. He strapped one over his shoulder, and one to his ankle, for the Beretta and the .22, respectively.

It was time to take matters into his own hands.

Chapter 49

Kevin gave up trying to reach Lauren on her cell. . . and reached, instead, for the comfort of the bottle.

He poured a snifter of Hennessey, neat. He didn't want so much as a single ice cube to dilute the potent cognac.

He was planning to get completely torn up. He couldn't deal with the thought that he had destroyed his marriage.

Alcohol offered only a short-term refuge from his pain, but right now he didn't give a damn about dealing with this long-term. He just wanted to shut down his brain, like switching off the ignition in a car.

As he was taking his first sip, his cell phone chirped.

He grabbed the phone, hoping that it was Lauren, calling back to say that she'd changed her mind, she was coming home—she didn't want a divorce, she wanted to work things out . . .

But it wasn't her. It was Cliff, the condo security guard.

"I got that answer for you," Cliff said. "Person who cut up your tire?"

In the maelstrom that had taken over his life in the past hour or so, Kevin had forgotten all about his request for Cliff to review the surveillance tapes to see who had slashed his tire and planted the bloody knife and photo in the trunk. The answer could clear up everything.

Kevin put down the snifter. The drink could wait. He wanted to be clearheaded for this.

"Who is it?" Kevin asked.

"Well . . . I think you'd better come down and take a look at it."

"I'm on my way."

When Kevin stepped off the elevator and into the lobby, Cliff motioned for him to come around the corner of the circular granite desk.

"It took a while for me to run through the tape," Cliff said. "But I got it."

As Kevin stood over his shoulder, Cliff indicated a screen on the far right of the bank of six monitors. It depicted a frozen view of the garage; Kevin's Jaguar was visible in the center of the display.

Cliff clicked a button on the video control console. The tape began to advance, at normal speed.

When Kevin saw who approached his car, he felt as if the floor had fallen from underneath him, like one of those thrill rides at an amusement park.

"I don't believe it," he said.

"You know who this is?" Cliff asked.

Kevin nodded. He sucked in a ragged breath. "I just don't believe it."

"The tape don't lie," Cliff said.

"No, it doesn't," Kevin said. He straightened. "Only people do."

Kevin began to walk away.

"Where you going, young buck?" Cliff asked. "I could lose my job for showing you this. You ain't gonna go off and do something crazy, is you?"

"Of course not," Kevin said. "Why would I ever do anything like that?"

He smiled. Shrugged. Cliff appeared to relax.

Kevin always had been a good liar.

Chapter 50

As twilight fell over the world, Kevin arrived at the mansion in Lithonia. He parked in the circular driveway that curved around a spouting fountain, at the base of the steps that led to the ornate double doors.

He could have driven to the house blindfolded. He'd visited many, many times over the past several years.

But never under these circumstances.

He opened the glove compartment and took out the .38. It was loaded. Climbing out of the car, he stuffed the gun in the waistband of his pants, against the small of his back.

Inside the house, soft light burned in several of the windows. The resident was home.

He looked around, warily. The house stood on four isolated acres of wooded land; night creatures sang in the growing darkness. Otherwise, he seemed to be alone.

He approached the front door. He rang the bell. Soft, melodic chimes played within.

Kevin couldn't wait for the door to open, to see the look on this person's face when Kevin said, *I know what you did.*

After a minute or so had passed, no one had answered.

Kevin tried the doorknob. Unlocked.

Forget good manners. No more time for that shit.

He pushed open the door and stepped inside. He walked in, hand wrapped behind him, ready to pull out the gun.

He found someone on the floor in a spacious room called the grand salon.

The man was sprawled across a Persian rug. Blood leaked

from a gash in his abdomen. He pressed a blood-soaked handkerchief against the wound.

But he was still alive.

Kevin came to stand above him.

"You," Kevin said.

Oliver Holmes, fighting for his life, looked at him, and his eyes told Kevin everything.

Kevin knelt beside Oliver. Although Oliver was bleeding badly, Kevin made no move to help him.

Oliver's betrayal cut too deep, like a blade in Kevin's own flesh.

"You found out," Oliver said in a tattered voice. "How?"

"Surveillance tapes from the parking garage at my condo," Kevin said. "I saw you slash the tire and plant the knife and the photo in my trunk."

Oliver closed his eyes. "I *told* her we were eventually going to make a mistake; the plan was much too intricate . . ."

"You told who? Eve?"

Oliver winced, nodded.

"How the hell do you know her?" Kevin asked.

"Met her, out and about in the city . . . Brother Kevin. I'm old, but I ain't dead . . . yet."

"You and Eve are fuckin'?"

Oliver managed a proud grin through his pain. Oh yes. Dear Eve has given me . . . new zest for life . . ."

Kevin was sickened. This man, his mentor, his father figure, had been fucking that crazy bitch? He couldn't believe it.

"Did she do this to you?" Kevin asked.

"I . . . refused to go along with her game any longer. You don't . . . tell a woman like her no."

"What the hell is this all about, Oliver? What's this game she's been playing with me?"

"Revenge."

"Revenge for what?"

"You . . . the other two boys. What you did to her . . . many . . . years ago."

Kevin shook his head. "I don't know what you're talking about. I've never met Eve in my life."

"Andre Green . . . Jason Simmons . . . you."

"We didn't do anything to her. We didn't even *know* her."

"I had pledged to help her, supplied the resources. Justice . . . must be served, Counselor."

Kevin turned away, paced across the room. Oliver was helping Eve? He just couldn't wrap his mind around that fact. He couldn't accept that Oliver, the churchgoing man of high morals, his goddamn father figure, had agreed to help a woman who was certifiably insane in her sick mission to get even with him and his old childhood friends . . . when they had done nothing wrong.

"Where is Eve now?" Kevin asked. "Where can I find her?"

But Oliver ignored him, his attention focused on his effort to get up. Too weak, he crashed back to the floor. He reached out for Kevin.

"Help me . . ." Oliver begged, face oiled with sweat.

"You betrayed me, betrayed our friendship, for a piece of ass," Kevin said. "Fuck you."

Kevin turned away. He walked out of the house, Oliver's pleadings following him outside.

Kevin got in the car and sat behind the wheel. He was shaking.

Oliver had turned on him . . . Jesus, if he couldn't trust Oliver, he couldn't trust anyone. Everyone was a suspect.

The image of Oliver, bleeding to death, paraded through Kevin's thoughts.

I can't do it. I can't leave him in there to die like that.

Kevin burst out of the car and ran back to the house, banging open the front door with his shoulder.

Oliver was no longer on the floor. Kevin found his cell phone, the prepaid one that had been taken from him at the hotel, lying on the rug where Oliver had been. He jammed it in his pocket.

At least he'd learned who'd been sending him text messages.

But where had Oliver gone?

Kevin began to search through the house, calling for him.

He couldn't find him anywhere. How could the man have

209

been fighting for his life only a couple of minutes ago—and now be gone?

A lucid thought burst through his haze of confusion and fear.

Oliver and Eve were playing him. Again.

Just like the setup at the hotel.

He hadn't actually *seen* Oliver's supposed gut wound, he recalled; Oliver had concealed the apparent injury with a blood-soaked handkerchief. The "blood" could have been replicated with red corn syrup, like they used in the movies.

Hadn't Oliver been a drama teacher before entering law school? Wasn't he famous around the firm for his theatrical flair?

"Fuck," Kevin muttered.

He heard a car engine, and ran to the front door.

Oliver's black Cadillac-Escalade was roaring down the driveway, away from the house and into the night.

Chapter 51

Alone, Kevin decided to take advantage of the opportunity to search Oliver's house. Perhaps he could find something that would shed light on Oliver and Eve's relationship, and this scheme of theirs.

He started, as seemed appropriate, in the bedroom.

It was a huge, lavishly appointed master suite, boasting a king-size bed draped with crimson sheets, white carpeting, a sitting area with leather club chairs, and a marble fireplace. A long oval mirror adorned a wall.

Beside the mirror, the double doors to the walk-in closet beckoned.

Kevin moved inside the closet and switched on the light. The area was nearly as large as Kevin's entire bedroom: racks of dozens of Italian suits, over a hundred pairs of shoes, golf shirts, and casual slacks . . . . Oliver could have donned a different outfit every day for an entire year and never once worn the same clothes twice.

A satiny, burgundy curtain hung at the rear of the closet. Curious, Kevin slid it aside.

"Oh, shit," he said.

There were more clothes racks and shelves back here. Those on one side of the closet were full of S&M paraphernalia: leather chaps, driver caps, vests, studded collars, chains, gloves, bullwhips, combat boots.

The other side of the closet contained women's clothes, shoes, and accessories. Dresses and blouses, pumps and sandals and flats, purses and hats.

Kevin bent and examined a pair of black pumps. They were huge—large enough to accommodate Oliver's size-thirteen feet.

"You've gotta be kidding me," Kevin said.

He'd thought he'd known Oliver well. As this night had proven, he didn't know the man at all.

Everyone had a secret life.

Disgusted, Kevin left the closet.

Next, he entered Oliver's home office. It was a large, airy space, with a panel of windows that overlooked the private lake in the rear of the house. A gigantic, L-shaped oak desk dominated the center of the room.

He settled into the leather executive chair behind the desk and began to open drawers.

In the top drawer, he found a black, leather-bound address book.

Now, this could be helpful. Oliver was old school; he kept names and addresses on paper, eschewing the BlackBerrys and PDAs that attorneys at their firm favored.

Kevin began to flip through the book. In the K section, he found a name, number, and street address for Dr. Eve Kennedy.

Doctor?

But she was the only "Eve" listed in the book. It had to be her. Black Venus.

What field of study could that crazy-ass woman possibly have earned a doctorate in?

She had an Atlanta address that Kevin recognized as the Grant Park neighborhood.

Kevin stuffed the address book in his back pocket. He swept through the rest of the house, but he discovered nothing else of interest. Oliver's house was so enormous it would have taken hours to do a detailed search, and he didn't want to waste any more time there.

He'd already found what he needed most—Eve's location.

He couldn't wait to see her again.

Kevin left the house and went to his car. When he reached to open the door, he heard a thumping sound.

It came from the trunk.

Kevin's heart thudded.

There had been no such noise coming from his car before. That meant, while he was inside talking to Oliver, or searching his house, someone had deposited something in his trunk.

The last time he'd found something in his trunk—the bloody knife and the yearbook photo—it had rocked his world. He had the feeling that another jarring discovery awaited him.

He moved slowly to the rear of the Jaguar.

Another muffled thump—as if someone was trapped inside, banging the lid with a desperate fist.

Standing several feet away from the car, Kevin pressed the button on the key chain to unlock the trunk.

Another thump from the trunk's prisoner knocked the lid all the way up.

Kevin peered inside.

It had been almost twenty years since Kevin had seen him, but he never would have forgotten the face of his old friend, Jason Simmons.

Chapter 52

Jason looked nothing like the proud, handsome brother Kevin had seen grinning in the family photo at Mrs. Simmons's house, earlier that day.

He looked like a prisoner of war.

His wrists and ankles were bound with duct tape. Another swatch of tape covered his lips. His unkempt hair was matted with dirt. His face, darkened with unchecked beard growth, was streaked with more dirt, blood, and dried snot. He wore a hospital patient's gown soiled with grime, blood, and other substances Kevin preferred not to think about.

And the smell—Jason stank as badly as if he'd spent the last week swimming in sewage.

Kevin covered his mouth, to stem the gag reflex.

The last twenty-four hours had been full of so many shocking incidents, it was a miracle that he still had his sanity.

"Jesus," Kevin breathed. "What happened to you?"

Jason's eyes were terrified, as if he were remembering what had happened. Tears tracked down his cheeks, winding through the crud. He murmured something behind the tape.

Kevin gently removed the tape from Jason's mouth.

Jason gasped—and then vomited all over his gown.

Kevin had never seen a more pathetic, revolting scene in his life. Without being told, he knew that Eve was responsible.

"Let's get you out of here and get you cleaned up," Kevin said. He tore away the duct tape binding Jason's ankles and wrists.

"K-Love?" Jason asked, in a ragged voice, as if his vocal cords had been mangled. He blinked. "That you, dog?"

K-Love. His nickname from back in the day—tagged on him because of his suave way with the ladies. Kevin had not heard that name in years.

"It's me," he said. "Put your arms over my shoulders so I can get you out of here."

But Jason's hands went, strangely, to his groin. Whatever he felt there made his eyes widen like saucers.

Jason opened his mouth and wailed.

Kevin dragged Jason, who, after screaming, had gone limp and mute, inside Oliver's house. He took him to the guest bathroom, on the first level.

"You've gotta take a shower," Kevin said. "Then I'll get you some clothes and take you to Grady, get you checked out."

Jason only lay on the bed, curled in the fetal position. He trembled

Watching his old friend, Kevin decided that he didn't want to know what Eve had done to him. He just didn't want to go there. He was struggling to stay on an even keel himself.

But he could imagine what could make a grown man scream like that.

He turned on the shower. Then, leaving Jason on the bed, Kevin went to Oliver's master suite, to get some clothes out of his walk-in closet. Oliver was heavier than Jason, and the clothes would fit loosely on him, but he didn't have any alternatives.

Maybe one of those dresses . . .

A lunatic laugh bubbled at the back of his throat, and he fought to hold it down.

He found a white sweat suit, Nikes, and an unopened pack of boxer shorts and socks. He bundled them in his arms and carried them downstairs.

Jason had crawled into the shower stall; the door hung open, mist drifting from inside. Jason sat curled up in the corner, warm water beating down on his head. His eyes were dazed. He still wore the filthy patient's gown. Grime swirled down the drain.

"Man, you can't get clean wearing that thing," Kevin said. He stepped inside the shower and grabbed the edge of the gown. He began to pull it over Jason's head.

Jason gave him no resistance. He was as helpless as a baby.

Kevin threw the wet gown on the floor behind him. Although Jason was curled in a ball, Kevin glimpsed the man's groin. The region was heavily bandaged, as if he'd undergone some kind of surgery.

Nausea reeled through him, and he quickly looked away from that part of his friend's body.

He took a clean towel, squirted a stream of shower gel into it, and used it to wipe down Jason's head, arms, chest, legs. Foul water continued to gurgle down the drain.

How long had Eve had this man? It would have taken several days, maybe a week or two, for him to get so bedraggled.

After soaping and rinsing Jason off several times, Kevin earned him out of the shower. He started to towel him off—when Jason snatched the towel out of his grasp.

"I can do it," he muttered. "Give a brother some privacy, aiight?"

"Okay, I left some clothes for you on the bed. Soon as you get dressed, I'll take you to Grady."

Jason nodded groggily. "What's the date, man?"

"Huh?"

"The date."

Kevin glanced at his watch. "July twenty-third."

"Fuck," Jason said softly. He started to cry. "Nine goddamn days in there."

Kevin wanted to ask, *Nine days in where?* but he kept his mouth shut. He left the room, to give his friend the privacy he'd requested.

But the .38 holstered behind his back seemed to be burning a hole in his flesh. He wanted to cock the hammer and take aim. At Eve. No man deserved to suffer the way Jason had suffered, the way he himself had been suffering since he'd met her. Whatever she mistakenly believed they had done to her, they didn't deserve this.

He wanted to kill her.

About ten minutes later, Jason shuffled out of the guest bedroom. The sweat suit was a little baggy on him and the shoes appeared to be a size too large, but they would have to suffice.

"Got anything to eat up in this joint?" Jason asked.

Kevin had anticipated that Jason would be starving. The guy's cheeks were sunken in, as if he hadn't been eating well.

He tossed Jason a large bag of tortilla chips.

"That's about all I could find in the kitchen," Kevin said.

Jason tore into the bag with his teeth and began to stuff chips into his mouth, with the frenzy of a man eating his first meal in days.

"I thought this was your crib?" Jason asked, between mouthfuls.

Kevin shook his head. "Long story, man."

"I got one of them, too," Jason said. He bowed his head, shuddered, and when he looked up, he was crying again. "Like you wouldn't believe."

Chapter 53

As Kevin drove away from Oliver's estate, Jason, riding in the passenger seat and eating another bag of chips, told him what had happened.

He met Eve at a club in Decatur, he said. Although he was married, he wasn't happy, so he was fooling around on the sly, picking up a female here and there. The minute he saw Eve sitting at the bar, in a tight-ass black dress that hugged every luscious curve, he knew he *had* to have her.

"Sounds familiar," Kevin said, nodding.

After he'd bought her a couple of drinks and they'd shared some small talk, she invited him to come to her house—which Jason, with hindsight, realized was actually Oliver's mansion, not hers. He'd thought it kinda strange that a woman like her would take home some guy she'd just met at a club, but he couldn't resist the siren song of the pussy he knew he was going to get. He followed her to the house, and soon after they got undressed, she drugged him, yanked a hood over his head, and beat the shit out of him with a whip, until he passed out.

"That wicked shit is tame compared to what happened later," Jason said. "I woke up, there was blood everywhere, broken glass and shit, like someone had gotten the shit kicked out of 'em—and it wasn't me. Next thing I know, a cop's at the door—"

"Detective Garrett?"

"Yeah. How'd you know?"

"I met him, too. But anyway, go on."

"He tries to say they got a call, and I'm responsible for a

218

murder, and that I better produce the body, or else he was gonna send my ass back to the joint. You know I did some time, back in the day?"

"Your grandmother told me." The fake cop's threat must have been especially frightening and convincing to him, Kevin figured.

"But they didn't have shit on me. I hadn't done anything. But I start finding these clues, I'd guess you'd call them— some old picture of me, you, and Andre. Start getting weird-ass messages on my celly. I don't know who's behind all this shit, right? I thought Eve was dead, somebody had offed her and was trying to set me up for it, you know? So I'm going nuts, go stay at my grandma's crib to lie low for a minute, thinking of breaking out for good—till some big knuckleheads run me off the road one night and drag me out of my ride. They take me to this big, old crib. And guess what? Eve came in. She wasn't dead. It was all a ma'fuckin' game to her. Bitch was trying to make me go crazy."

Jason finished the bag of chips, balled it up, and threw it on the floor. Kevin kept his car meticulously clean, but he didn't bother to say anything to Jason. The guy had been through enough recently.

Jason gazed out the passenger window. His voice was soft, haunted. "She locked me in a fuckin' cage, man. Treated me like a dog—made me sleep on straw, gave me a bone, even . . . even fed me dog food. Can you believe that shit? Jason whirled to face Kevin, his nostrils flaring.

"She won't get away with this, trust me," Kevin said.

"And the other thing she did . . ." Jason glanced at his crotch, then looked away, tears sliding down his cheeks. He sniffled. "Can't even say, man."

"Why is she doing this to us?" Kevin asked. "That's what I don't get. We don't deserve any of this shit."

Jason nodded gravely. "Oh yeah, we do, man."

"What the hell did we ever do to her?"

"First off, her name ain't really Eve. That's some new shit. Her old name is Nikki. Nikki Waters."

"I don't remember a Nikki Waters."

"That's 'cause she was ugly back then, man. Coke-bottle glasses, nappy hair, chicken legs, no tits or ass. A goddamn ugly duckling—bitch grew up into a *helluva* swan."

"That's the truth," Kevin said, thinking of Eve. "But I'm still drawing a blank on Nikki."

"You remember the Nasties? How we'd take girls to the woods behind the school football field, get 'em drunk and high, then fuck around with 'em, pop their cherries?"

The Nasties. Kevin smiled at the memory.

"All right, I remember that," Kevin said. "All the girls loved that stuff, though. They wanted to be with us—we ran that school."

"Right. But we picked only the fine girls for the Nasties. We had high standards, remember? But then one of us—I think it was 'Dre—said we should pick an ugly bitch for a change. Somebody who wouldn't get no dick unless a nigga was feeling generous."

"So we picked Nikki?"

"You did." Jason pointed at him. "You said, 'She looks like a dog, but pussy ain't got no face.'"

"Damn." To hear what he'd said now . . . it sounded so cold. "I think I'm starting to remember now . . . we coaxed her into the woods, gave her some beer, and then we got interrupted."

Jason snapped his fingers. "Bingo. You remember who interrupted us?"

"Wasn't it some guy, said he was her uncle or something?"

"He said that, but he wasn't really her uncle," Jason said. "He was Herbert Robinson."

"Who's he?"

"He was a child molester, man."

Kevin suddenly felt queasy.

"We handed Nikki over to him and ran away," Jason said. "He took her to his crib and kept her all night. You can fill in yourself what happened to her."

Sweating, a chill sinking deep into his bones, Kevin pulled over to the side of the highway.

Silence hung between Kevin and Jason. The only sounds were the cars and trucks *whooshing* past on the highway, the Jaguar rocking slightly in the air currents.

"Jesus Christ," Kevin said. "I . . . I . . ."

"I didn't know what to say, neither," Jason said. "When she told me, I *couldn't* talk—but I don't wanna get into that."

"She blames us for what happened," Kevin said.

"If we hadn't taken her back into those woods, that sick ma'fucker never would've gotten her," Jason said. "Yeah, dog— *she blames us.*"

"But we didn't know. We didn't do it on purpose."

"I hear ya. But she doesn't see it that way. I don't think she's ever been right in the head since that shit went down. You remember that she got sent to a different school maybe a week later?"

"No," Kevin said.

"Neither did I," Jason said. "She refreshed my memory on all this shit when she locked me up."

"Shit." Kevin wiped greasy sweat from his face. "I still can't believe all this."

"It's real. She's getting her revenge. In the worst way."

"What happened to 'Dre?"

"She ain't gotten to him." Jason shrugged. "'Dre's been in the joint for ten years now, nigga ain't getting out for maybe another ten. He robbed a liquor store and mowed down the clerks—some Arab cats. He already had a record long as my arm, so . . . that was the end of that."

"Why'd she wait so long to get back at us? Why not sooner?"

"I don't know how that crazy bitch's mind works, man. She didn't say. You'll have to ask her yourself."

"I'm going to see her tonight." He gave Jason a frank look. "I'm going to end this, once and for all. If you're up to it—"

"Fuck that!" Jason said. "I don't ever want to be within a hundred feet of her crazy ass!"

"Okay, that's cool, no problem."

"I don't wanna go to no hospital, either." He sighed heavily. "Just . . . just take me home."

"Where do you live?"

"You know, my grandma's crib."

"Oh yeah, right." Kevin shifted, into drive and rejoined the flow of traffic.

Neither he nor Jason spoke for the remainder of the trip. They had been friends almost twenty years ago, had taken different paths in their lives and evolved into completely different people.

One thing, however, never would change: their shared involvement in the tragedy that had befallen poor Nikki Waters, aka Eve Kennedy, aka Black Venus.

He could almost understand why she was doing this to them, could almost empathize with her desire for revenge.

Almost.

Chapter 54

Marcus was confused.

He'd followed Kevin from his Midtown condo to an estate in Lithonia, certain that the asshole was going to meet a woman for another rendezvous. But, parked far away from the entrance to the mansion and using his Bucknell binoculars to watch the proceedings, Marcus witnessed some strange shit going down.

Kevin went into the house. While he was in there, a gray van rolled around the corner of the estate. Two black men, one young and built, the other middle-aged and broad, climbed out of the van and dragged something large and bundled in black cloth out of the cargo area. They opened the trunk of Kevin's Jaguar with a key, and dumped the package—whatever the hell it was—inside. Then they drove away.

Marcus had an unsettling feeling about what the guys had deposited in Kevin's trunk.

Several minutes later, Kevin stumbled outside, looking furious. He started to get in the car—and then, a couple of minutes later, he went back inside the house.

Shortly after that, a Cadillac Escalade roared down the driveway. An older black man was driving.

Marcus ducked out of sight when the SUV passed by.

Kevin was involved in some weird shit. But what was it?

Marcus was going to keep watching, and following. In the end, it didn't matter to him what Kevin was doing. The guy was an asshole, his existence preventing Marcus from having Lauren all to himself, and Marcus was going to take care of him.

Chapter 55

Kevin pulled up in front of Mrs. Simmons's place.

"Wanna come in?" Jason asked. "Grandma probably got a big-ass Sunday dinner on the stove. Probably a pot roast, potatoes, greens, peach cobbler."

"No, thanks. I'm going to take care of business."

Jason shook his head and regarded Kevin sadly.

"You crazy as hell," Jason said. "Man, you better leave town or something. Don't fuck with her. It ain't worth it—and I'm *proof*." He lowered his gaze to his crotch, touched it gingerly. A tremor shook him. "I can't ever. . . . Look, just don't go, aiight?"

The front porch light blazed into life. Mrs. Simmons's wide shadow filled the doorway.

"Your grandmother's waiting for you," Kevin said.

"Well, it's been real, catching up and all." Jason gave Kevin a pound. "Stay true."

"Stay true," Kevin echoed, repeating their motto from back in the day.

Jason climbed slowly out of the car. He started to head across the walkway, and then turned back to the car, motioning for Kevin to lower the window.

"If you want to warn me out of going again, don't waste your breath," Kevin said.

"Wasn't gonna tell you that," Jason said. "I was gonna tell you—if you serious about that shit, soon as you get a chance, kill that crazy bitch. Or she'll fuck you up for the rest of your life."

Then Jason swung around, pulled up the baggy sweatpants, and shuffled to his grandmother's house. Although he was only in his early thirties, he looked like an old man, with his best days well behind him.

Chapter 56

Eve couldn't have been happier. Everything was going so well. So perfectly.

It was proof that her ambitions were in accord with universal law, that she had what amounted to divine approval.

Karma was finally on her side.

Eve stood at the bay window in the master bedroom of her house, holding a chilled glass of Chardonnay. The shower was running in the bathroom behind her. Oliver Holmes, her benefactor in her great mission, was visiting, and the rules that she laid down for her many lovers applied to him, too: He had to shower before she would be intimate with him.

Veils of darkness draped the world outside the window. The full moon, clothed in tattered clouds, occasionally peeked through and relieved the blackness. But she didn't need moonlight to ascertain whether Kevin had arrived. The motion-activated lights along the driveway would blaze into life when he neared, as he inevitably would.

Then the game would reach its final conclusion. Almost twenty years of torment would finally end.

Although her reflection in the glass, to an onlooker, would have portrayed a beautiful, grown woman, when Eve looked at herself, she saw a rail-thin girl of thirteen with nappy braids, lips too full for her pinched face, and thick glasses.

She saw Nikki Waters.

C'mon, baby, it'll be fun . . .

With sweetly worded enticements, Kevin's crew of teenage rebels had lured her into the dense woods beyond the school football field. Nikki, unaccustomed to anything but negative attention from the popular, wild trio of boys, but yearning to be accepted, to be told that she was beautiful, went along willfully.

She'd heard whispers from the other girls about what the boys liked to do with the girls in the woods. They drank beer. They smoked weed. They kissed.

They had sex.

Nikki had never drunk alcohol (save for a sip of whiskey she'd stolen from her aunt's glass one night), had never smoked weed (not counting the contact highs she got from her aunt's raucous parties), and had never been kissed, and definitely had never, ever had sex. No one wanted to kiss her, or touch her in an intimate way. She was Nikki Waters, after all, one of the ugliest girls in the school, attending classes to a daily torrent of hurtful insults.

You so ugly, when you was born yo mama left you at the hospital . . .

Yo lips so big, you could cool off a barbecue grill with one blow . . .

Yo so skinny, yo mama used to call you "rake . . ."

So when Kevin, Jason, and Andre had visited her table at lunch in the school cafeteria, where she would always eat a peanut butter and jelly sandwich in solitude, Nikki had braced herself for another round of merciless teasing. She had never anticipated the sugary words that had tumbled out of their mouths.

Girl, you looking fine today. Like an angel. We just had to come sit with you.

Hmmm. Your lips are so juicy, I get chills looking at you.

You got the best body I've ever seen, baby. Can I get fries with that shake?

Nikki had been taken aback. She was convinced that they were putting her on, setting her up for a big joke.

But secretly, she'd hoped that they were being honest.

Then Kevin said: *You wanna meet us behind the bleachers at the football field after school?*

In spite of her hope, she was unconvinced, and she automatically declined. But the boys—Kevin most of all—had kept begging.

C'mon, baby, it'll be fun.

She'd gotten up from the table and left. But feeling their eyes on her. Wondering if looking at her really turned them on, as they said it did.

Later that afternoon, she found a note that had been slipped inside her locker.

Will you kiss me after school? Kevin

The note had made her bubble with excitement. When the final school bell rang that day, Nikki found herself waiting behind the bleachers, in such a daze she barely remembered walking there.

The boys had shown up soon after.

Hey, baby, we were hoping you'd change your mind. Let's go do this.

She followed the boys through the wall of tall trees, and into the forest. As they walked, Kevin wound his arm around her narrow waist and pulled her close. He whispered sweet stuff in her ear, his lips so close she could smell the cherry Jolly Ranchers on his breath.

A cleared-out area in the woods was littered with beer bottles, cigarette butts, and candy wrappers. Andre began to clear out the area; Jason opened his knapsack and took out a bottle of Old English; Kevin opened his bag and produced a frayed blanket, which he spread on the ground with the extravagant manner of one whipping out luxurious Egyptian cotton sheets.

Have a seat and chill, baby.

The four of them sat in a circle on the blanket. Jason started to guzzle the beer, but Kevin swiped it from him—*ladies, first, man*—and handed it to Nikki. She paused, still unable to believe that she, Ugly Duckling Nikki, was here with these pretty young boys, and then she tipped the bottle.

As the first sip of warm beer hit the back of Nikki's throat, a man's voice thundered from somewhere close: *What the fuck are you little niggas doing to my niece?*

Nikki choked on the beer, spat it out, and stained the front of her blouse. The boys jumped to their feet, eyes wide and scared.

A large man dressed in oil-spattered denim overalls stepped out of the shrubs. Coal-black, he wore a grimy Atlanta Braves cap. His eyes were like bullets.

He'd said she was his niece, but Nikki had never seen this man in her life. But her family was so crazy and screwed up . . . maybe he *was* her uncle, one she hadn't yet met, someone that her aunt Rose had sent to come get her. Nikki had never even met her own daddy and barely knew her mother—why should she have met all her uncles?

But something in the man's dark eyes planted a thick lump in her throat that kept her from talking, made it hard to even breathe.

This here's my niece. Get the hell out of here before I kick all of your asses.

The boys scattered, grabbing up their things and running off into the woods.

Wait! Nikki cried, finally finding her voice. *Don't leave me here!*

But the boys had gone.

The man turned to her and grinned. Several of his front teeth were missing; but he had a gold tooth, the metal twinkling like a nasty secret.

She tried to run, but he caught her easily.

Come to Uncle Herb, sweetheart. Uncle Herb's gonna treat you real nice.

But later, after "Uncle Herb" dragged her to his car, a rusted-out Ford, and drove her to his shotgun shack of a house, he hadn't been nice at all.

He'd given her the longest, most terrifying night of her young life.

A week later, her aunt transferred Nikki to another school. That was her way of dealing with what had happened. Nikki did not get psychiatric counseling—she got a school transfer and a lecture from Aunt Rose that had imprinted itself on her brain forever.

It's bad what happened to you, but that's the way of the world, and the sooner you learn, the better. Men are like dogs, baby—all they want is to fuck. Fuck a kid, fuck a grown woman, fuck a grandmama with one foot in the grave and the other on a banana peel. It don't matter to them dogs, Nikki—they'd fuck a hole in the wall if that was all they had around. 'Cause of that, a woman can have a lotta power over a man, but she gotta learn how to use it. If she don't, she's gonna be used, hear me?

Nikki had heard her aunt Rose, all right. At the school she'd transferred into, she was no longer known as Ugly Duckling Nikki.

She became known as Nasty Nikki.

She would do anything, sexually, with a boy—or boys. It didn't matter. What mattered was that soon after the word got out about her total lack of inhibitions, the boys craved her with a need that verged on a drug addiction. Their desire for her translated into power. As her body began to fill out and her beauty blossomed, her power multiplied tenfold.

When she turned eighteen, she changed her name to Eve Kennedy. Kennedy, because it sounded like American royalty, and she considered herself a queen ruling men. Eve, because that was the name of the first created woman—the first woman to manipulate a man into doing what she desired.

Men bought Eve clothes from boutiques and sent her on shopping sprees in New York and Paris. They bought her expensive cars. They paid for her luxury apartment and all of the furnishings. A wealthy, older white doctor with a taste for freaky black women funded her undergraduate degree, pulled strings to get her accepted into med school, and even paid for her MD degree, too.

She chose the field of psychiatry, to gain additional insight into men and ready access to the pharmaceuticals that she could use to control them.

In spite of the power she wielded over men and all of the benefits it had brought her, Eve battled with depression. It culminated in a nervous breakdown, a year ago.

Her therapist—unlike Aunt Rose, she had the good sense to see someone—advised her that she had not dealt with the childhood trauma that had set her on her sexually explicit path. The psychologist tried to talk her through the pain, to break through it via in-depth counseling.

But Eve, in a flash of insight, had discovered a better way.

Revenge.

She would take revenge on the three boys who had placed her in harm's way. She would take revenge on the man who had molested her, all those years ago.

Her new mission eradicated her depression, infused her life with fresh purpose and direction.

Hiring a detective—he offered his services for free in exchange for several of her brain-busting blow jobs— she tracked down the four individuals. The molester, "Uncle Herb" Robinson, had died years ago in prison. One of the boys, Andre, was currently in prison (ironically, the same one in which Robinson had died). But Jason and Kevin were free, still in Atlanta, still playing their games with women.

She would get Jason, but Kevin was the grand prize. He was the one who had pursued her the most, who had coaxed her into joining them in the woods.

C'mon, baby, it'll be fun.

Her detective friend told her about Oliver Holmes, Kevin's mentor. On a tip from the detective, she approached Oliver on a Saturday afternoon at an art gallery featuring an exhibit of Jacob Lawrence's work. Oliver was a widower, lonely and sexually frustrated. By that evening, she had him bent over his bed, his bare black ass in the air as she spanked him with a Ping-Pong paddle. (Later, she discovered his penchant for dressing in women's clothing; the strange tastes of men never failed to amuse her.)

Oliver treated Kevin like a son, and was initially reluctant to help her. But frequent servings of spectacular, sexually depraved activities, dispensed over a couple of weeks, won him to her side. (She had his nose so wide open that he knew she freely had sex with other men, and he didn't care at all, so long as she fulfilled his desires. He even allowed her the use of his home for some of her "dates.")

With Oliver's generous backing, her plans for revenge crystallized. Thanks to him, she had access to Kevin's home, his office, his computers . . . everything she needed to execute a major mind-fuck.

Some of the other theatrical props—the pig's blood she'd spilled on the floor at the hotel, the bloody knife (also dipped in pig's blood)—she secured through her own sources.

She couldn't remember the last time she'd had so much fun.

The bathroom door opened behind her. Jarred out of her thoughts, she blinked. Her reflection in the bay window was once again Eve Kennedy, the irresistible seductress who would soon have the ultimate revenge against her childhood tormentor.

"Is he here yet?" Oliver asked.

She turned. Oliver came out of the bathroom, wearing a white terry cloth robe and house slippers.

"Not yet," she said. "But I've heard that he's on his way."

Two other men, guys Oliver had hired, were assisting them. One of them had posed as a security guard at the Ritz-Carlton; the other had acted as an Atlanta homicide detective. The men were actual actors, desperate for work, and happy to earn a tax-free knot of cash for their role in her little game. They had been tailing Kevin since last night and phoning in regular reports on his whereabouts.

"Good." Oliver smiled. "Then we've got a little time together."

"What do you have in mind?"

"Well . . ." Oliver grinned sheepishly. He had the nerve to be embarrassed by his own desires. It annoyed Eve, but she would play along.

"I think I've been a bad boy." He cleared his throat, his voiced tinged with hesitant expectation. "I think I . . . need a little discipline."

"Of course."

It was Oliver's favorite fetish, after dressing in women's garments.

A tall rosewood cabinet beside the dresser contained Eve's bedroom tools. She opened the double doors. An array of whips, chains, spikes, masks, clubs, gags, cuffs, and other instruments hung inside.

Eve selected a long wooden paddle. The business end was perforated, which contributed to a satisfyingly painful sting when it connected with bare flesh.

Oliver had set up a mini-camcorder on the table near the bed. Like many men, he enjoyed recording their sessions, and watching them later.

She smiled for the camera.

Oliver unbelted his robe and dropped it to the floor. His dick, nestled in a thatch of gray pubic hair, was already erect and throbbing—all three inches of it, anyway. His tiny dick explained his penchant for having everything jumbo-sized—big SUV, big house. It amused her.

Oliver bent over the side of the bed, his dark, wide ass thrust in the air.

Approaching him, spinning the paddle in her fingers, Eve thought about her Aunt Rose. How right she had been. A man would do anything to have his erotic buttons pushed. Even a wealthy partner in a prestigious law firm was not above the lowest form of sexual debasement.

Oliver glanced over his shoulder. Anticipation gleamed in his eyes.

"Make it hurt," he said.

"Don't I always?" Eve smiled sweetly.

She beat Oliver's ass like he'd stolen something.

Chapter 57

Sometime after eleven o'clock that night, Kevin located Eve Kennedy's house.

It was a huge, old Victorian, ivory with black shutters, bringing to mind a Gothic house in a ghost story; it sat far back from the winding, tree-lined road, the yard enclosed by a chest-high, wrought-iron fence topped with sharp spikes. Large oaks and maples flanked the property, like giant guards.

Soft golden light glowed in an upstairs window. Although curtains veiled much of the window, he could make out moving shadows.

Instinct told him that the people inside were engaged in a sex act.

So Eve was home, and she wasn't alone, either. Oliver's Escalade was parked in the driveway that led to the unattached garage.

The thought of Oliver and Eve together drew a band of anger across Kevin's chest. He'd trusted Oliver with so much . . . he couldn't understand how the older man could betray him. Just for a piece of ass. Years of friendship flushed down the toilet, for sex.

After this, he would never trust anyone again.

Kevin parked a few houses down from Eve's place. He didn't know whether they were expecting him or not, but he decided it would be wise to attempt to take them by surprise.

He opened the glove compartment.

The .38 waited inside.

He hesitated to reach for the gun. If he took the revolver

with him to Eve's house, someone was probably going to get hurt. Guns and rage were a combustible mix. He had to be prepared for the possibility that in the next few minutes, he might become a felon. He might go to prison and serve hard time.

Then he thought about Jason, hobbling into his grand-mother's house, his manhood permanently severed from his body, his spirit broken forever.

Fuck that. I'm not letting this bitch do that to me. This is self-defense.

He grabbed the gun.

He would deal with the consequences of his actions later.

He got out of the car, slid the gun into his waistband, and made his way toward the house.

Chapter 58

While Eve was whipping Oliver's ass, she heard a car cruising slowly past her house, as if the driver was studying her home.

She stopped the paddle in midswing. Oliver, lying on his stomach on the bed, his buttocks purple and quivering, looked over his shoulder at her. His eyes were teary; she'd been punishing him for a good fifteen minutes.

"That him?" he asked, short of breath.

"It has to be. Hardly anyone drives past at this hour of the night. I chose this location because it offers privacy."

Oliver turned over. Moving caused him to wince; he tenderly massaged his buttocks.

"So what's the plan?" he asked.

"Go to the guest room and keep the door shut. I'll let you know when I need you again."

Oliver nodded, like an obedient little boy. He was an influential man in the legal world, but as Eve had learned, the most powerful men were often most amenable to allowing a woman to dominate them. Running the world was a burden; letting a woman order you around in the bedroom was a welcome respite from that stressful life.

"Will we be able to be together again tonight?" he asked.

"You're a glutton for punishment, aren't you? I'll see how I feel after I get Kevin squared away. No promises, dear. Now get out of here."

Oliver dutifully gathered his robe and the camcorder. She smacked him lightly on the butt as he left the bedroom, and he smiled. A few seconds later, she heard him enter the guest room down the hallway and shut the door. He would probably review the video of their session—and get excited all over again.

Men.

Eve extinguished the candles in the bedroom. She turned on a lamp outfitted with a blood red lightbulb. A crimson glow suffused the room.

Red put her in the mood to mete out intense pain to a man (which many men, in their bizarre way, loved). Whipping Oliver was merely a prelude to tonight's main activity.

She tiptoed to the window and peered through the curtains.

She saw Kevin slithering across the yard. He slid from one tree to the next, trying to conceal himself as he neared the house.

A smile curved across her face.

Oh, baby, I can't wait to see you again.

She watched Kevin a moment longer, and then she stepped away from the window.

It was time to unleash the dogs.

Chapter 59

After he scaled the fence, Kevin was sneaking toward the house with the stealth of an assassin, plotting ways that he might get inside without alerting Eve to his presence— when a series of harsh white lights suddenly powered up at the front of the house, eradicating the darkness.

Motion-activated lights, he thought. *Shit.*

He was only about twenty feet away from the front door, but he froze, feeling as exposed as a bank robber trapped in a police searchlight. Ducking behind an oak tree, he dug his fingers into the bark. He couldn't afford to give away his presence, not this soon.

He waited. After perhaps thirty seconds, the lights switched off. A tide of darkness washed over the property.

He peeked around the corner of the thick trunk.

The front door of the house yawned open. It hadn't been open before. Was Eve on the threshold, watching him? Darkness filled the doorway, preventing him from seeing who might be near.

Then he saw two large, four-legged creatures vault through the doorway, like animals leaping through a hoop. One animal was light-colored, the other was dark. Their eyes glinted like silver in the murkiness.

Dogs.

Kevin's heart rose into his throat.

Snarling and snapping, the dogs thundered toward him.

He had the gun, but the dogs were coming at him so fast that there was no way in hell he could drop both of them with a bullet before one of them took him down. The lights, activated by the running dogs, blazed into life again, and Kevin saw that the dogs were enormous, resembling pit bulls on steroids, and their flashing teeth looked sharp enough to tear him to pieces within seconds.

Operating on a pure drive to survive, Kevin followed his first impulse: He started climbing the tree.

It was a mature oak, with lots of branches, so he found ready handholds. He pulled himself off the ground and several feet into the air, just as the slavering canines came within striking distance of the tree.

"Fuck y'all!" Kevin shouted.

The dogs barked angrily. The white one jumped—the damn thing had a vertical leap like LeBron James—and snagged the cuff of his jeans between its teeth. Weighted down by the large animal, his fingers ached; he started to lose his grip on the branch overhead.

"Get off me!" he screamed.

But the dog had locked its jaws on his pants, nostrils flaring furiously, saliva frothing from its lips.

Risking a fall to the earth below, Kevin took one hand away from the branch and dug in the waistband of his jeans. He grabbed the gun, and swung the butt at the dog's skull.

There was a loud *thunk* as the metal connected with the dog's bricklike head. The dog released him and dropped to the ground, shaking its head as if clearing away dust.

Kevin pulled his legs up, resting them on a bough that was out of the dogs' reach.

As the canines continued to snap and leap futilely beneath him, Kevin looked up, studying the tree's wingspan. One of the thick, leafy branches came to within five feet or so of the house's second level.

A plan began to brew in his mind.

He stowed the gun in his waistband.

He started to climb.

Chapter 60

Eve sent Snow and Storm into the night, fully expecting them to capture Kevin. The animals had been schooled by a professional dog trainer, and obeyed her commands implicitly. She had ordered them to detain Kevin, not kill him.

But Kevin, damn him, climbed the tree and ascended out of their reach.

As she stood just inside the doorway, she watched Kevin scale the branches. He disappeared in the thick cover of leaves, climbing with an agility that amazed her.

What was he doing?

She studied the oak tree, and the realization struck her, bringing a smile to her face. Kevin was more resourceful than she had anticipated.

She called the dogs inside, and hurried upstairs.

Chapter 61

High on fear-fueled adrenaline, Kevin scaled the tree with a skill that bordered on superhuman. The dogs had vanished, their final barks echoing in his ears.

Stopping with his legs wrapped around a branch, Kevin surveyed his surroundings.

He estimated that he was about thirty feet above ground. During his undergrad days, he had worked in home construction one summer, spending a good portion of the time working on roofs. Heights didn't frighten him, but only a fool would be reckless this high in the air. A fall to the ground would break his neck for sure.

He shifted to face the house. The branch that extended to within five feet of the second floor stretched in front of him, like a gnarled gangplank.

Okay, let's do this.

He gripped a bough overhead, steadied his feet on the branch below, and began to inch forward.

Leaves brushed across his face, and twigs trailed down his arms and back, like groping fingers. A fat drop of sweat rolled into his eye, and he blinked rapidly to clear his vision.

He resisted the compulsion to look down. But as he moved farther away from the solid security of the trunk, he could feel the space opening up beneath him, could sense the tug of gravity, threatening to pull him down if he slipped.

Stay focused.

His shoe slipped on a bristling patch of leaves. He locked his arm around the branch above, swaying for an agonizingly long moment.

"Fuck."

Finally, the tree stabilized again.

He was near the middle of the bridge, as he had come to think of it. He looked toward the house, studied the window that he planned to break to get inside, eyed the ledge that would support him. Almost there.

He began inching across the bough again.

The branch began to bend and crackle underneath him. He was near the end of its length; it couldn't support his weight. He had to make a jump for it.

He focused on the ledge. Less than ten feet away.

He edged forward a little more.

The branch began to crack.

Keeping his eyes on his destination point, he leaped.

He landed on the side of the house, directly onto the target ledge. He groped madly, got his hands on the rain gutters overhead. One of his feet was on the ledge; the other was suspended in the air. He carefully placed his other foot on the ledge.

The ledge was about six inches wide. Not much room to maneuver, but enough.

The window was only a couple of feet away.

He moved closer, and then dug into his waistband and got the gun. He swung the butt of the revolver toward the glass.

The window shattered, the sound loud in the night. Shards of glass tinkled to the roof below.

Kevin used the gun to knock away the remaining slivers of glass in the frame, so he wouldn't cut himself when he climbed through it. Then, bending low, he gripped the edges of the window and looked inside.

Oliver stood in front of the window, wearing a white bathrobe.

"What the . . . " Kevin's lips parted in surprise.

Oliver grabbed Kevin and hauled him inside.

Chapter 62

Oliver flung Kevin onto the hardwood floor. Kevin landed hard on his shoulder, fiery pain blazing down his side.

The fall had knocked the gun out of his fingers. Oliver stepped toward the revolver and picked it up.

He leveled it at Kevin.

"You never should have come here, brother Kevin," Oliver said. "You should've left town."

Woozy, Kevin sat up. The bedroom contained a full-size bed, a dresser, a desk, and a large-screen television. An amateur video played on the screen: a side view of a black woman Kevin recognized as Eve, dressed in a dominatrix outfit, and using a paddle to spank the dark, fleshy buttocks of a man. The man grunted loudly with each resounding *thwack;* he looked over his shoulder at his punisher, a rapturous grin on his face.

Oliver?

Kevin looked from the TV, to his old friend.

"I can't believe you, man," Kevin said. "You betrayed me so you could get that bitch to beat your ass?"

Embarrassment flushed Oliver's face. "That's not me."

"The hell it isn't. I saw your face. All these years I've known you, I never would've imagined that you went for that sick shit."

"Shut up!" Oliver said, raising the gun.

Kevin slowly got to his feet. "I spent some time in your house, *brother* Oliver. I went into your closet. Guess what I found behind your secret panel?"

243

Beads of sweat rolled down Oliver's face. His hand that held the gun trembled.

Kevin advanced toward him.

"What would the partners think if they knew that you liked to wear women's dresses and shoes?"

"Please, don't . . . tell anyone." Tears leaked out of his eyes.

"I used to admire you," Kevin said. "You were the father I never had."

Oliver looked away, lowering the gun. His shame was too great for him to face Kevin like a man.

It was exactly what Kevin had been counting on.

He seized Oliver's arm and attempted to take the gun. Oliver was a large man, heavier than Kevin, but old age and indulgent living had slowed him down. Kevin easily wrested the gun out of his grasp.

"Don't shoot me," Oliver said, hands raised in surrender. "I'm sorry, brother, I couldn't help it—"

Kevin thumped the gun upside Oliver's head. Oliver slid heavily to the floor, unconscious.

Kevin picked up the camcorder and popped out the miniature cassette. He stuffed it into his pocket. As evidence of Oliver's fetishes, it might prove a useful blackmailing tool later.

He found a leather belt in one of the dresser drawers. He used it to bind Oliver's wrists behind him. He wanted to keep Oliver out of the way until he finished what he had come there to do.

Holding the gun with the muzzle pointed skyward, he slid to the bedroom door. He opened it.

The darkened hallway beckoned.

He was certain that Eve was there. But where was she?

This was her house; she would be comfortable here, in her territory. And he couldn't forget about the vicious dogs. They had fallen silent—meaning that she might have brought them back inside, to hunt him.

Eve held every advantage. It had been an act of madness for him to come here.

But what other choice did he have? She had pushed him to this, and he wasn't going to go out like a punk.

And he sure as hell wasn't going to wind up like Jason, castrated for the rest of his life.

Steeling himself for anything that came at him, Kevin crept across the threshold and moved deeper into the house.

Chapter 63

Oliver had failed her. Eve was disappointed, but not surprised. He was getting up in age, capable of performing in the bedroom, thanks solely to Viagra. He hadn't stood much of a chance against her hard-body prey, Kevin.

The thought of Kevin, drunk on adrenaline, muscles pumped, skin oily, made her almost unbearably horny.

Concealed in the shadows, Eve slid her fingers to her pussy and touched her warm wetness. She stroked her clit, till eddies of pleasure rippled through her. She stopped just short of giving herself an orgasm.

First, she wanted to see Kevin.

She double-checked that her weapon was operational, and waited for her prey to enter her lair.

Chapter 64

Moving silently and deliberately, gripping the gun, sweat trickling down his back, Kevin wandered down the long hallway, checking inside each room he passed. He looked into a bathroom, a home office, a laundry room, and yet another bedroom. All of the rooms were sparsely decorated, clean. He found no sign of Eve's whereabouts.

The door at the end of the corridor was the only one he hadn't checked out. Soft red light leaked from underneath, as if a pool of blood were just on the other side.

He remembered the blood on the floor in his hotel room, shook his head to clear the disturbing image.

He heard a faint noise coming from inside, too. Music?

He put his ear to the door. Listened.

He heard, playing softly, a classic Marvin Gaye song. "Let's Get It On."

Kevin scowled. Was Eve taunting him?

He opened the door.

Red light, shining from a brass lamp on the other side of the room, revealed the chamber to be a large, master bedroom suite. Hardwood floors. Ornate, hand-carved ceiling fan. A king-size poster bed sat in the center of the room, covered with black sheets.

Red rose petals were scattered across the bed, looking, in the crimson luminescence, like bits of bloody flesh.

Kevin stepped across the threshold, red light bathing his skin.

Other furnishings included a large rosewood cabinet, a

matching bureau on which sat a molded plastic black case; an overstuffed chair, a sheer red negligee dangling from the arm; and a wall of mirrors. Kevin caught his own red-tinted reflection, saw the sweat streaming down his face and his anxious posture, and had to look away.

The music came from a turntable standing beside a big, flat-screen television.

Kevin also noticed a leather-bound photo album on the bed, half buried beneath the rose petals. He brushed aside the rose petals and opened the book.

The first page featured baby photos of a child that had to be Eve—aka Nikki Waters. She had been a small, pale child, with a smear of dark stringy hair, and bulbous eyes. She certainly wouldn't have won any baby beauty pageants.

He looked around, confirmed that he was still alone, and continued turning pages.

Additional pictures showed Nikki growing older: a shot of the toddler in diapers, eating a banana; the preschool-age girl with Afro puffs, wearing a red jumpsuit; the child at maybe seven years old, with gigantic thick-lensed glasses that covered half her face . . . Kevin kept flipping forward.

When Nikki hit her late teen years, things got interesting.

The Coke-bottle glasses were gone. Her hair was long and luxurious. Her body had filled out.

A photo with SWEET SIXTEEN written in neat handwriting underneath showed Nikki sitting on a chair that resembled a throne. She was naked, her legs spread. A teenager was bent in front of her, his mouth pressed to her pussy. Nikki's hand cupped the back of his head, and she wore a grin of mischievous delight.

Further photos depicted Nikki—maybe she'd begun to call herself Eve at this point—indulging in more acts of debauchery as the years passed. A twenty-first birthday spent carousing in the bedroom with three well-muscled men and another black woman; Eve at twenty-five, dressed as a dominatrix and clenching a bullwhip between her teeth; in her late twenties, licking clean a man's dick; at thirty, wearing a mask and holding a gray-haired man by the roots of his hair as she rode astride his body like a cowboy.

The next-to-last photo showed Kevin and Eve in the hotel room at the Ritz; he lay on the bed, her teeth attached to his neck as she bit him hard enough to draw blood.

Kevin's neck, still ringed with a bruise, throbbed at the memory of the pain. The crazy bitch must have set up an automated camera in the room, without his knowledge.

The Marvin Gaye song ended. With a soft click, the turntable arm lifted and replaced itself on the cradle.

The only sound in the room was Kevin's racing heart.

He turned another page, to the last photo.

It was the old picture of Kevin, Andre, and Jason. In the version Kevin had seen earlier, a red X had been marked across Andre's and Jason's faces.

In this one, his face had been marked, too.

"All because of you," a soft voice said, close to him.

Kevin looked up.

The wall of mirrors—actually, he saw now that it had been a closet—had opened. Eve had walked out, wearing one of her black leather dominatrix outfits that exposed her nipples and her clean-shaven pussy.

She was aiming a gun of some kind at him. There was *a pop*.

Kevin began to raise the .38 . . .

Twin probes, trailed by wires, launched from her weapon and attached to the front of his shirt.

"Too slow on the draw," she said, as thousands of volts of electricity suddenly surged into Kevin's body.

He dropped his gun and fell face-first onto the bed, jerking and twitching.

Chapter 65

Oliver came to with a terrible headache.

He lay on the floor in one of Eve's bedrooms, his wrists tied up behind his back. Shards of glass covered the area rug near his head.

His memory of what had happened, foggy at first, quickly cleared.

Kevin and Eve. The showdown. Kevin had brought a gun, but he would be no match for Eve. She was the most dangerous woman he had ever met in his life.

That was partly why she drove Oliver crazy. That, and her stunning looks.

Oliver's desire for her overrode his guilt at how he had betrayed Kevin. Every man had a weakness, a kryptonite. His happened to be named Eve. He was helpless to resist her.

He tried to loosen his bonds. It felt as though a leather strap had been used to confine him. A belt, maybe?

Sitting up, he grunted, rubbed his wrists together to generate enough perspiration to lubricate his flesh and make it easier to slip out. He managed to get two of his long, thick fingers around the tip of the strap. He started to work it back and forth. The movement chafed the tender flesh of his wrists, but the belt slowly began to loosen.

Within a few minutes, Oliver had worked himself free.

He stood, his muscles aching. There was a knot on his temple that felt as large as a golf ball.

Kevin had given him a helluva pop with that gun. He was

going to be in a world of pain tomorrow—and it wouldn't be the erotic pain that he enjoyed.

He looked to the television. Before Kevin had broken into the room, he had been watching the video recording of his recent encounter with Eve, reliving the exquisitely pleasurable session. A check of the camcorder showed that the tape compartment was empty.

Kevin must have removed the tape while Oliver had been unconscious. Fear razored through Oliver. If that tape got into the wrong hands, his legal career was over.

He had to find Kevin.

He found Kevin—and lovely Eve—in the master bedroom. The room was awash in red light. Eve had Kevin sprawled on the bed, the probes of a stun gun fixed to his shirt. Poor sap.

Eve whipped her head around at Oliver's intrusion.

"What do you want?" she snapped.

Oliver glanced at Kevin. He saw the anguish in his friend's eyes, the drool dripping down his chin as the electricity tortured his trembling body.

Oliver had to look away.

"He took my videotape," Oliver said softly.

Eve sighed, as if dealing with a troublesome child.

"I'll take care of it," she said. "Get out of here. I'm busy right now."

"Where are the dogs?" He didn't dare to go downstairs if those wild mutts of hers were on the loose.

"I put them in their kennels. Now go home!" She turned away from him and resumed her terrible work on Kevin.

Oliver gave a last look at his friend.

Kevin watched him. His eyes pleaded for mercy.

Oliver lowered his gaze, backed away, and shut the door. This was none of his business, not anymore.

But the look in Kevin's eyes stayed with Oliver as he left the house.

Chapter 66

Kevin was at Eve's mercy.

He lay on the bed, quivering from the aftereffects of the stun gun. Involuntary spasms shot through him. He had lost all muscle control: When he tried to get up, or tried to kick Eve away, it was as if he were fighting against concrete.

When Oliver entered the room and saw him, Kevin fought for control of his body, failed, and tried to appeal to Oliver with his eyes, to let Oliver know that he would forgive him for everything if he would only help him out of this. But his efforts were in vain. Although Oliver clearly looked troubled, he left the room, like a rebuked child.

It was then that Kevin realized the depth of his trouble. No one was going to save him. Eve could do anything she wanted to him. Anything.

At the moment, she was stripping his clothes off him. There was nothing sexual about it; she might have been undressing a doll. She removed his shoes, his socks.

"I left out the photo album to show you the course of my life," she said. "Pretty wild, huh?"

Kevin, lacking control of his vocal cords, couldn't have responded if he'd wanted to. He uttered only a guttural "*uhhh.*"

She yanked off his pants, continuing her monologue.

"I love sex, but you know what I really enjoy? The power it gives me over men. You men will do anything for a piece of pussy. Look at what you did, Kevin. You married a beautiful woman, you're a successful attorney, and now you're about to lose everything—all because you wanted some ass on the side."

She ripped away his shirt, tore off his T-shirt.

"Men are dogs, just like my auntie told me. I knew you would fall into my trap. You couldn't help yourself. Enticing you with kinky sex was the perfect way to lure you in."

She began to roll down his boxers.

Please, God, Kevin thought. *Help me.*

"You know why I want revenge, don't you? I'm sure your old road dog, Jason, told you everything—I left him with instructions to do that. Boy, I had fun with him! Anyway, Kevin, it's because of the situation you put me in that I wound up on the path that I did. How would I have turned out if you and your friends hadn't handed me over to that sick man? I might have grown up to be a nice girl, an old-fashioned southern belle. Instead of a whore."

His boxers were around his ankles. She took his dick in her hand and squeezed. Due to the electrical shocks he had sustained, he was barely able to feel the pressure.

Eve grinned.

"But you know the crazy part? I like being a whore— *love* it. But growing up, I was prone to frequent bouts of depression, feeling suicidal. Eventually I had a nervous breakdown—yes, I did—and I went into therapy. Know what I learned?"

She slid her fingers to his balls and tickled them. Kevin tensed, involuntarily.

When she squeezed hard, he let out a thin scream. Sweat pooled on his chest. He'd definitely felt *that.*

"I learned that I won't be healthy until I come to terms with my past. Until I deal with the demons lurking in my subconscious, if you will. Well, I figured out *who* the demons are. I'm destroying them, one by one."

Kevin's testicles ached. With the pain, sensation had begun to seep into his body again. He could wriggle his tongue, curl his finger. *Yet* he still felt weakened, as if sludge filled his muscles. He was in no condition to fight against Eve. She was not a frail woman; she was tall, in splendid physical condition—and she had the strength that only the certifiably insane possessed.

Eve placed her hand against his cheek, almost tenderly. Her eyes glistened.

"It's rather sad, actually," she said. "If we were different people—if you weren't a dog and I weren't a whore— you and I might have had a life together. We might've had a happy home, a family."

A sardonic smile twisted her face.

"Yeah, right. You would've been cheating on me, fucking anything with two legs. Then we still would've wound up in a situation like this. I don't believe in tolerating any shit from a man, Kevin. I believe in punishment. The pain and reward system. Works well for both dogs and men."

You're out of your mind, Kevin wanted to shout at her, now that he had regained partial control of his body, but he kept his mouth shut. Let her think that he was still immobilized. It gave him an advantage.

Eve turned away and strolled to the bureau. She picked up the large, plastic black case and brought it near the bed, placing it on the glass nightstand.

What was she doing?

She opened the case.

He caught a glimpse of metallic instruments, glimmering in the reddish light.

She lifted an item out of the case: a long, hypodermic syringe. It looked like something a veterinarian would use to give an injection to a horse.

His jaws clenched. He couldn't let her stick him with that thing.

As she stabbed the needle into a vial of clear fluid, a loud crash came from somewhere downstairs.

Eve looked up, frowned.

"Don't go anywhere," she said to Kevin. "I'll be right back."

Chapter 67

Marcus couldn't wait any longer. He had to know what was going on inside that house.

He'd followed Kevin all over Atlanta. He couldn't figure out what this guy was involved in. Some kind of drug deal? He had no clue.

Marcus followed him to the large Victorian house in Grant Park, maintaining a safe tracking distance and staying abreast of the proceedings with his high-powered binoculars.

When Kevin scaled the fence and climbed the tree to avoid a duo of vicious hounds—and then broke a window to get inside the house, like a star of an action movie—that was when Marcus decided he'd had enough of sitting on the sidelines. It was time to get involved.

Intuition told him that if he didn't act soon, he would lose his shot at Kevin. His boy was obviously involved in some dangerous shit. Marcus wanted to get a crack at him, before anyone else did.

But there was the problem of the dogs. Big, snarling dogs always complicated his investigative work. He had a canister of mace designed especially to repel canines, but he was hesitant to use it in this situation. He just didn't know what he was dealing with here.

As he sat there mulling over the possibilities, someone solved his problem. The dogs made a beeline inside the house, as if summoned by their master, whoever that was. Marcus saw only a silhouette of a person—he couldn't determine the individual's gender—standing within the doorway. The dogs vanished inside. The door closed.

But something—intuition, again—advised Marcus to wait.

Maybe twenty minutes later, the Cadillac Escalade parked in the driveway—the same one from the mansion in Lithonia—came roaring onto the street.

Marcus ducked down in the seat to avoid detection. But he got a quick look at the driver: It was the same older black gentleman from the mansion.

Marcus didn't know what had just transpired inside, and he didn't care.

He'd had enough of waiting.

He picked up his Beretta. He hurried down the street toward the house. Like Kevin, he found the gate locked, so he climbed the fence.

The front door of the house was locked, too.

What he was about to do would cause him to lose his investigator's license, but he figured he had long since crossed the line of what constituted ethical behavior for a private detective.

He kicked the door down.

Chapter 68

What was going on downstairs? Had Oliver disobeyed her command and returned to meddle?

Eve wasn't sure. But whatever was going on down there, she wasn't happy about it. She was *so close* to exacting her revenge on Kevin. She hated to be pulled away from her work. Kevin was currently incapacitated, thanks to the stun gun, but the effects would eventually wear off. She didn't want to have to restrain him again.

From the top of the spiral staircase, she could see the entry hall. The front door yawned open, the hinges damaged.

The sound she'd heard must have been someone kicking the door in.

But who? Police? They would have announced themselves first; they didn't just knock down doors.

She tightened her grip on the syringe. It contained a dose of an anesthetic that would make Kevin pliable to surgery. Although intended for Kevin, she was willing to use it on anyone who dared to invade her home.

She removed her stilettos—they were sexy but it was impossible to move fast and quietly with them on—and she crept down the stairs in her stockinged feet. She drifted into the hallway, as silent as a ghost. The first level was dimly lit, but she knew this house so well she could've navigated it with a blindfold over her eyes.

She could smell the intruder. A young man. She smelled his musk in the air, his sweat.

A pleasant tremor passed through her. She could get horny

at the oddest times. She slid her finger to her pussy, caressed herself.

She entered the living room.

"Don't move," a deep man's voice said, just beyond the archway.

He pressed a gun against her temple, the muzzle as cold as a block of ice.

Chapter 69

Kevin didn't know what had happened downstairs to distract Eve, but he was determined to use the opportunity to gain the upper hand on her crazy ass.

Although he had gotten back his muscle control, moving was still difficult. His body felt as though he had been ground through a shredder. Nausea cramped his stomach. When he raised his head, dizziness spun through him, as if he'd just stepped off a carousel at an amusement park.

Hurry up and get going, damn it. The bitch could be back any minute.

Gritting his teeth, straining and grunting, he sat up on the bed. The effort drained sweat from his pores.

He looked to the black case on the nightstand. It contained what appeared to be surgical instruments.

He saw the scalpel, nested in the middle of the tools. He reached for it.

And lost his balance.

He pitched forward, his hand striking the case, and everything clattered to the floor.

Chapter 70

Marcus couldn't believe the woman who had walked into the living room. Acting on reflex, he had pressed the gun against her head before taking stock of her appearance.

When he did, his jaw came unhinged.

She was incredible.

She was tall and long-haired, possessing a body too perfect to be believed. She wore a skimpy, black learner outfit that had cutouts around her nipples and her pussy—where currently her finger resided, stroking softly.

Marcus closed his mouth, licked his lips.

He had figured out what Kevin was doing here. The man was trying to get his freak on. Looking at her, Marcus couldn't blame him one bit.

He wondered if she was Black Venus, the woman from the Internet that he'd been planning to meet Something told him that she was. She looked like a goddess.

"Like what you see?" she asked, in a husky voice that sent a chill of pleasure along his spine.

He finally found his voice. "My beef isn't with you. It's with Kevin. What's going on here?"

"Lower the gun, honey, and I'll tell you."

Marcus hesitated. Something wasn't quite right here. Tearing his gaze away from the sight of her questing finger in her pussy, he noticed that her other hand was behind her back.

As if she was hiding something . . .

A clatter from above drew Marcus's gaze away from the woman, to the ceiling. What was going on up there?

The woman moved swiftly.

Grinning, she jammed something into his neck. A needle. *Oh, Jesus . . .*

His knees weakening, he dropped to the floor, the gun thudding beside him. A heavy numbness spread through his body.

"I've injected you with an anesthetic," she said. "It won't hurt you, but it will keep you still for a while."

She bent down, studying him closer.

"My, aren't you a sexy one?" she said. She slid her hand to his groin. "And quite well endowed. I'd love to enjoy you, sweetheart. But I have business upstairs first. One man at a time—at least, tonight. I'll leave you with a taste to whet your appetite."

She pressed her guilty finger to his lips and smeared her juices across them. Then, smiling devilishly, she picked up his Beretta and sashayed away.

Chapter 71

Eve's house was, she thought, a hotbed of activity tonight. First Kevin, and now the handsome stranger who'd broken inside, seeking Kevin for some unfathomable reason. Well, perhaps not so unfathomable; knowing Kevin's ways, he had probably slept with the stranger's wife or girlfriend, and now the man desired revenge.

He would have to wait his turn.

The clatter from upstairs that had distracted the intruder had to have been caused by Kevin. Her boy must've regained partial control of his body. She would have to hurry to resume control of him.

As she ascended the steps, she dropped the man's fearsome-looking gun on a table. She loathed firearms. She preferred injectable drugs and instruments that required intimate contact.

She tapped her finger against the needle. The syringe contained enough anesthetic to pacify Kevin. Perhaps she would inject him, take him downstairs, and then return to the sexy stranger. It had been her original intent to fix Kevin immediately—her desire to torture him exceeded her patience—but she wasn't anything if not adaptable. The intrusion was a welcome chance to incorporate a bit of unexpected pleasure into the evening.

At the top of the stairs, she slid on her stilettos. She arrived at the bedroom and pushed open the door, red light bathing her flesh.

Kevin had knocked her tool case onto the floor. Her precious instruments covered the hardwood. She noticed, immediately, that the surgeon's scalpel was missing.

Kevin was gone.

Chapter 72

It took all of Kevin's fortitude to keep quiet. His breaths wanted to roar out of him; his hammering heart banged in his ears, so loud that surely Eve must hear it; and with the plentiful dust bunnies so close to his nostrils, he struggled to keep from sneezing.

He had hidden underneath the bed. He lay flat on his stomach, arms curled in front of him, gripping the scalpel in his right hand. He was nude except for his boxer shorts; he felt sweat oozing from his pores and seeping into the hardwood floor, as if he were a wet sponge.

The black bed skirt ended about four inches above the floor, giving him a partial view of the room beyond.

As he looked around, Eve's black stilettos crossed the bedroom's threshold. He heard her release a quick burst of shocked breath.

That's right. I've been in your little box of sicko tools. Now come closer.

Kevin had regained most of the control of his body, though moving caused his tender muscles to ache. But he was willing to endure the pain for a shot at Eve.

He wondered what had happened downstairs. The crash had sounded like a smashing door. Could it have been the police? He usually despised the cops, but he prayed that they would help him here.

But if it had been the police, how was Eve back up here again so soon?

Eve walked slowly around the bed. She was too far away for him to swipe at her leg with the scalpel.

As he inhaled, a dust bunny got lodged in his nostril. He stifled a sneeze, rubbed his nose against his sweat-slick arm to clear his airway.

Eve was at the mirrored doors of the walk-in closet. She paused in front of them.

Kevin realized that he could see himself reflected in the mirror, crammed underneath the bed like an immature teenager playing hide-and-seek.

If he could see himself in the glass, then Eve could see him, too.

Oh, shit.

Eve spun around. She marched to the far wall.

Kevin remembered a tall cabinet stood over there. He heard her open the doors.

What is she getting out of there?

Eve knelt to the floor.

"Peekaboo," she said in a tinny, child's voice. "I see you."

She lashed a whip toward his face, as if she were trying to beat a rodent from underneath the bed.

The leather popped against Kevin's cheek. He cried out, and as he scooted backward to get away, he bumped his head against the bed frame.

Eve snapped the whip at him again. It burned against his forearm, like a tongue of fire.

Jesus, she's like Indiana Jones with that fucking thing.

"Come out, come out, come out," she sang sweetly.

But Kevin still had the scalpel.

As she flicked the whip at him again, he snagged the tip in his hand, gritting his teeth against the sharp pain, and held it tight. He jerked Eve toward him.

Thrown off balance, she fell to the floor with an "*uuuhhh.*"

Kevin surged like a snake from underneath the bed. Leaping forward, he slashed at her with the scalpel, going for her throat.

But Eve rolled away, bringing up her arms protectively. The

sharp blade zippered down her forearm. Blood spouted, dark red in the crimson light.

Eve shrieked.

Kevin pounced on top of her. She squirmed frantically beneath him. He pinned her shoulders to the floor.

"Crazy fucking bitch!" he shouted.

She bucked her knee into his crotch. Pain exploded in his groin and spread in a nauseating wave throughout his body.

Eve pushed him off her. She got to her feet.

"This crazy bitch is more than capable of handling you," she said. Although her forearm bled, she seemed unconcerned—proof that she was every bit as crazy as he thought.

Through his haze of agony, Kevin saw her heading for the bureau, where the syringe waited.

Tears rolling down his cheeks, growling like a beast from the effort to move, Kevin managed to rise on his knees. He raised the scalpel, thinking fuzzily of ramming it into her spine, severing her spinal cord.

Eve whirled and kicked him in the mouth. His lip burst like a ripe fruit. She kicked him again, in the jaw, like an abusive owner might kick a dog. He dropped heavily to the floor. He could feel a painful welt swelling on his face.

Got my ass kicked by a woman, I can't believe this.

Holding the syringe, Eve sat on him, pressing her knees onto his lungs. He couldn't breathe. He lacked the strength to push her away.

Blood ran down her forearm and dripped onto his shoulder. He worried about contracting some sort of disease from her—though that should have been the least of his worries, at the moment.

"Let's get you to the basement now," she said.

Kevin remembered Jason's harrowing account of living in a cage in her cellar. Fresh terror stoked his chest. But he was powerless to fight. He'd had his chance, and lost it.

Eve inserted the needle in his neck.

Chapter 73

Marcus lay on the living room floor, blinking slowly, pulling in deep breaths. Unable to move, thanks to the drug, but conscious and alert, he had resigned himself to thinking about his predicament.

It was, he decided, Kevin's fault that this had happened to him. If Kevin had not been screwing around on Lauren, Lauren never would have come to Marcus for investigative assistance; he never would have fallen in love with her; she never would have broken his heart; and he never would have launched his vendetta on Kevin. The chain of events started and ended with Kevin's infidelity.

For that reason, Marcus was still going to wipe him out. The woman had taken his Beretta, but he had a .22 in an ankle holster, his backup piece.

He stared at the fingers of his right hand. They were splayed. If he could only wriggle a finger . . .

He concentrated.

Soon, his index finger moved.

Chapter 74

Eve was dragging Kevin through the house by his feet. Like a dead body she planned to dispose of somewhere.

He was completely incapacitated. The drug she had given him had robbed him of control of his body. He was numb, like a rubber dummy.

Eve had wrapped a bandage around her wounded forearm. Gripping his bare feet, she dragged him down the hallway; the carpet burned against his exposed back. She pulled him to the staircase.

Hey, take it easy! he wanted to shout at her, but he couldn't speak.

Taking him feet first, she pulled him down the stairs. The back of his head thunked against each riser. He could hear his teeth clacking together. He was grateful, for once, for the numbness, because the pain of the rough descent down the steps would have been intense.

They reached the bottom of the stairs. She dragged him across the hardwood floor.

Although Kevin was unable to turn his head, in his peripheral vision, he saw another black man, dressed in dark colors, lying on the floor in the living room. The guy who had knocked down the door? He seemed to be incapacitated, too.

Kevin got only a quick glimpse, but the guy looked familiar . . .

The guy Lauren was fucking, he thought. *The private investigator. What the hell is he doing here?*

He looked to Eve.

"Oh, you saw that guy in the corner of your eye?" Eve asked, speaking for the first time in several minutes. "He came for you. *You* must've slept with his wife, or some such thing."

No, no, no. That motherfucker slept with my *wife, damn it!*

Eve only smiled, shook her head. "You men. You never cease to amaze. He's a tasty-looking piece. After I get you squared away, I'm going to have some fun with him."

Her madness knew no limits.

They reached another door. She opened it.

It was the basement.

He slid down the hard wooden staircase, head knocking against the steps.

* * *

When Marcus heard the woman dragging Kevin down the steps, he stopped his efforts to move, and played possum.

She pulled Kevin onto the first floor, and into the hallway. She only glanced at him, briefly, and them murmured something to Kevin that Marcus couldn't hear.

As soon as they were out of sight, Marcus went back to work.

He could move all the fingers of his hand.

And now his arm . . .

Chapter 75

The basement was like a dungeon. Dank, dark, festooned with cobwebs. The bare, weak lightbulbs did little to relieve the heavy shadows.

Fear festered like a tumor in Kevin's gut. As Eve dragged him across the dusty concrete floor, he'd begun trying to move. But it was pointless. Whatever she had injected into him had deadened his muscles to halt his voluntary control.

Eve took him to yet another door, this one painted red. When she opened it, he saw a steel cage that resembled something you might find chimpanzees frolicking in at Zoo Atlanta.

"I had this confinement chamber custom-made," she said. "It heightens the excitement of the bondage and submissions games I like to play—and has come in handy for dealing with you and Jason."

Kevin strained to speak. He had to talk sense to her. Somehow.

A word fell from his lips, softly: *"Please."*

Eve didn't hear him; or if she did, she chose to ignore him. She swung open the cage's door, the metal moving with a soft squeak. She pulled him inside.

He saw gleaming iron bars, a ragged blanket, a bed of pine straw, metal feed bowls mounted to the cage wall. A gnawed femur bone lay in the corner.

Jason's words surfaced in his mind: *Treated me like a dog— made me sleep on straw, gave me a bone, even.*

The stench made Kevin want to vomit; the fetid odor of piss and shit clotted the damp air.

"I haven't had time to hose the place down," she said. "Guess you'll have to cope with that."

She dragged him to the layer of pine straw and finally dropped his feet.

"Whew." She dusted off her hands. "That was hard work."

He only looked at her. His face was wet. It took him a moment to realize that he was crying.

Eve knelt. She cooed to him as if he were a puppy: "Aw, poor little doggie. I'm gonna feed you and give you water, yes, Mama will. Little doggie will be just fine."

She cupped his crotch and squeezed hard. Alarm shot through him, but he felt only a dull pressure.

"Later, Mama's gonna neuter you. Yes, she will. She'll fix you, and you won't mess with no more bitches again, uh-huh. You'll be a good little doggie, yep."

If Kevin had use of his hands, he would have ripped out her tongue.

Eve rose. She walked to the door of the cage.

"Bye-bye, doggie," she said, and waved at him.

Sudden gunfire boomed, the harsh report almost puncturing Kevin's eardrums.

Eve slumped to the floor, her body sprawled in the doorway.

The man Kevin had seen lying on the floor in the living room stepped over Eve's body and entered the cage. He held a small pistol.

Kevin did not know whether he was looking at his rescuer—or his executioner.

"It stinks to high heaven in here," the guy said, surveying the cage with a frown. "What kind of crazy shit are you and this woman into, man?"

"Help me . . . " Kevin wheezed. "Please."

"What did you say?"

Kevin tried to raise his head, managed to lift it maybe a centimeter. *"Please . . . help me."*

"Help you?" The man grinned. When Kevin saw his death's-head grin, his stomach sank. He was in far worse trouble here than he'd ever been with Eve.

"You never deserved Lauren," the man said.

Then he shot Kevin.

*   *   *

As Oliver was driving home, guilt overcame him.

He shouldn't have left Kevin at Eve's house. He never should have assisted her in her vengeful scheme. He represented himself to the world as a moral man, an upstanding Christian. Yet he had succumbed to the temptations of the flesh.

When he looked in the Escalade's rearview mirror, he saw not his own brown eyes, but Kevin's anguished, pleading gaze.

That did it.

He turned around. He drove back to Eve's house.

Rushing inside—the front door sagged on its hinges, as if struck by a battering ram—he raced upstairs. In the bedroom, he saw Eve's instruments littered across the floor, and dark droplets of what could only be bloodstains, but no Kevin, or Eve.

Before leaving the room, he searched Kevin's pants, which lay on the floor. In the back pocket, he found the videotape of his discipline session with Eve.

"Thank you, Jesus," he said, and kissed it before depositing it safely in his own pocket.

Next, he ran to the basement. Fortunately, Eve's dogs were still contained in their kennels. They glared at him as he raced to the cellar doorway.

He found Kevin inside the man cage (Oliver had willingly spent a few hours inside it once, to his everlasting shame), blood leaking from his chest. He was barely conscious.

What in God's name had happened here? This was beyond anything Eve had promised to do to him.

Oliver picked up Kevin, slung his arm over his shoulder, and carried him to the stairs. It took some work, but he got Kevin inside his SUV, laying him on a blanket across the seats in the back.

"Hang on," Oliver said. He mashed the accelerator and burned down the road. "I'm taking you to the hospital."

"Where . . . is. . . . Eve?" Kevin asked in a reed-thin voice.

"I don't know where she is. I didn't see her in the house."

Kevin slumped onto the seat.

"This may be the wrong time to bring this up," Oliver said. "But since I did come back to get you and probably saved you from bleeding to death, I was hoping that you could forget all about what you learned about my . . . private life."

Clenching the steering wheel, Oliver glanced at Kevin in the rearview. Kevin raised his head slightly, nodded.

"Deal," Kevin whispered.

Oliver closed his eyes and prayed. *From this day forward, I'm cleaning up my act, Lord. I promise.*

Oliver relaxed his grip on the wheel and drove Kevin to the hospital.

Chapter 76

Three days later, Lauren visited Kevin in his private ICU room at Grady Memorial Hospital.

Kevin had been shot with a .22, a smaller caliber, which, luckily for him, offered a greater possibility of survival and full recovery. The bullet had narrowly missed his lung. The surgeon had removed the smashed metal jacket of the bullet from his chest and sewed him up. He would always bear a scar. But at least he was alive.

He hoped the opposite was true of Eve.

Kevin dimly remembered seeing the crazed private investigator shooting Eve. He remembered seeing Eve drop to the basement floor. But after the guy turned the gun on him, his memory got fuzzy. Had Eve gotten up on her own? Oliver had reported her missing when he returned to rescue Kevin. Or perhaps, after shooting Kevin, the investigator had moved her body and hidden it somewhere. Was Eve in another hospital, recovering from her injuries?

Was she in this same hospital?

Kevin had no idea. Not knowing the madwoman's fate spawned endless nightmares for him.

But the days were better; he spent them entertaining numerous visitors. Oliver (still looking ashamed), several of his friends and colleagues—even his mother came by. His mom, smoking a cigarette, surveyed him lying there in the bed and remarked that now that he had a gunshot wound, he had proven that he was just like his daddy, in every way. "And where's that high-yella heifer of yours?" she had asked.

Kevin didn't know. He hadn't seen or talked to Lauren since their argument at the condo, before everything had gotten crazy. He'd tried to call her several times, and she never answered her cell phone, and when he called her parents' house, they always said she was unavailable. He left messages telling her where he was, and asking her to come see him.

He'd almost given up hope of ever talking to her again—when she suddenly appeared in the doorway on Wednesday afternoon.

"Hi," she said. She carried a bouquet of bright flowers.

"I'm so glad to see you, baby," Kevin said. He started to climb out of bed.

She hurried to him, setting the flowers on a nearby table.

"Take it easy, stay on the bed," she said. She adjusted the pillow underneath him and helped him to lie back down.

"Damn, you look good," he said. Lauren wore a yellow sundress, her hair was freshly styled, long and curly, and her skin had a healthy, bronzed tan.

He tried to kiss her. She turned her head, giving him her cheek. Like he was a family friend, and not her husband.

As she settled into the bedside chair, he noted that her ring finger was bare.

"I'm sorry to hear about what happened to you," she said. "What happened, exactly? You weren't clear in your messages."

"It's not worth rehashing," he said. "Let's just say that I got what was coming to me, and leave it at that."

She nodded; she didn't disagree, he noted.

"You were lucky to survive," she said.

"Truly, I was. I feel as if I've been given a second chance. An opportunity to do right by everyone—by you, most of all."

Her lips were firm. "I've already spoken to a divorce attorney, Kevin. The process is in motion. I'll have the paperwork soon for you to sign."

"I don't want a divorce, baby. Lying here, fighting to survive . . . I can see the error of my ways now. I'm a changed man."

"You're a changed man, huh?" She crossed her arms over her bosom.

"Absolutely. Swear to God. And I love you."

Lauren studied his face, as if searching for fault lines.

A nurse rapped on the door.

"Time for the meds," the nurse announced, marching inside holding a glass of water and a small cup that contained the capsules Kevin was taking to aid the healing process.

Lauren started to rise out of the chair.

"No need to leave, ma'am," the nurse said. "This will take only a sec."

The nurse was an exotic-looking young woman. Her name was Tamika. She had been his primary nurse since he had been admitted to the hospital, and he had begun a low-grade flirtation with her.

When he took the cup of meds from Tamika, their hands touched. She smiled—and winked.

Kevin felt the familiar rush of arousal surge through his body.

Before I check outta this place, I have to arrange some private time alone with this cutie.

He popped the capsules in his mouth and chased them with the water, grateful for its coldness. He needed something to cool him down.

When the nurse left, Kevin turned back to Lauren. She was shaking her head, ruefully.

"What is it?" he asked.

"You say you love me," Lauren said. "I think you do, in your own warped way. But you haven't changed, Kevin."

"What're you talking about? I swear I've changed, sweetheart. I was at death's door and now I'm alive. How could I not be changed?"

"That's a good question—one you need to seriously think about," she said. "Instead of scheming a way to have sex with your nurse."

"Huh?"

"It was all in your eyes, in your body language. Do you think I came down with the last drop of rain? *I know you.*"

"You're wrong," he said, but his denial sounded unconvincing, even to his own ears.

Lauren gave him a cynical, you-know-better smile. She got out of the chair.

"You're leaving already?" he asked. "You just got here."

"It took only a few minutes for me to see what I needed to see—once a dog, always a dog."

"I'm not a dog. I'm your husband, who loves you." He reached for her hand.

She moved away.

"My attorney will be in touch soon," she said, and left him in the room, alone.

* * *

Late that night, Kevin awoke to see someone drawing the privacy curtain around his bed.

He sat up suddenly, the abrupt motion causing a spike of pain in his tender chest. A human shape flitted behind the gauzy material.

"Who's there?" he asked. His heart pounded.

"It's your nurse," a muffled voice answered.

"Tamika?" he asked. His erection stirred.

He heard a clinking sound, like metallic instruments moving on a tray. That all-too-familiar noise made his mouth dry.

"What're you doing?" he asked, his voice holding a note of fear.

The curtains parted.

Eve stepped inside. She wore green hospital scrubs, a surgical mask dangling from around her neck.

As Kevin gaped at her, certain that he was having a nightmare, she pierced his arm with a syringe and injected a clear fluid into his bloodstream. He immediately lost control of his body.

"I'm preparing you for surgery," she said.

She slid the mask over her mouth and moved her hand to his groin, feeling him through the patient's gown, and slowly began to laugh.

About Brandon Massey

Brandon Massey was born June 9, 1973 and grew up in Zion, Illinois. He lives with his family near Atlanta, Georgia, where he is at work on his next thriller. Visit his web site at www.brandonmassey.com for the latest news on his upcoming books.

Made in the USA
Lexington, KY
07 August 2017